4

FOREST OF SOULS

AN ELA OF SALISBURY MEDIEVAL MYSTERY

J. G. LEWIS

For my friend Meredith Waring, animal lover extraordinaire, who makes me laugh and is always (unsuccessfully) trying to convince me to end my books on a cliffhanger.

ACKNOWLEDGMENTS

I am very grateful to Rebecca Hazell, Betsy van der Hoek, Anne MacFarlane and Judith Tilden for their careful readings and excellent suggestions. Many thanks also to the marvelous Lynn Messina. All remaining errors are mine.

CHAPTER 1

*S*alisbury, March 1227

ELA, Countess of Salisbury and High Sheriff of Wiltshire, needed a nap. All morning long she'd navigated her way through a gaggle of local disputes and upsets, pronouncing remedies and fines and punishments. Her grand carved chair had never felt harder or her back stiffer.

Yet here came two more red-faced farmers, already arguing with each other as they approached her dais in the great hall of Salisbury castle. And the general din—of servants, children, local villagers and garrison soldiers milling about—had grown so loud she couldn't hear herself think.

"Silence!" she called, with force that surprised her.

"Silence!" echoed John Dacus, her co-sheriff, a few years her senior, his shiny dark hair flecked with gray and his kind brown eyes showing a look of perpetual surprise. His words bounced off the timbered ceiling into the sudden hush, emphasizing the effectiveness of her own plea.

Even the two farmers paused their haranguing and stared at her like she'd grown another head. Formerly barging past each other, they now hesitated as if each hoped the other would go first.

"Wilf Crowder." She recognized the older of the two. A solid, stolid man she'd bought some fine sheep and a productive sow from in the past. "What brings you here today?"

"The ancient boundary of my land has been tampered with." His words exploded into the air. His thick gray hair curled about his neck, mingling with his rough beard. Long exposure to wind and cold had roughened his cheeks. "My neighbor"—he spat the word— "has stolen a piece of my land."

"Lies! The boundary lies where it always has been." The younger man—thirty-five years old, perhaps—thrust himself forward. His light brown hair was cut so that it hung just above blazing blue eyes. Ela didn't recognize him and racked her mind for who owned the land next to Wilf Crowder's farm.

"Your name?" she asked, when he did not produce it.

"Bertram Beck, my lady. And old Crowder has forgotten where the boundary lies. And why shouldn't he? It runs through the woods under a thick layer of leaves. His memory deceives him."

"Or so you hoped," growled the older man. "Except that every inch of this land is drenched with the blood and sweat of my family, who've owned it for nigh on a hundred years. Don't think I don't know every twig and every puddle like it's a sheep in my flock. He's built a fence of branches ten rods or more on my land."

"Why would I want to steal a few yards of woodland? I have twice the land you do."

"There's no accounting for greed," said Crowder, looking straight at Ela. "Some men are never happy with what they have and are always looking to snatch from another man's table."

Ela held up her hand to silence them. "This matter should be easy enough to resolve. The boundaries of the land were noted in the Domesday Book. We shall consult the records and determine the original boundary. We shall also consult the records for recorded sales of the properties in question to see if any part of the land has legally changed hands."

"I bought my farm in full from the previous owner," said Bertram Beck, the younger farmer.

"Rue the day he sold his good land to a stranger," blustered Crowder.

"I've made good use of my farm." Beck looked smug. "I have twice the flocks you do and better stock, too."

Crowder's arm twitched like he wanted to punch his young neighbor in the face.

"Silence." Ela held up her hand. This had deteriorated into a squabble, and the matter would not be resolved today. "Once the records are reviewed, Sir John"—she indicated Dacus, her deputy—"or I shall visit the property and determine the true location of the boundary. In the meantime please refrain from addressing the matter as I don't wish to hear of an assault charge being pressed against either one of you."

"But he's running pigs in my woods," protested Crowder. "And their rooting is destroying what was left of the ancient boundary ditch that marked the properties."

"There's no ditch." Bertram Beck looked bored. "Never was."

"There was a ditch and berm, dug who knows how long ago, running along the western edge of my property."

"And when do you believe this encroachment began?" Ela already found herself favoring Crowder.

Who suddenly looked sheepish. "I've been busy with my flocks these past few years and haven't studied that bit of woodland for a while. My hip pains me, and it's up a steep hill with a thick stand of brambles that—"

Ela held up her hand again to stop him. "I see. And what made you suddenly notice that the boundary was moved?"

"One of my sheep strayed and got stuck in a thicket up there. I had to climb up to free him, and I saw his woven willow fencing and his pigs rooting all over my land."

Bertram Beck appeared uninterested in the whole proceeding. He clearly thought he was in the right. Possibly because a man who neglected a border of his land for several years might just deserve to lose it to a more assiduous neighbor.

"Each man shall mind his business, and the pigs shall stay where they are for now," said Ela. "Within a week I shall visit the property myself we shall determine the true boundary."

Wilf Crowder looked like a keg about to explode, but perhaps he should have looked to his boundaries earlier. Old age was an affliction, but surely a son could walk the border for him. There was no excuse for such neglect. Ela had the boundaries of her own manors walked at least once every six months and the corners and edges marked with cut stone where the natural boundaries weren't obvious.

She looked over their heads, to where a distressed looking woman cradled an injured piglet in her arms. "Who's next?"

THE FOLLOWING DAY, Ela sat at the main table in the great hall, breaking bread with her children. Her son Stephen had just begun boasting about his new falcon's hunting prowess when Bertram Beck was announced.

He's going to attempt to bribe me, thought Ela. She'd learned that such attempts to buy favor were the norm, not the exception. She deliberately took another bite of mushroom tart and chewed it thoroughly, then sipped her watered wine, before rising to address him.

She walked across the hall to where he stood, waiting, cap on his head when it should have been in his hands. "Good morrow, my lady," said Beck with a deep bow.

"God's blessings upon you, Farmer Beck. What brings you here?" She kept her expression pleasant.

"It's about the matter of the boundary to my farm." His hand crept to the tooled purse that hung from his belt.

"I imagined it would be." It could be entertaining to watch how men approached such an awkward matter as paying for favors. Some had great skill and made the matter seem a natural business transaction or even a compliment. Most were like Beck and fumbled awkwardly, wondering how best to incriminate themselves without causing offense.

"I hope that the matter can be resolved without wasting your valuable time," he wheedled.

"Indeed."

"I imagine it would be a great inconvenience for you to ride all the way out to my farm when you're so busy being sheriff and all."

"Fortunately I enjoy an opportunity to ride in our glorious countryside." Winter had eased its icy grip on the land but the weather was brisk enough to enjoy a good pace without working her horse into a lather. If she had to sit in this hall all day, she'd lose her mind.

Beck blinked, blue eyes wide with alarm, hand now clutching his purse. "I thought, perhaps—" He stammered the last word. "That two pounds would save you the trouble of the journey." He pulled open his purse and reached inside, fingers rustling among the coins.

Two pounds was a good sum. More than most farmers would have at their disposal on any given day. Enough to raise her eyebrow. "Did you think you could buy my favor in this case, Farmer Beck?"

"I…I…" He pulled out his coins and started counting them.

"Put your coins away. The course of justice cannot be bought and paid for but must be determined by following the letter of the law."

His face fell. He clutched the coins in his fist. "Perhaps a donation to the poor of the parish?"

"A donation to the poor of the parish would no doubt be most welcome. I'm sure Bishop Poore could put your coin to good use for his school or the almshouses he's building."

Ela hoped that her reputation for being incorruptible would spread and she'd receive fewer of these proposals. On the other hand they did give her a good indication of who was honest and who was not.

Beck let the coins fall back into his purse. "So you'll be coming to look at the boundary?"

"Indeed I will, and I shall be on the alert for further attempts to pervert the course of justice." She lifted her chin and looked down the length of her nose. Beck, though sturdily built, wasn't much taller than her. "So beware of any attempts to disturb the ground and obfuscate the process."

"My pigs have already turned up the ground to a great degree, as pigs do," he mumbled.

"No doubt they have," she said drily. "But ancient boundaries are hard to obliterate. Good day to you."

Two days later, Ela set out with John Dacus and a phalanx of castle guards. She rode Freya, her gray horse and friend through many trials, and Dacus rode a big, sturdy bay whom he spoke to as if it were a person. The bay had a white blaze and four gleaming white stockings and clearly liked Dacus as much as he liked his horse. This warmed Ela to both of them immeasurably.

Dacus had been installed as her co-sheriff, not an unusual arrangement but one that she had initially opposed. It was so instinctive for men to defer to another man—instead of a woman—that she worried she'd end up being treated as his handmaid. Dacus, however, had quickly won her over with his kind, avuncular manner and by saying—in so many words—that even if they shared the title of sheriff, he considered himself her deputy.

A knight with battle experience, Sir John was a fine rider and had impressed her children with his falconry skills and swordsmanship. He'd cheered Ela with his willingness to engage with her young ones.

"The farms are up at the end of this lane, my lady," he called. "I studied the map, and it's the only way to get there without riding over the fields."

The fields were wet this early in the spring. A farmer wouldn't appreciate anyone riding across his land and leaving deep pocks in the mud, so they'd resolved to ride there by road.

They trotted along, bells jingling on their harness, breath visible in the cold air. As they topped a rise they saw a good-sized farmhouse hunkered along the road, weathered oak beams crusted with moss but with the thatch freshly laid and clean. The farmyard looked neat, with the chickens contained in one woven enclosure and the geese in another.

"Which farm is this?" asked Ela.

"Wilf Crowder's. Been here his whole life, from what I

hear." Dacus wasn't a native of Salisbury but he'd managed to familiarize himself with the surrounding area. "Has a good reputation as a husbandman and a fair dealer at the market."

"Yet has not the time to maintain the boundaries of his land."

Dacus rode closer to her. "That does strike me as odd, my lady. Would not a change of ownership on the property next door cause any man to check and defend his borders more closely?"

"Indeed it should," agreed Ela. "Though his excuse of old age and infirmity is not without merit. Does he have no son to take over the farm?"

"None living."

"Unfortunate. Perhaps he should take an apprentice who could one day inherit from him." Ela was still seeking homes for a small group of orphans she'd rescued from a child slaver. "But that's a matter for another day."

They rode up to his door, and he appeared out of a wattle-and-daub outbuilding and doffed his cap. "My lady."

She told him to lead the way, but his progress—on foot— was so slow that eventually she asked him to point to the disputed boundary and agreed to meet him at the upper portion of his land where it lay hidden in a copse of trees.

The leaf litter of the previous autumn had mostly faded into the soil, which had yet to be punctured by patches of spring shoots. The area of woodland spread out over an almost table-like area at the top of the hill that descended down into the neighboring farm. "There would be fine views from up here," observed Ela, "if not for the trees. It's almost as high as the castle mound." Between the trunks of oak and beech she could make out glimpses of the white walls of her castle shining in the morning sun across the fields.

As they rode through the woods she saw the boundary erected by Beck, a fence of stakes and woven branches. Past the fence, the trees were pollarded and some even felled, as well as the ground much disturbed by the foraging of pigs.

"You say there should be an ancient ditch here? It seems a strange place for one," said Ela to Dacus. "Surely a ditch should be in a low spot."

"According to the Domesday Book there was an ancient settlement up here." They reined their horses to a stop. "Hundreds of years old. The ditch was probably defensive like the one around your castle."

"That makes sense given the high location with good visibility over the area. It would make a good place for a fort, and if the ditch is as wide and deep as ours it should be easy to find the boundary. The hills and valleys around here are littered with the remains of our predecessors. I've heard of farmers ploughing up gold and gems as well as potsherds or the boss of an old shield."

The nearby remains of the great stone circle and the vast mound that her own castle stood on were a constant reminder that their land had been inhabited by an ancient race of men who'd left their mark all over the landscape.

Dacus commanded the guards—who'd been furnished with picks and shovels—to start digging in what looked to be the most likely place for the original boundary: the highest ridge with the best vantage point in all directions.

Bertram Beck came storming up the far side of the hill on his dappled gray horse as the men bit into the soil with their tools. "What are you doing?" He gestured at the men digging more than two hundred feet on his side of the erected fence. "This is my land!"

"We're here to determine whether it is or not," said Ela. "You're welcome to help with the digging."

"You should be digging on his side, not mine! If anything the boundary has encroached the other way."

"Hardly," said Ela. "It's clear to us that he hasn't so much as cut kindling up here in a decade. You, on the other hand, have been making tidy use of these woods."

"And why shouldn't I? It's a fine woodland and a crime to waste the excellent wood it provides."

Ela couldn't help but agree with him. If this wood lay on one of her manors she'd have men actively managing the growth for maximum productivity.

"His use or neglect of the property is not your concern, Farmer Beck. His ownership is. We seek the remains of a ditch buried beneath the surface. That's the legal boundary as it's recorded in the Domesday Book."

"There's nothing up here but trees and birds. I haven't found a single brick or timber."

"Sir John tells me that you're a newcomer to the area," said Ela. "Those of us who've spent our lives here are more familiar with the forts and barrows of our ancient ancestors. Rest assured that we'll find evidence of the former structure that marks the boundary."

The guards were set to digging in a variety of likely locations, each man with an axe to break the ground—not that the pigs hadn't done most of the work already—and a shovel to dig through the recently disturbed layers.

THE MATTER WAS NOT EASILY RESOLVED. One man turned up some shards of broken pottery, which, as was quickly observed, could be scattered anywhere and didn't indicate the presence of a boundary wall.

Another found the remains of an old well, which they realized was relatively recent, no more than fifty years old. The digging continued.

The third discovery proved even less helpful.

"I've found a skeleton," called one guard. Ela turned to see him holding up a leg bone. She quickly crossed herself.

"Put that back! It's disrespectful to the dead." She shuddered at the thought of someone plucking one of her leg bones from the soil a thousand years from now and holding it up to curious eyes.

"Surely they were heathens, my lady?" offered John Dacus softly. "And don't suffer the same compunctions as ourselves."

"I suppose you're right." Ela approached the spot, past the brow of the hill and probably on Beck's side of the true boundary. "Do dig carefully, though."

A skull, complete with teeth, stared up at her from the damp pit surrounded by freshly dug soil. Usually proud of her strong stomach, Ela found herself oddly unsettled by the sight. "I wonder if we should remove him to the cathedral yard and give him a decent burial."

Dacus looked at her. "Would his soul not be well settled wherever it may be? Valhalla perhaps?"

"But such a place is a delusion," said Ela. "His soul must be traipsing the valleys of hell. Perhaps we can speed his passage to Heaven." She'd want someone to do the same for her if she'd lived her life in ignorance.

They agreed that the body should be removed, and one of the soldiers unfolded a blanket on the ground to collect the bones.

"If treasure's found, it's on my land," called Bertram Beck.

"If treasure's found it can be claimed by the king," retorted Ela. "And the entire purpose of our visit is to determine where your land ends and Wilf Crowder's begins. We've not yet determined the boundary."

Crowder stood silent, not looking at all optimistic. Ela could easily see how he'd have trouble getting up here. The steep chalk hill leading up to this area of high ground was better suited to sheep and goats than old farmers. The approach from Beck's side was more gradual, across a field planted with winter rye.

Ela could see that Beck managed every inch of his land with care. "Perhaps, if the land does turn out to be part of Wilf Crowder's farm, you could offer him a sum to part with it."

"I'd rather give up my own spleen than sell a single rod of my land to him! This farm was passed down to me by my father." Crowder crossed his still-burly arms over his chest. "I'll not let this arrogant young whippersnapper look down on me from the top of it."

Ela sighed. "Once the body is safely disinterred, we'll locate the boundary and it can be marked with stakes until you erect a new fence."

The skeleton, removed from the ground bone by bone, grew back into a fleshless man on the red and gray woven cloth. "The bones are well preserved for a man who must have been dead for centuries," observed Ela. The sight of them being plucked from the damp earth and arranged together—finger bone by finger bone—like a child's puzzle, unnerved her.

"Perhaps it's the body of a great king who's lain here in state among nature's glories, waiting for this perfect moment for us to find him," expounded Dacus, his brown eyes shining. "And God, in his wisdom, knew that bringing us here today—"

The guard doing the digging let out a blistering curse and jumped back, causing Ela to spook like a horse. He looked up at her, face suddenly white. "This body ain't ancient at all."

CHAPTER 2

*T*he guard lifted something from the soil. Ela could see it wasn't another bone. It glimmered slightly in the sunlight shining through the leafless branches of the trees above them.

"What is it?"

"A knife. And not an ancient one either. It's got a wooden handle in good repair."

"That'd be long gone if it was five hundred years old," exclaimed Dacus. "Let me see it."

The guard handed Dacus the knife and he wiped it off on the inside of his cloak hem, revealing a blade flecked with rust from its time underground.

Ela glanced at Bertram Beck, who looked irritated. Then at Wilf Crowder, who looked alarmed. "Did you know this was up here?" she asked.

"The knife? I've never seen it before."

"Are you sure?" Ela held out her hand and Dacus placed the cleaned knife in it. It had a sturdy wooden handle with carved finger grips and a medium-length blade. Apart from a somewhat unusual finger grips, it was the kind of knife any farmer might have for his daily tasks—anything from slitting a lamb's throat to slicing an pear. She held it up for Crowder to see.

He shuffled forward and peered at it. "I've seen that knife before." He looked up at Ela. "It belonged to Oddo."

"Who's Oddo?"

"The man what owned the land before this one." He jutted his chin at Beck. "The one that sold it to him."

Ela blinked. If this knife belonged to the farmer who'd once owned the land, then perhaps he'd been killed with it and these were Oddo's bones spread out bare and white on the cloth at their feet. Perhaps Bertram Beck had killed him and buried him here before claiming the land he lay in. "We must summon the coroner."

GILES HAUGHTON RODE up the hill on his bay palfrey just before midday. Ela was glad of her fur-lined cloak given the length of time she'd now spent on this windy hilltop in the March cold.

"A dead body?" He jumped down from his horse and removed his hat, revealing his silvered hair. "Yet the hue and cry has not been raised?"

"The time for urgent action has unfortunately passed." Ela indicated the skeleton laid out on the cloth. "At first we thought we'd found the bones of an ancient up here on this site of an old barrow or hill fort, but the discovery of a relatively new knife makes that unlikely."

Haughton squatted near the bones and surveyed them. He grasped the skull—teeth still in it—and turned it over in his hands. "Ancient bones wouldn't be in as good a state as this. I've been called in before for bones that turned out to be a hundred years old or more, but these are likely less than ten years in the ground. Were there no clothes or burial cloth?"

Ela glanced back to the guard who'd been quietly excavating the hole all this time.

"Nothing in here yet but the bones and the knife," he said gruffly.

"Perhaps they disintegrated in the ground like leaves," suggested Ela.

"Not this fast," said Haughton. "There'd be traces left at least. Most likely someone didn't want to throw away good clothes. Or his clothes could have been removed to hide his identity. Without garments it's hard to tell a king from a peasant, I'm afraid."

"We've found a knife." Ela asked the guard to hand it to him. "Buried with him. I'd imagine it's the murder weapon. And Wilf Crowder here says this knife belonged to his neighbor Oddo the Bald, who sold the land to Bertram Beck some eight years ago."

"Oddo, aye, I remember him. A good man and well respected at the market. I've bought a ham off him more times than I care to admit." He looked at the bones. "I suppose there's a good chance this is him, then. How was his absence not noticed?"

"He sold this land to me eight years ago, fair and square," protested Beck, who'd been pacing impatiently on what he claimed was his land, eliciting annoyed squeals from his pigs. "He was alive and well. Got too old to farm and moved away."

Haughton frowned. "I don't remember him being that old. Younger than I am right now, I reckon. Then again, that's not saying much. Where did he move to?"

"What do I know? I'm not his keeper. I paid thirty pounds for the place with a hundred head of sheep on it."

"What did you do before you became a farmer?" asked Ela curiously.

"I was a man of business." Even he didn't sound convinced.

"Where?" asked Ela.

"Up north."

Ela felt the hair on the back of her neck prickle with irritation at his evasive attitude. "I've spent considerable time in the north, accompanying my husband at the side of his brother the late King John. Could you be more specific?"

"West Yorkshire," he mumbled.

"Which town?"

"Beeston."

"And why did you leave?" It was hardly the norm for anyone to just pack their belongings and move to another part of the country.

Bertram Beck paused, lips pursed, for a moment. Ela could tell he was trying to think of a good lie.

"My father was hanged for something he didn't do."

Ela found herself startled into silence. If that was a lie it was an outrageous one. And as sheriff she could verify it quite easily with a few days' notice. "And how did that event bring you to Salisbury?"

"I traveled for a while and eventually I settled into the Bull and Bear in Salisbury. When Oddo the Bald put his farm up for sale, I bought it."

"What was your father's name?"

"I prefer not to say." His confidence had returned.

"You're a murder suspect. You'll tell me his name or spend the night in the jail."

He frowned. "Everard le Bec."

Ela didn't recognize the name, but from the sound of it he was likely a minor noble.

"And what was he accused of?"

16

"I don't even know. It was all lies. They wanted his land. I left before they could find something to hang me for." She could hear anger seething in his voice. Strangely enough she believed him.

And she'd certainly heard of sheriffs who'd wage a war of intimidation on someone to take his property by force. Her reviled predecessor, Simon de Hal, for example.

"I see. So Oddo was alive and well when he sold the property to you?"

"He could hardly have sold it to me if he wasn't." His arrogance had returned, and again Ela felt that prickle of dislike for Bertram Beck. Had he created the opportunity for the sale by some foul means?

Ela turned to Wilf Crowder, his neighbor. "What do you know of this sale?"

"What would I know? Tried to buy the land from old Oddo myself more than once over the years. Told me he'd rather be dead than sell to me." He gave a pointed look at the corpse. "Apparently he got his wish."

Ela blinked. "You were enemies?"

Crowder let out a sharp guffaw. "We never came to blows. I'd say we were rivals. Grew the same crops, raised the same animals, sold them in the same markets. I will say that he never tried to encroach on my property by moving the boundary. I suppose I should have appreciated him for that." Now he shot a glare at Beck, who returned it with interest.

"If you wanted his land and he wouldn't sell to you, that might give you a motive for murder," suggested John Dacus, who'd been watching quietly.

Crowder laughed. "Except that I still don't have the land, so what good did it do me?" The old farmer certainly didn't look too worried at this sudden charge of murder. He seemed to find the circumstance more amusing than anything else. "If anything, young Beck here has more of a motive. Turns up here out of nowhere, and buys himself a fine farm that just happens to come on the market? All a bit too convenient if you ask me."

"How many years ago did you take over this farm?" Ela asked Beck.

"Eight years." His sarcasm was gone. "But I had nothing to do with this and no idea this body was up here. Do you think I'd have let my pigs root around in this soil if I knew a body was buried just under the surface?"

"The body was down too deep for pigs to disturb it," observed Ela. "But perhaps disputing the boundary and invoking men with shovels up here to examine the soil would be unwise if you knew there was evidence of murder concealed here."

"See! I didn't know."

"But you're admitting that you moved the boundary?" Ela saw an opportunity to resolve at least one issue.

Beck hesitated for a moment, as if trying to decide which way to incriminate himself. "This is my land."

"In all fairness it was Wilf Crowder who started the boundary dispute," interjected Dacus. "He brought the complaint to the castle and Beck turned up to dispute it."

"Which tells you that I didn't kill anyone," cut in Crowder, who'd been standing silent and stolid this whole time.

Ela studied Wilf Crowder. His back was bent from years of hard labor, but he looked a strong and sturdy man, capable of killing another if he wanted to badly enough. And eight years ago was a long time at his age. He'd have been a man in middle age at that time. "You admit that Oddo the Bald was not a friend of yours."

"I do. He knew I wanted to buy the land from him, and he sold it to another. What friend would do that?"

"And how do you have such a stash of riches to buy the neighbor's farm?" she asked. His clothes, though good, were worn and discolored by the sun and soil. He didn't look like a man with coffers of silver buried under his hearth.

"I've worked hard and saved all my life. And my father before me. He tried to buy the land from Oddo's father, but he wouldn't sell either."

An idea occurred to Ela. "If Beck here were to hang for murder and his land go up for sale, would you try to buy it?" Perhaps Crowder—knowing the body was here—had seized an opportunity to put Beck within reach of the noose for it.

Crowder looked thoughtful for a moment. "Now? Nay. I'm too old. I can barely manage the farm I have." He sighed. "But I'm damned if I'll let that young whippersnapper run his pigs over the land I do own."

Ela wondered how many years those pigs had been doing just that before he noticed them. "Farming is a hard life for an older man. Do you have plans to retire?"

"And do what? Sit in a chair and whittle myself a new handle for a knife I'll never do more than pare an apple with? I'd rather drop dead up here chasing a stray sheep."

Understandable. Ela didn't much relish the prospect of a life of idle contemplation either, even if it would offer unlimited opportunities for prayer and meditation. She recognized this as a weakness in her character but understood his feelings well.

"If you have enough money saved that you could buy a neighboring farm, perhaps you could hire a young man or two to do the more demanding parts of your work?" she suggested.

"I've done that in the past, and they're nothing but trouble. No, I'd rather do things my way, even if I'm slower than I was."

Ela realized she'd strayed off course again. They were here to determine a boundary, and this body had upended their plans. She turned to the group of soldiers a stone's throw away who'd been digging while they talked. "Has the digging unearthed the original boundary ditch of the barrow up here yet?"

"Aye, my lady," said one soldier, a man in middle age with a weathered face. "The ditch is right here." He pointed to the disturbed ground at his feet. "Easy enough to see when you hack back at the brush."

Ela picked her way through the wooded tangle to the area of excavation. Sure enough, cutting away the snarl of brambles and straggling saplings and raking aside years of accumulated leaf litter had revealed the contours of a distinct ditch twenty feet wide and at least ten feet deep, running along the side of the hill and curving around it.

She looked at her co-sheriff. "Sir John, do you agree that this appears to be the boundary ditch of the ancient earthwork?"

Dacus stared at the sloping ground, where the leaf litter and the dark earth it crumbled into were now scraped back to reveal the native white chalk beneath. "It certainly seems that way."

"This ditch is the boundary between the two farms." She looked at Beck. "And amply demonstrates that you moved the boundary five or more rods to the south of where it should be. We shall mark the trees so you don't make the same mistake again."

"And don't cut the trees, neither!" commanded Wilf Crowder, who stood some distance away. "Does he get no fine or punishment for taking and despoiling my land?"

"If you knew when the trespass started, perhaps you could charge him a lease fee," said Ela.

"But he doesn't, because he hasn't been up here in the entire eight years I've owned the farm," said Beck. He looked at Crowder with disdain. The younger man with his thatch of light hair didn't seem much cowed by being discovered in his theft of what likely amounted to almost an acre of land, in a long strip along the boundary. Perhaps he felt entitled according to the childhood adage of *finders keepers, losers weepers*.

Truth be told the laws of society sometimes operated along those principles—in the siege of a castle, for instance.

"Sir John and I will discuss the matter of punishment for the theft of this land." She didn't want him to think he'd simply get away with it. That might encourage him to try it again. "In the meantime, we have the more pressing matter of a dead body in our midst."

"A murdered body," rumbled Giles Haughton. "Because the man hardly stripped himself naked and fell on his own knife up here in the forest."

"How can we be sure it's his knife?" asked Ela. "Or even if this is Oddo the Bald?"

"It does seem likely that it's him," said Haughton, rising from the body. "Given the location and the fact that he disappeared from these parts at the time Beck took over this farm." The body lay on land now owned by Beck.

"But if he sold his land he might have simply moved elsewhere," argued Ela.

"He might have. Or he might not have had the opportunity." Haughton tilted his chin at Beck. "It would be my recommendation to arrest this man."

Beck paled.

Ela hated arresting people. To deprive a man of his freedom was a responsibility almost akin to taking his life in her estimation. Especially since conditions in the dungeon lent themselves to sickness and premature death. And putting a farmer in the jail meant letting his farm go to ruin and presented the problem of what to do with his livestock while he was locked up.

Also, although she respected Haughton's accumulated

wisdom, she'd noticed that sometimes it made him too quick to jump to a convenient conclusion.

"We're assuming this body belongs to Oddo the Bald—just as we're assuming the knife is his—based on the conviction of his neighbor Farmer Crowder. We must find out the truth by means other than hearsay."

"'Tis a shame no skin or hair remains," said John Dacus. "The lack of the latter seems like it would be good identification based on the man's name."

"Can you tell how long he's lain here?" asked Ela of Haughton.

"I'd say he's been here no less than six years. It would take that long for all the flesh to turn into earth. If he were in a coffin the process would be arrested and he might still have skin and hair. Contact with the moist ground speeds up the process of decomposition."

"Whoever it is has lain here for years, and no one raised the hue and cry over his absence." Ela looked at Wilf Crowder. "Did you know of your neighbor's intention to sell up and leave?"

Crowder shrugged. "We weren't on speaking terms."

"Did he have no children who might have expected to inherit?"

"He had three daughters and a son. Where they are now, I have no idea," said Crowder.

"We must find them. It's odd that he wouldn't pass the land to his son. Was his son not much of a farmer?"

"How would I know?" Wilf Crowder looked irritated by this line of questioning. "As you can see the brow of this hill separates our farms so I can't even see his unless I climb up here. And I wasn't calling on Oddo for a jug of ale."

"We must bring the skeletal remains of Oddo's body back to the mortuary for examination. Perhaps you can determine the mode of death."

Haughton looked amused. "With not an ounce of flesh left on his bones to examine and a sharp knife found buried just inches away, I don't think there's much to discover."

Dacus also looked like he was about to chuckle, then he glanced at Ela and thought better of it. Both Crowder and Beck appeared to hold their breath. As well they might, since she had—admittedly scant—grounds to arrest either or both of them on suspicion of murder.

"Neither of you must leave Wiltshire for any reason." She stared at Beck. "Which means you must not go back to Yorkshire or travel from our shire on any pretext, including trade."

Bertram Beck scowled. "For how long? I take my pigs to the market in Southampton."

"You had better find a nearer market for your pigs," she retorted. "Or face arrest." Beck had already proven himself a man who felt that laws were for other people.

"And the same goes for you, Wilf Crowder."

"Where would I go?" he lifted his gnarled hands as if holding up an empty basket. "I was born on this land and I intend to die here."

SOLDIERS MARKED the trees with crosshatches from an axe before Ela, Haughton and Dacus turned to ride down across Wilf Crowder's farm and back to the castle.

A veil of cloud had settled over the winter sun casting an eerie glow over the landscape.

"I know you think I should have arrested Beck," said Ela to Haughton once they were out of earshot of Crowder's house.

"It just seems so likely that Beck killed Oddo in order to take over his farm."

"We have no evidence of that whatsoever." Ela hated when people jumped to conclusions. "We haven't had a chance to examine the documents for the sale. What if it's all in order?"

"And what if it isn't? Beck was a stranger to these parts. He just turned up and moved in and no one asked any questions. A few short years later he's so confident that he's got away with it he starts to break yet more laws by taking his neighbor's land. People who commit one crime will often commit another, in my experience."

"I appreciate your hard earned wisdom, but I take very seriously the prospect of depriving a man of his liberty." She looked at Dacus, who'd said little this whole time. "Sir John, what are your thoughts on the matter?"

John cleared his throat and looked awkward, which gave Ela the idea that he agreed with Haughton. "I'm not sure, my lady."

"We don't even know if it's Oddo's body!" she exclaimed, growing exasperated.

"That does seem likely, though," said Haughton mildly, looking ahead down the road.

A horse appeared round the bend at full canter, which startled all of their horses into shying. Ela recognized the rider as a young guard from the palace. He slowed his horse to a trot and hurried up to them.

"Edgar, what's amiss?"

"It's Hilda, my lady. She's gone into labor."

"God be praised." The poor girl was so heavy she could barely catch her breath this past month.

"Something's gone wrong, my lady, and the midwife is too ill to come. They sent me to fetch you."

Ela's heart clenched. "Go fetch the doctor!" She gathered up her reins and cantered all the way back to the castle with fear pounding in her veins.

CHAPTER 3

*T*he birth of Hilda's baby had been anticipated for nine very long months. Ela's lady's maid, Hilda was not the hardest worker or even competent, but she'd earned Ela's affection with her natural curiosity and ebullience. She was also the niece of Sibel, Ela's trusted longtime lady's maid, who'd recently left to marry. When Hilda became pregnant by a much older male guest in Ela's house —who was then murdered—Ela vowed to protect the girl and her baby as much from of a debt of loyalty to Sibel as for her affection for the girl. She'd even managed—through legal machinations—to secure her dead lover's manor for Hilda and her baby, since the unborn child was the manor's rightful heir.

If it lived.

The castle courtyard bustled with its usual activity as Ela rode up, perspiring in her cloak. She jumped down from her horse and handed it to a guard. Albert the porter parted the fray for her as they hurried toward the tower of family rooms, where a chamber had been set aside for Hilda to deliver her baby.

"What's amiss, Albert?" she asked as they climbed the stairs two at a time.

"I'm not sure, my lady." At the top of the stairs, a scream pierced the air. The door to the chamber stood open and Ela rushed in to find Hilda on her hands and knees on the bed, her long light brown hair loose. "Help me," she cried. "The pain—" Her words broke off into a terrible scream as she collapsed into the bed.

Ela's looked around in a panic. Hilda's labor hadn't started when she left the house this morning, although that was hours ago. Elsie, her other maid, stood white-faced in the corner, looking like she was about to burst into tears. "Where's the midwife?" Ela asked her.

"She broke her leg, my lady," stammered Elsie.

"Has Sibel been sent for?" Elsie stared at her. Ela turned to Albert. "Send a messenger with a horse to bring Sibel here at once."

Hilda had stopped screaming and risen back into the strange hands-and-knees posture. She peered up at Ela again through strands of sweat-soaked hair. "Help me," she said softly.

Ela removed her cloak and threw it on a chair, since Elsie seemed to have turned to stone. She plucked a linen cloth from a pile at the end of the bed and wiped the girl's forehead. "I've sent for the doctor. He should be here soon. When did your pains start?"

"I don't know—" Hilda gasped. "A long time ago. It hurts so much I can't breathe."

"I know, my sweet, I've been there eight times. You'll get through it." So far nothing seemed amiss, except for the missing midwife. "Who else has attended you?"

"Cook was here. Then she—" Hilda paused to scream, then pant, before she continued. "Then she muttered something under her breath and ran away."

What? That made no sense. Cook was a wise older woman who'd born four children of her own. Why would she run off? "Would you mind if I take a look at you?"

Hilda stared at her. Ela walked around the bed and lifted the girl's shift to see if the baby's head was crowning. She half expected to see the head nearly out, since the girl seemed in such an advanced stage of labor.

But it wasn't. Everything was closed up tight like the castle vault. Ela swallowed. "Hilda, dear, can you lie on your back for a moment?"

Hilda's response was another blood curdling scream, followed by more panting and more screaming. The sound of Elsie's sobs rose to join it. "Elsie, can you go find Cook?"

She pushed Hilda onto her side and lifted her gown to examine her belly. With hands used to feeling the position of her own babies, she quickly realized that Hilda's little one was not yet turned head down.

Hilda stared up at her, gray-blue eyes wide with terror. "Am I going to die?"

Ela swallowed. "Of course not." They could turn it. At least she hoped they could. "Where's the doctor?" she called to Becca, another maid and the only person left nearby. "And fetch Petronella." Her oldest daughter still living at home was inexperienced but sensible and kept her head in a crisis.

"Can you stand up and walk around? That might help the baby to drop into position." Trota of Salerno recommended this for difficult births in her book on medicine for women. Ela had a prized copy of the text that her husband had bought for her in London.

Once again Hilda's scream ripped through her. Why was she having contractions, and so hard, when her womb hadn't opened yet? Nothing seemed right about this situation. Ela wanted to scream herself, but that would hardly help Hilda's nerves.

When the contraction passed, Ela tried to help Hilda upright. Her feet tangled inside her gown and she almost fell, but finally managed to stand. She clung to Ela, shaking like a willow. "Help me."

"I'm trying, my love. Take a step." Together, they lurched forward. "Now another one." They managed another two before Hilda doubled over with a shattering scream, almost knocking her to the stone floor. Ela held her as her contraction shook her from head to toe, wringing her out like a sponge. As she felt it ebb from the girl's body, and prepared to grasp a few moments relief, she sensed something hot and wet on her toes.

Hilda's water had broken.

"I'm bleeding," stammered Hilda. She too noticed the quantity of warm liquid running down her legs.

"It's not blood, it's the fluid from around the baby. It's a normal part of the birth." But it also meant that time was running out. Once the water broke, the delivery had to proceed fast or her humors could become unbalanced and make her ill. "Let's walk another step." Where was that damn doctor?

Footsteps on the stairs heralded the arrival of Cook, red-faced and carrying a steaming jug. Elsie followed behind her with fresh linens.

"The baby's head isn't down," said Ela.

"I reckoned so," said Cook brusquely. "So I went to brew a batch of marigold and flax to help relax her muscles."

"Good idea." Though she wasn't sure how much of a good idea it was to leave the suffering girl alone with only other striplings who'd never borne a baby.

They wrapped the steaming hot poultice in fresh linens and laid it over Hilda's huge belly. She writhed and protested at the heat, but Ela and Cook reassured her it would help her baby settle into position.

Would it? Only God knew the fate of Hilda and her baby.

Petronella stood against the wall, gazing at Hilda in horror. "Petronella, please pray a rosary for the smooth delivery of Hilda's baby and the health of both mother and child." Ela said it brightly as if it were a perfectly natural labor room request. Cook was the only person there old and experienced enough to know it wasn't.

"Of course, Mama." Petronella settled herself quietly into a corner on her knees and began murmuring the familiar and reassuring words under her breath.

Hilda screamed her way through several more contractions, and the baby remained stubbornly stuck in the wrong position. Where was the doctor? "Is there not another midwife to be found?" Ela asked Cook, who was unusually quiet.

"Our one from the town is laid up with a broken leg."

"Is there only one?" This seemed hard to believe.

"There used to be two others, but they've moved up the road to New Salisbury."

Of course. Half the businesses that served the village inside the castle walls had picked up their casks and barrels and trundled down the road to the spacious new town. "Stay with her."

Ela hurried outside and gave detailed instructions to Albert, who still hovered there anxiously, to send multiple messengers out to New Salisbury in search of a midwife and, if possible, to return with more than one. In a situation like this it was hard to predict who'd have the required expertise to turn the baby before it died in the womb.

Especially now that Hilda's water had broken.

"And please find out where the doctor is, then report back." In the worst-case scenario—or perhaps the next-to-worst-case scenario—the doctor might cut the baby from Hilda's womb. Hilda wouldn't survive such an operation, but

it would be better to save the baby than for both of them
to die.

Ela crossed herself and murmured a Hail Mary along
with Petronella, trying to keep her expression calm and
steady for poor Hilda.

"Am I going to die?" the girl asked again tearfully.

"Of course not, my pet. But it can't hurt to pray for God's
help." She wondered if they should call for a priest. "How
long ago did your pains begin?"

"Hours," rasped Hilda.

"Before the bells for Sext," muttered Cook. "It has been a
few hours."

*I'm not going to call for a priest. She's going to live and so will
her baby.*

"Let me have another look at you, Hilda. We'll see how
things are developing." Hilda's water breaking should have
helped her womb open.

The girl's gown was already lifted to apply the poultice. A
linen napkin covered her private parts. Ela moved the napkin
aside and peered in between the girl's legs. Almost immediately Hilda began to writhe and strain and scream with the
force of her next contraction. Ela felt between her legs, and
tried to hide her fear when her hands wrapped not around
the smooth ball of the baby's head but the sharp crook of its
tiny elbow. It was presenting arm first.

"Cook, have you seen a midwife turn a baby?"

"Never. Can't be done." Cook's red face had a terrible
expression. Usually irascible and cantankerous, she looked
like she was about to burst into tears.

She thinks Hilda's going to die.

"I've seen it done when I was a girl in Normandy,"
insisted Ela. "The midwife turned it with her hands." She'd
been a child and didn't actually see it happen, but all the
women in the castle talked of little else for a week.

But she didn't know how, and where was the doctor?

Ela removed the rapidly cooling poultice and the cloths wrapping it, and palpated Hilda's belly, determining the exact position of the baby. Things had improved. The head now pointed down, but down and out to Hilda's left side. Instead of the crown of its head, the elbow of its left arm jutted down into Hilda's pelvis. Its legs lay curled together and tucked up into the right side of Hilda's belly.

"The head is here, see? Not so far from where it needs to be." But how to move the elbow without alarming Hilda? "Let me reach in and feel around a little."

"Is my baby all right?"

"Yes," Ela answered before she was confident of the answer. She hadn't actually felt the baby move. Labor and delivery could be quite literally a fight between life and death and keeping the girl's spirits up was half the battle.

She reached for the tiny elbow again and pinched it gently, hoping to spark some reaction in the baby. Nothing.

Hilda cried out as another contraction wrung her out like a rag. Ela waited for it to pass, as she couldn't move the baby while Hilda's whole belly clenched tight as a drum.

If the baby was dead, Hilda would lose the manor at Fernlees, since her only claim to it was through her baby. Her reputation would be forever tarnished by an unwed pregnancy—diminishing her marriage prospects—and she'd have no baby to love.

Ela cast a glance at Petronella, praying faithfully in the corner, eyes closed, lips moving and fingers sliding over her plain wooden rosary.

Hilda fell back, gasping, as the contraction loosened its cruel grip on her. Ela quickly bent over her and thrust her fingers back inside the girl. She'd dilated further, which would be a good sign if the right part of the baby was coming out of the opening.

31

Ela managed to reach her fingers in far enough to grasp the baby's arm. Focusing all her energy on it, she pushed—slowly but firmly—trying to guide the baby's arm away from the opening.

"Cook, place your hand on the baby's head,"

Cook hurried into position, looking flustered. "How do I know where the head is?"

"It's right here." Ela put her hand on it. "Now very gently guide it toward the opening."

Cook looked doubtful. "What if the cord is wrapped around its neck?"

If the cord is wrapped around its neck they'll both die. Ela banished the thought. "It isn't. At least I don't think so."

"It might be. That's why she's in so much pain and the baby won't come down."

Ela froze. She had a point.

"Let me feel for the cord." Ela had seen her cowman stick his entire arm inside a cow and grab hold of a stuck calf. Surely she could feel for the cord around the baby's neck? Of course Hilda's opening wasn't the same size as that of a cow weighing twelve hundredweight.

Gritting her teeth, Ela reached her fingers in as far as she could. Luckily she had small hands and, reaching around above Hilda's left hip, she could feel the baby's shoulder, then its neck. And no cord.

"The cord isn't around its neck, praise be to God. Try to gently push the head down. She's opening up and we need to get the head into position to come out."

Her hand fully immersed inside Hilda, Ela gripped the wet baby as best she could and pulled, trying to get the arm away from the opening so the head could come down toward it.

"It moved!" exclaimed Cook. Ela pulled with all her

might, trying to jostle the baby to the side. Was the baby moving of its own accord or because of their movements?

As she asked herself the question the baby's tiny arm pulled backward from her, out of the dilated opening, and Ela quickly moved her hand and shoved it to Hilda's right side as hard and fast as she could. The slippery flesh slid over her palm as the baby turned and the elbow popped back up into Hilda's belly.

"Yes!" exclaimed Ela. "Push Cook, keep pushing!" The cook, face beetroot with distress and exertion, pushed on the baby's head with both hands as if she were kneading bread. Ela palpated Hilda's belly, trying to shift the baby's body enough for the head to descend down into the opening. "We're getting close, perhaps—" She was about to suggest that Hilda stand up to assist the baby in descending, when Hilda was gripped by the cruel fist of another contraction.

"Your baby's moving, Hilda." She heard the emotion in her own voice. "It wants to come out. It won't be long now."

Hilda's cries rang through the room. Even Petronella looked up from her prayers for a moment before lowering her head and continuing. Ela kept her hands on Hilda's stomach, trying to keep the baby from shifting back into the position they'd just moved it from.

As soon as the contraction subsided, she wiped her hands on a piece of clean linen. "Rise up, Hilda. Let's get you up and walking again."

"I can't," protested Hilda.

"Yes, you can," retorted Cook. "With us here to help you." She and Ela lifted the girl up and, supporting her under each armpit, they managed to raise her heavily to her feet on the wood floor.

"Take a step," implored Ela. "Your baby is trying to come out of your womb and we need to help it. Babies have been making this same journey since Eve's first delivery, and yours will find its way." She wanted to convince herself as much as Hilda.

Hilda winced with every step. "I'm being punished for my sins," she moaned.

Quite possibly, thought Ela. "Every woman since Eve has said the same," she said instead. Poor Hilda had been tempted down the path to sin by a worn-out knight who most certainly knew better. Ela sometimes wondered if Eve really talked Adam into eating the apple or if it was actually his idea and she just quietly took the blame. "You're young and strong. You'll get through it."

Another contraction buckled Hilda's knees. "Let me check you again." They helped her back onto the bed, and as soon as the contraction subsided, Ela lifted her shift and felt around her belly and in between her legs. "The head is down and in the opening!" she cried with relief. "Everything is going to be fine!"

At that moment she heard a flurry of footsteps on the stairs and Albert announced the arrival of local doctor Philip Goodwin, an older man with years of experience and a long, kind face beneath his thick white hair. "Good day, my lady," he said with a slight bow. "I came as fast as I could. How is she progressing?"

"Rapidly. The baby was upside down, but it's now turned into the right position."

"Babies have a way of doing that. They just like to give everyone a good fright first." The doctor peered between Hilda's legs—which seemed awfully inappropriate, him being a man. Ela had never needed a doctor at her deliveries and was eternally grateful for that right now. "The head is crowning." He looked up at Hilda. "Are you ready to have a baby?"

Poor Hilda, exhausted and wrung out already, didn't manage a reply.

"Let's keep her walking around slowly," suggested Ela. She didn't want Hilda to lie down and have her progress slow down. Her fierce contractions had already wrung the strength out of her. It would be better to get the baby out of her as soon as possible and let her rest.

Hilda's screams rent the air again. The doctor, to his credit, knew all the right soothing things to murmur. Then suddenly her moans grew deeper.

"Do you want to push?" asked Ela.

Hilda made an affirmative groan, and they helped her back up onto the bed. "Wait for your next contraction, then push with all your might," said Ela.

"I'm not sure why I'm needed here," said the doctor mildly. "You seem to have the situation well in hand."

"I'm glad of that, to be sure. When I sent for you I was miles away studying a boundary dispute in a wood. I didn't know what to expect. And when I got here the poor girl was all alone. The midwife has a broken leg and the cook had gone to make a poultice."

Hilda's energy for screaming seemed to have no limits. She screamed her way through every contraction, and now, with the baby's head crowning, she screamed her way in between them as well.

Finally the baby's head emerged. Ela held Hilda's hand as she bellowed. The shoulders followed, and suddenly the baby all but popped out—red and shiny—into the doctor's waiting hands. Hilda collapsed back on the bed like she'd just been clubbed.

"It's a boy!" exclaimed the doctor. "A fine, healthy boy." The doctor slapped the baby's slippery bottom, and it let out a yell of protest.

"You have a son," Ela said softly to Hilda.

A tiny smile crossed the girl's mouth. "His name is Thomas," she whispered. "Thomas Drogo Blount."

Ela frowned. She didn't want this bright young life named after his father, a scoundrel by any account, if an amiable one. But she didn't want to quarrel with Hilda now. "He's lovely. And so big."

The doctor cut the cord, then Cook took the baby and wrapped him in a length of linen. She wiped his face with water from a jug on the floor. "He's a boisterous one," she said with a smile. "And has a head of hair already. Just look at him!" The baby kicked against his linen covering.

"I'm so tired," said Hilda.

"You must nurse him," said Cook, bringing the baby closer.

"Maybe later."

"You really should nurse him now," said Ela. "It will help you expel the placenta."

"The what?" Hilda's eyes wouldn't stay open.

"The afterbirth. It has to come out as well." Ela never relaxed after a delivery until the afterbirth came safely out in one piece. She'd heard too many stories of women delivering a fine baby, then bleeding to death in the hours afterwards. "And Cook's right. Nursing somehow makes it easier."

Ela unlaced the top of Hilda's shift, and Cook put the baby at the girl's breast. The infant instinctively rooted for her nipple and quickly latched on. Hilda winced and looked like she wished the baby would just leave her alone.

"Put your arms around him, my dear," said Cook gently.

"I'm too tired." Hilda's eyes didn't open.

"Welcome to motherhood," said Cook. "Only a few more years and you'll get a good night's sleep again." She and Ela laughed.

Hilda managed to wrap her arms around the baby, and her eyes cracked open enough to gaze on him with reassuring maternal affection. "He is handsome isn't he?"

"He is," said Ela.

"And now I really am mistress of Fernlees."

"Indeed you are, and young Thomas" — Ela was already resigning herself to the name— "is its little master. I hope you'll be very happy there."

"I know I shall." Hilda looked up at Ela, her eyes slate blue in the dim light. "And all thanks to you, my lady."

At that moment Sibel arrived, summoned from New Salisbury, and with her husband behind her. She exclaimed with joy at the sight of the baby, and Hilda alive and well. "We were so worried. We heard something had gone wrong."

"The baby was head-up," said Ela. "But he turned himself at the last moment."

"It's a boy!" Sibel gazed at the baby, then kissed Hilda on the forehead. "And he's a sturdy one. Well done my pet."

"Do you think my mam will come visit him?" said Hilda drowsily.

Ela froze. Hilda's parents hadn't spoken a word to her since they'd learned of her unwed pregnancy. Her mother was Sibel's sister. Ela glanced at Sibel.

"I'll be sure to tell her the happy news, and I hope she will." Sibel's nervous expression suggested that this was by no means a certainty.

The doctor produced a small phial of frankincense to provoke sneezing in Hilda, with the promise that it would help expel the placenta. After some time, the placenta passed and the doctor pronounced himself satisfied with Hilda's condition and went away.

Cook returned to the kitchen, and Sibel and Elsie washed Hilda with cool water from a fresh jug.

Dusk had fallen while Hilda labored. Servants brought lanterns to hang on the wall, and Petronella offered to stay with Hilda and keep her company. Ela went to her room, where Becca, another serving girl, lit candles then helped her wash and change into fresh clothes.

Thus refreshed, Ela descended the stairs and headed for the great hall, hoping there'd soon be something to eat despite Cook's long absence from the kitchen. But when she walked into the hall her thoughts were interrupted by the sound of a man's raised voice.

Ela recognized Wilf Crowder, who she'd left on his hill earlier that day.

A furious Wilf lifted a fist in the air. "He's only moved the bloody river!"

CHAPTER 4

"Guards!" Ela was in no mood to be yelled at by an angry farmer. He needed to respect the peace of her hall. Besides, the evening was no time for business of this sort.

She had the guards walk him over to one side of the hall and seat him at a table where some soldiers were rolling dice. She'd instructed Gerald Deschamps, commander of the garrison troops, that that the soldiers must comport themselves quietly even while off-duty, and not become drunk and rowdy.

Ela took some time to drink a cup of watered wine and eat a small plate of nuts and dried apricots with a fresh pastry. She was in danger of becoming lightheaded after the day's exertions on an empty stomach.

She beckoned to Sir William Talbot to join her. "Praise be to God, Hilda and her baby are safe."

"Praise indeed. The good tidings spread fast." His expression turned serious. "Sir John took charge of the knife from the burial site."

Was her old friend Bill jealous of the trust she placed in

her new co-sheriff? Bill had been at her side for most of her life and was her closest friend in the world now her husband was gone. Neither of them knew John Dacus well enough to be sure of him, though he'd made a good impression so far. "And what of the bones?"

"They've been brought to the castle mortuary under Giles Haughton's watch."

"Where I hope they'll be guarded under lock and key. We still need to verify their identity. We should be able to determine the approximate height of the deceased by laying them out on the table." A ghoulish pursuit, to be sure.

"It seems almost certain that the bones belong to the former landowner." Bill took an offered cup of wine.

"Which means that the purchaser is under suspicion." She cast a glance at hoary old Wilf Crowder, who looked out of place among the young soldiers. "Perhaps we should arrest him tomorrow. Wilf Crowder has accused him of moving the river."

Bill burst out laughing. "I doubt any but God himself could move a river."

"You'd be surprised." Ela wiped her hands on a napkin. "It's quite common to reroute water to improve drainage in a marshy district or to bring water to a dry one. And rivers have been used as boundaries since ancient times."

"So moving one is a way to gain more land for yourself on one side of it." Bill shook his head. "But how could he have done that much digging without Crowder noticing until now?"

"We don't know if he has. It's all hearsay until we see the site. However, it's clear that he's been taking advantage of Crowder's age and growing infirmity."

"And one can hardly fault Crowder for being too old to manage his farm," said Bill.

"I'm not so sure. He's too stubborn to hire help, though he

could well afford it. Imagine if I tried to be sheriff of Wiltshire but refused to hire anyone to assist me?"

"So you think Beck has some right to take control of land that's being neglected?"

Ela sighed. "I didn't say that. However, I must admit that is rather how my mind works. I hate to see neglect cause a property to fall into disrepair."

"Can a woodland fall into disrepair?" Bill had an oddly mischievous look in his eye.

"Yes," she said curtly. "Thick undergrowth can render it impassable. And many trees produce more useful wood if they're pollarded regularly to encourage new growth." She stared at him. "Are you about to ask me if a river can fall into disrepair?"

"I wouldn't dare." Humor danced in his eyes. "But you've had a long day. Would you like me to get rid of Crowder for you so we can postpone the matter until you're well rested?"

"I'd be most grateful if you'd put him off until tomorrow. Hopefully neither he nor Beck will kill the other before then. Arrange a time for us to visit this mysterious rerouted river."

Bill approached the farmer and in his usual affable style managed to convey the information—then calmly ushered him out the door. Ela was petting the head of her greyhound, Greyson, and feeding him a morsel of walnut when the porter made a surprising announcement.

"ALL WELCOME BARONESS IDA."

Ela rose to her feet and cried out with pleasure. It had been some months since she'd seen her eldest daughter. The move from her manor at Gomeldon and all the business associated with assuming the role of sheriff had kept her from traveling for pleasure.

"Ida, my love! No one told me you were coming."

Ida walked toward her with a serious expression on her pretty face. "If I told you I was coming you'd have come up with a lot of excuses why now wasn't a good time to visit."

"Have I done that?"

"Absolutely."

"I apologize profusely. You're always welcome to visit, and I'm delighted to see you." She instructed the porters to carry Ida's baggage up to one of the guest rooms. "Come, have something to eat and drink. We're all rather tired. Hilda had her baby today."

A strange expression crossed Ida's face. "Who's Hilda?"

"I haven't told you about Hilda?" Had she really not confided in her daughter for so long? They sat at the table nearest the fire, and Ela called for more wine and some shortbread. "Hilda is Sibel's niece who came here to be my serving girl after Sibel left to marry, but she became pregnant."

Ida gave her cloak to a servant and arranged herself daintily on the bench. "Hilda's married?"

"No, I'm afraid she isn't. It's a long story involving a very unsuitable man who's now dead. But I took the girl under my wing and we've all been anxiously awaiting the arrival of her baby."

"Oh." Ida's lips pressed together.

"What's the matter, my sweet?"

"Nothing."

Her face contradicted her words. Ela knew she'd have to battle her own fatigue and pry Ida's worries out of her. "How are things at home? Did you have hard work to persuade your husband to let you visit me?"

Ida shrugged. "Liam is always hunting or playing cards with his friends. I doubt he'll even notice I'm gone."

So that was it. "Oh, my sweet. He's still a young man, and

they're drawn to such pursuits at that age. He'll settle. You'll see. Wait until your first child comes along. He'll mature overnight."

Ida took a swift sip of the wine that was placed before her. "If that ever happens."

"It will. Don't worry."

"We've been married for years."

"You're still young." This was too intimate a conversation to have in the great hall, where anyone could listen in. "You've many years yet."

"What if I'm barren? Liam might leave me and take a new wife."

Ela wanted to dismiss her worries as foolishness, but she could see the pain in Ida's eyes. And men had deserted a good wife for less. She leaned in and spoke softly. "Your father was as wild as they come as a young man. Always ready to drink and carouse or spoiling for a fight to test his skills—no thanks to his brother, the king."

The late King John had been a true thorn in Ela's side during those early years. He moved his household constantly throughout his kingdom and kept his much-loved half-brother, William, at his side, depriving her of her husband's company unless she wanted to sit through long evenings of carousing at a strange hearth.

Ida leaned in and whispered, "What did you do to get pregnant, Mama? I hear there are tricks a woman can use."

Ela blinked. The oldest trick known to womankind was to have sex with another man, but she'd never suggest that to her prim eldest daughter, even in jest. And it was far too early in their marriage to be sure that her husband was the problem. "Well, there is one thing you can try—"

"Ida!" Stephen came bounding up to his sister and threw his arms around her, closely followed by his brother Richard. The little ones, Ellie and Nicky, heard their cries and came running, followed by their barking and jumping pet dogs which followed them everywhere.

Ida greeted her siblings warmly and bounced Ellie on her knee. Ela could see she was so ready to be a mother that she could taste it. She could remember those anxious early years of marriage when she was past her fear of sex and of getting pregnant and so eager to be a mother that every new monthly bleed filled her with despair.

"Hilda had her baby!" cried Ellie. "Hilda's my new bestest friend."

"And mine," shouted Nicky. "She plays ball with me and chases me even though she's big as a house."

"She won't be big anymore," said Ellie. "Not now the baby's come out."

"She'll be too busy to play ball for quite some time," said Ela. "And too tired as well." She hoped Hilda wasn't in too much pain. Everyone talked so much of the pain of child-birth, but no one mentioned how sore one could be after-ward. "You must be gentle with her."

"Will she let me hold her baby?" asked Ellie. "I'll be very gentle and won't drop it." Ellie had a bedraggled poppet trailing from one hand, and she snatched it up into her arms and rocked it.

Ela saw tears well in Ida's eyes. "Ida, let's go upstairs to your bedroom and make sure the maids are unpacking your clothes properly."

"I'm coming too!" yelled Ellie.

"You stay here and help your brothers finish this plate of shortbread, my pet."

Ela took Ida's hand. "We'll go to my solar," she said. "And talk in peace."

ONCE INSIDE, Ela set her lantern on her writing desk, closed the door and gestured for Ida to sit in a chair by the empty fireplace. The fire up here wasn't usually laid until shortly before bedtime, and she debated whether to call a servant to light one but decided against it. She pulled up the chair that usually sat beside her bed and took Ida's hands in hers.

"Did I ever tell you how many years it was after I married your father before I became pregnant with you?"

"But you married as a child. No one expected you to have a baby."

"It still took a long time once I was old enough. And I lost more than one baby. I don't think I've ever told you that, have I?"

Ida looked startled.

"It happens to many women. Almost all of us, truth be told. That I have eight living babes to love and raise is a blessing that I shall never cease thanking God for."

Ida was silent for a moment. "Maybe God is punishing me."

"For what?"

"For my sinful thoughts."

Ela smiled. "Sex within marriage is natural and holy. It's the source of life and blessed by God. It's a good thing to be attracted to your husband and to want to have sex with him."

Ida looked mortified, eyes cast down to the floor. Then she met Ela's gaze again. "But I don't always want to have sex with my husband."

"Is he unskilled?"

"I think so. He's clumsy and sometimes it hurts. Sometimes I feel he half forgets I'm there and that I might as well be the wood bedpost he's banging himself against." Tears sprang to her eyes.

"Oh, my love." Ela wanted to hug Ida, but her daughter held herself rigid. "What you describe is so common in

45

marriage. No one schools decent and pious young men in the art of lovemaking. They really should be trained in it as they are drilled in the arts of war."

"It's not like I could teach him. I don't know anything about it myself. Except that whatever we're doing it won't seem to make a baby."

"In a way it's reassuring that he hasn't been schooled in the bed of a courtesan. Some young men develop exotic tastes that confound their wives. Dear Liam is a clean, innocent young man just as you are a pure young woman."

"If only prayer alone were enough to make a baby," said Ida tearfully. "Then I'd have at least three by now."

"Prayer alone won't fill your belly, but there are some things a woman can do to help the man's seed grow into a baby."

Ela gave her daughter a handkerchief to dry her tears. Once Ida calmed down, Ela straightened her fillet and stroked her cheek. "I truly believe that enjoying the act makes it more likely to be successful."

"But how?"

"You must tell him what you want."

"You mean what I don't want." Ida bit her lip. "I wish he'd stop hammering at me like I was a nail."

"Tell him to be softer, ask him to go slower. And don't wait until you're abed to do it. Mention it softly over a cup of spiced wine in front of the fire. Build anticipation. Tell him what you'd like him to do to you."

Ida blinked. "Won't he think I'm…"

"Wanton?" Ela smiled. "Such desire is a welcome thing in a wife. For most men at least. And Liam is a kind husband, is he not?"

"He is busy and travels much but still tries to be solicitous of my needs."

A knock on the door made Ela start. "Yes?"

It was Albert, the porter. "It's the coroner, my lady."

"Now?" She turned to Ida. "This feels like the longest day of my entire life. Can nothing wait until tomorrow?"

"Shall I send him away?" asked Albert.

"No, no. That wouldn't do. I'll be right down."

Ida's face fell. "Already? We only just started talking."

"Then you must stay for long enough that we can do all the talking we want." She squeezed her daughter's hand. "And one day soon you'll discover all the demands on a lady with a busy household filled with children."

She rose and followed Albert down the stairs. She didn't like to leave Ida feeling abandoned, but she didn't want to encourage self-indulgence, either. And what could be so urgent as to draw Giles Haughton away from his own hearth after dark?

CHAPTER 5

$\mathcal{N}$ow that darkness had fallen and the hard work of the day was largely done, an atmosphere of gaiety filled the hall. Members of the household and the garrison soldiers alike all celebrated the safe delivery of Hilda's baby.

Haughton greeted Ela with a nod. "I hear the little one is safely arrived."

"You'd think the next king had been born to hear the merriment in this hall." Ela worried that all the jubilation—over the child of a servant, no less—would make Ida feel even more anxious about her empty womb.

"This babe's arrival was long awaited, I know. And the last I heard you were summoning a doctor with some urgency."

"I am relieved that both Hilda and the baby are fine. As you know, the occupancy of Fernlees depends on it. But why are you here so late?"

He frowned and inhaled. "I've laid the bones—the body from the hilltop—out on the table in the mortuary. Nearly all of them were present. It strikes me that Oddo was a tall man with broad shoulders and a solid chest. This man is of a smaller and slighter build."

Ela stared. "If it's not Oddo, then who went missing all those years ago and has been unremarked upon since?"

"He would have died before my time as coroner, but I didn't hear of anyone reported missing and never found."

"And you couldn't be mistaken about how the bones are arranged?"

Haughton cleared his throat, and she realized she'd offended him. "Not about the broadness of his collarbone and ribs, and the length of his arm and leg bones. I remember Oddo. I didn't know him well, but he would come into the Bull and Bear from time to time. I can still see him in my mind. Even this man's face seems narrower."

"If Oddo lives, we must find him."

"Indeed we must. And he could be the killer. What better incentive for a man to sell the land he's farmed for years than that there's a dead body you've just murdered soaking blood into it."

Ela shuddered. "Surely guilt would make a man less likely to sell it for fear the crime would be discovered?"

"No doubt there are other bodies up there at the ancient site—men who died a thousand years ago or more. Perhaps the killer hoped this one would be taken for an artifact from a former era."

"And we might have, if it wasn't for the knife found with him. So we have a mystery body on disputed land."

"And no one seems to know where Oddo went. I've asked a few people, and one suggested he had a daughter who lived in Winchester. Perhaps he went to live with her."

"The daughter's name?"

"I don't know. But it should be in the baptismal records at the local chapel. She was born on that farm. The whole family should be recorded there. I'll go first thing in the morning and ask the priest."

"Excellent plan. In the meantime I'm utterly wrung out. Come see me tomorrow with the news you find, and we can plan how to proceed."

"At your service, my lady." He gave a slight bow. Giles Haughton often had an air of mocking amusement. Ela was never sure whether to be offended by it or to enjoy the familiarity.

"And I at yours, Sir Giles," she said, with an arch look. "Oh, and did I mention that Wilf Crowder now accuses his neighbor of moving the river?"

ELA BEGAN the next day with her usual rounds, making sure the boys were sweeping the castle paths and tending to the pigs and chickens; that the garrison guards were at their posts, not still lolling around drunk.

She had two guards follow behind her as she made her rounds. She half resented the intrusion but it had become necessary after she was attacked on her morning rounds the previous spring. Any regular routine could be observed and rendered her vulnerable to attack by her enemies.

And as sheriff, charged with upholding the law and prosecuting evildoers, she would likely always have enemies whether she was aware of them or not.

Her guards even escorted her to the door of Hilda's chamber, where she found the girl fast asleep in bed with her baby at her breast.

"Hilda, how are you feeling?"

The girl's eyes flickered open, and she startled when she realized she'd fallen asleep holding her baby. She quickly gathered her gown to cover her bosom and pulled her baby close. The sleepy infant barely stirred. "Do you need me, my lady?"

"I do not. Elsie's helping me. You should rest and mind your baby. It's best for both of you to stay away from crowds for a few days while you build your strength. We don't want your baby to catch a cold when it's so fresh from the womb." Her eyes rested on the tiny infant, with its blotchy pink cheeks and rosebud mouth. She felt a tiny stirring in her own womb. "Goodness, isn't he precious?"

"Would you like to hold him?" Hilda lifted the baby.

"I'd love to." Ela gathered the sweet baby in her arms. He smelled like milk and fresh linens and that delicious newborn smell. "He's lovely, Hilda. And looks so strong and healthy after the scare he gave us."

"Was I in danger?" Hilda stared at her baby.

"A woman is always in danger until the baby and the afterbirth are safely delivered." Even then...but no need to scare Hilda, who—though pale—looked in good health and spirits.

"The doctor came, didn't he?"

"Indeed he did but thank Heaven all was put to rights before he even arrived."

"How soon can Thomas be christened?"

Ela stroked the baby's silk-soft cheek. "I'll speak with the priest. Perhaps he can do it today."

"His papa would be proud of him," said Hilda softly, gazing at her baby with her long-lashed eyes.

"To be sure. He lives on in his strong, healthy son, who can grow up to be a knight like his father." And could hopefully avoid the fate of getting injured and being reduced to poaching like his unfortunate sire. "You know Drogo Blount saved my husband's life?"

"I do. That's the only reason you put up with him."

"True," said Ela with a smile. She'd caught him taking

advantage of Hilda and she probably should have thrown him off the property right then, but she didn't. "He was a very amusing man."

"And handsome." Hilda looked at her baby in Ela's arms. "My baby's going to be handsome just like him."

"Looks aren't everything," scolded Ela. Hilda's own extravagant looks had brought her to this predicament. "What's in his heart is far more important."

"Oh, I know. That's why I want to get him baptized. So he can be a true Christian."

Ela smiled as she handed Hilda's baby back. Hilda took him and tucked him into her arms, supporting his heavy head with one expertly placed finger. Having helped raise a gaggle of younger siblings, Hilda had years of experience in the care of babies.

"Rest and eat well and let others wait on you while you recover your strength. I'll let you know when the christening is arranged."

ELA DESCENDED into the hall ready to break her fast. She discovered that Wilf Crowder was already in the hall waiting for her.

Ela ignored him for now. She took her place at the high table and ate some dried fruit and a nut pudding. She greeted her little ones and asked their tutor about their studies. It was time for Nicky to begin the study of Latin. She'd been reading him prayers and Bible passages in it since he was a newborn like Hilda's babe. Now it was time for him to learn how to read and write in the ancient tongue.

Wilf Crowder stood respectfully, cap in hand, waiting for her to finish breaking her fast. She rose from the table and ascended the small dais, where her official chair sat, then beckoned for him to approach.

"You have a new complaint against your neighbor?"

"He's stolen part of my meadow. He's moved the river to take a strip of my land for his!" The old man was agitated.

"Rivers do change course of their own accord."

"Not this one. He's dug out the sides and moved it over."

"That sounds like an awful lot of work for a strip of grazing." She had a hard time believing that Bertram Beck would go to the effort of digging down deep and long enough to move even a small stream. "What does he claim?"

"He says he dug some clay to line the floor in his new barn." He snorted. "But if that's the case he dug clay from my side as well."

"I shall have to come view the river and hear his side of the issue."

"He was in the wrong about the woods. You saw he moved the boundary up there."

"It does indeed appear that way."

"Some people aren't happy unless they're taking something from another. If a man will commit one crime he'll likely commit another," said Crowder grimly.

This was true. Ela had seen ample evidence of it. Still... "Stealing a few rods of forest is hardly the same as taking a man's life. But rest assured that justice will be done."

"How? Will he be made to pay me rent on the land he used?"

"That's unlikely. But look to the rest of your holdings. If I find land lying neglected I may well find a better purpose for it."

"The butterflies and the bees might have a purpose for it," muttered Crowder. "Or would you put them to work as well? The land needs to rest sometimes, just like an old man needs to rest."

Ela blinked. His insolence surprised her. And his wisdom. "I honor your age and experience and shall ponder what you say." Then she inhaled. "But these are new and different times where ownership is determined in a court of law as often as it is by generations of indifferent occupancy, so in future look to your boundaries *before* your neighbor steals them away from you."

She didn't want word getting around that hoary old farmers could tell her how to run the county or offer her barb-laden pieces of wisdom. And if half Wiltshire was occupied only by blue tits and butterflies, then how would there be enough food at the markets to feed the people?

"Bertram Beck might be the killer, though," insisted Crowder. "He's not from these parts. He just turned up here out of nowhere."

Ela held up her hand to silence him. "The matter of the corpse is under investigation. It seems likely that the skeleton we found belongs to someone other than Oddo." She didn't need him spreading false rumors. "The coroner is working to determine the dead man's identity."

Crowder's mouth hung open. "Not Oddo? Then who could it be?"

"Do you know where Oddo might have moved to, if he is still alive? Does he have any children in the area?"

"He had a daughter that married a tavern owner."

"Do you know where the tavern lies?"

He frowned. "Winchester, I think. Or was it Whitchurch? Her name was Agnes from what I remember."

This was progress. Both towns were an easy ride. "Do you know her husband's last name?"

"Can't say I do. And he had two other daughters as well. One married a baker who cheated people by adding sand to his loaves and lost his business because of it. Can't say where they are now."

"And the other?"

"How would I know? Nor his son, neither, though they say he joined the king's army and went overseas to fight."

"What was the son's name?"

"Simon. They call him Simon of Oddo. Useless lad."

"Useless? Yesterday you said you didn't remember him."

"I didn't remember anything good about him."

"Good morrow, my lady."

The sound of John Dacus's well-schooled voice in her ear made Ela turn around. "Ah, Sir John. Farmer Crowder has informed me that the border dispute is not yet resolved and we must visit his land again. Would you ride there with me?"

Truth be told she was dying to get out of the castle and take some fresh air.

"It would be my pleasure, my lady. Allow me to first escort Farmer Crowder back to his horse and cart." He led Crowder away, making pleasant conversation about the price of spring pigs, then returned to Ela. "Your horse is being readied. Is there anyone else who I should summon to attend?"

Ela frowned. Something nagged at her. "Giles Haughton, the coroner. New information has emerged since yesterday, and I'd like to make another study of the surroundings." Ela hesitated, not sure if she really wanted to open this jar of worms. "And I think we should call a jury."

CHAPTER 6

A bitter wind buffeted the castle mound as Ela and her co-sheriff waited outside the east gate for Haughton to join them. He rode up on his bay palfrey, face scrunched against the icy blast.

"I thought you should join us now that you've observed that the body is not likely to be that of old man Oddo. I've also asked for jurors to be summoned. We shall need their opinion on the matter of the land dispute as well as the dead body."

"I appreciate the chance to look at the scene now I've had time to ponder the circumstance of the death." They rode down the castle mound and onto the lane. "I do believe he was killed with the knife found with him. There are scrape marks on two of his lower ribs, and I suspect the knife was thrust between them."

"Are there marks on the knife itself?" asked Sir John.

"I removed what rust and tarnish I could, but I wasn't able to discern clear marks. Not that I was expecting them. Living ribs are not generally hard enough to scrape a blade."

"Do you still believe it was Oddo's knife?" asked Ela.

"It does seem to be." They rode through a small patch of woods, ducking beneath a low-hanging branch that glittered with ice. "He carved his own knife handle, and it was unique. When I showed it to the men in the tavern two of them confirmed it as his."

"It seems the tavern denizens can almost be called upon as a jury," said Ela drily. Why did Haughton spend so much time in a tavern? She hoped he wasn't developing a weakness for strong drink.

He let out a hollow laugh. "The men in there are mostly jurors anyway." He reined in his horse. "They'll likely be joining us after they've downed their ale."

The jurors were mostly older men who often had strong —even fixed—opinions on various local matters. Sometimes she felt they obfuscated the course of justice rather than smoothed it. "Do you think they can tell us much about this eight-year-old—or older—crime scene?"

"It's possible. Perhaps one of them recalls a dispute that might have left a man buried naked up in those woods." Haughton stared ahead at the brow of the hill before them, the knot of disputed trees almost a silhouette against the white sky. "And they may know more about the old quarrel between Crowder and Oddo that made Oddo sell his land to a stranger instead of his neighbor who's lived his whole life there."

"That is odd," said Ela. "I hope we have the chance to question Oddo himself about it. I've sent out messengers to look for him."

Instead of taking the long way around via the lane, they rode up along the edge of one of Farmer Crowder's pastures, keeping their horses as close to the hedgerow as possible so as not to churn up his grazing. But as they rode higher up the hill, toward the woods, three men came riding up behind them, passed them and crossed directly across the field, talking loudly. They wore hats pulled low over their foreheads and cloaks wrapped high on their necks.

These men surely weren't jurors, who would never ride right past her. Did Crowder finally hire some help? "Who are they?" Ela asked John Dacus.

"One of them looks like John Wheeler's boy. The red-haired lad."

"That was up on poaching charges last year?"

"But wasn't convicted due to lack of evidence. That's him. He has the same crooked way of riding."

"Summon them," said Ela to John.

"Hey there!" called Sir John, riding forward to address them. "Halt and address your countess and sheriff."

Ela watched as they slowed—with some reluctance—and peered curiously at her small party.

"Tell us your names," commanded John.

They stared at him. She noticed that people didn't take Sir John very seriously. He was too nice.

Ela rode forward. "He asked for your names, spit them out immediately or spend the night in jail."

Each of them mumbled his name, and sure enough, one of them was the aforementioned Wheeler. The other two were minor miscreants with misdeeds colorful enough that their names were also lodged in her brain.

"Why are you riding across Wilf Crowder's field when the land is in thaw and easily damaged?"

"Oh, is it?" said Wheeler. "I thought it was frozen." His voice had a mocking flatness to it.

"Why are you crossing it?" hissed Ela, stretching out her last shred of patience.

"Because Bertram Beck paid us to," he announced with a jut of his pimpled chin.

"He paid you to ride across Wilf Crowder's farm?"

"Twice a day. Once in the morning and once in the afternoon."

Ela glanced at Giles Haughton. Whose face was unreadable as a Saracen's script. "Why?"

"I dunno. We each get a farthing a day. Just for riding here."

Now Beck had gone too far. "You must stop immediately."

"But we have the right to ride here. He told us it's an ancient right of way dating back to the time of the druids. Goes right up the hill and into those woods."

Ela felt her eyes narrowing. "And where does this ancient right of way begin?"

"Down at the lane." Wheeler tilted his chin in that direction. "If you follow the lane and ignore the hedgerow but instead ride right through it, the path continues up here, as it must have done in the old days."

Ela blinked. Ancient rights of way could be a source of bitter contention. She had a tiresome one behind her manor in Charlton, which allowed carters to roll along an old track right by her grain storage barns and laid them open to theft or other mischief. Sometimes she wished they could just wipe these ancient passages from the face of the countryside.

But, if common grazing was the beating heart of the countryside, those old rights of way were its veins. Still... "What proof do you have of this path being ancient? There's no beaten track on this grass." The un-grazed winter field showed only a few hoofprints from their last two or three journeys this way. Certainly not signs of regular use over a long period of time.

"If you ride up to the top of the field you'll see there's an old stile there made from two great stones. Been there for donkey's years, I'm sure." Wheeler smirked.

"We shall ride up. And later we shall check the area maps." Not that the maps had every pathway on them. If Beck could somehow prove the path was ancient, he'd likely win in court even if she were the one making the decision.

Ela instructed Wheeler to lead them on the path, which he did with his head held at a jaunty angle. As well it might be if he was getting paid to take a leisurely ride twice a day.

Beck has declared war on Crowder. Again he sought to antagonize his neighbor with this bold act. But why?

At the top of the field, a straggly hedgerow separated the grazing from a knot of woods that topped the hill. Sure enough, there were two great stones, well buried in the earth, marking the top of the track and leading into the woods.

She hoped that the woods had closed over the path enough for her to declare it derelict and defunct, but in fact there was now a noticeable depression in the soil, almost like a ditch, that suggested the passage of thousands of feet had compressed the ground. And it had been recently cleared of undergrowth. The fresh-cut stalks of shrubs and weeds bristled along the path.

"Why would Beck want this path in use? His side of the hill is less steep, and he has easier passage from the lane down near his house."

"I dunno," said Wheeler. "Not my business, is it?"

His rudeness galled her. She resisted the temptation to threaten him with jail again. "It is your business to explain yourself if your sheriff should question you."

Wheeler's flat face didn't react. "You'll have to ask him his reasons yourself. He meets us up here and gives us the money of an afternoon."

Ela looked up to the top of the hill and sure enough she could see a man in a red tunic approaching through the trees and brush. He'd have some explaining to do.

Wheeler and his cronies rode with them up the hill and into the woods. "Here's the area where the body was found," called Haughton, as they were about to ride right over it. Ela had almost forgotten about the murder in her agitation over Wheeler's insolence and Beck's brazen efforts to disturb his neighbor.

"You examine it while I address Beck."

She rode up to the farmer, who sat on his own black horse just past the brow of the hill, red tunic almost blindingly bright in the morning light. He didn't look particularly surprised to see her.

"Good day, my lady. I see you met the men in my employ."

"You've employed them to upset your neighbor by traipsing across his grazing from what I can tell."

"No grazing at this time of year. The land is brown and bare." A cold smile crossed his mouth. "And it is a convenient route up to this hilltop where my woods lie."

"You stand accused of encroaching on your neighbor's property," snapped Ela. "Don't think there won't be consequences."

"It was an honest mistake. One oak tree looks much like another, and when the leaves fall and cover the land—"

"Silence. What is the meaning of this effort to aggravate and upset your neighbor?" She pinned him with a steady gaze.

"I don't want to upset anyone." Beck shifted in his saddle. "I just want to enjoy the full use of my land."

"And the land around it. What's this about the river? Crowder has accused you of changing its course." She wondered where Crowder was right now. He'd come to the castle with a donkey and cart and had to come back here by the road, while they'd rode across the fields. It might be some time before he made his way up the hill on foot.

"Moving the river?" he laughed. "As if any man could do such a thing. When rivers shift their course it's the work of God."

"Not always," said Ela coolly. "A jury has been summoned that will be riding up here."

Finally Beck's self-satisfied expression melted. "A jury? What for?"

"Perhaps you've forgotten that a dead man's skeleton was found in these woods."

"I don't see what the murder has to do with me. Oddo the Bald was alive and well when he sold this farm to me."

"The dead man is not Oddo the Bald. The coroner examined the skeleton, and it has a shorter, slighter build. Oddo was a man of large proportions."

"I don't know who it was. Nor do I care. I didn't kill him." Beck grew visibly ruffled.

"A jury of your peers can determine that. Until then you're as much a suspect as anyone."

"For killing a man I never even met?"

"If you say one more insolent word you'll spend the night in the castle dungeon." She raised her voice as she spoke. She knew she couldn't allow these men to disrespect her. "Don't speak unless you're spoken to."

He stared at her, no doubt wondering if she'd actually follow through. She silently dared him to try her.

He didn't.

"Now." She gathered up her reins. "Please lead me to the riverbank."

He looked like he wanted to protest, perhaps to ask which section of riverbank or argue that there wasn't a riverbank at all. But he glanced at her face and changed his mind. "This way," he mumbled.

They followed a winding track through the forest, back down from the brow of the hill and past a thick stand of brambles.

Ela heard the stream before she saw it. It sprung from the side of the hill and trickled down toward the valley. The brambles, red stems dusted with frost, hid it from view until they rode almost all the way down to bottom of the hill.

"It's hardly a river. The stream flows down here and between these fields," said Beck, gesturing with his hand.

The brambles ended abruptly, hacked back with a scythe, revealing a vista that shocked her so much that her horse spooked and almost dropped her in the shallow water.

CHAPTER 7

"You have completely changed the course of this waterway," Ela exclaimed once she found her voice.

River was indeed a strong word for the stream descending from the hill above them and flowing through the turned earth below. It probably slowed to a trickle in a dry season.

"I removed some material for the floor of my barn, but hardly any. The ground has been trampled by livestock," said Beck. He had the decency to look a little nervous. As well he might.

"I'd advise you not to take me for a fool." She walked her horse along the bank, taking in the scene. The dark, disturbed soil—devoid of plants—continued for some distance. From the look of it he'd shifted the water course about fifty feet onto Crowder's land, thus claiming the land on his side of it for himself. "Were you hoping that he'd take too long to notice this and that the plants would have grown back, obscuring your handiwork?"

"Probably sheep that trampled it," said Bertram Beck, through thin lips. "They come down here to drink."

"No doubt you drove them here for that purpose." Their hoofprints were clearly visible in the soft mud. "But it's clear that the earth is recently disturbed."

"You can't prove it." His greedy eyes flashed before he glanced away.

"The jurors shall render their opinion, and that will be proof enough." Where were they? Was Giles Haughton still nosing around the site where they'd found the body? Ela felt glad of her armed attendant. She wouldn't like to be alone here with Beck and his hired henchmen.

She heaved a sigh of relief to see two jurors walking over the brow of the hill on the opposite side of the river, accompanied by Wilf Crowder. She and Beck stood in silence as they approached.

"Good day to you, sirs." She greeted Stephen Hale, the cordwainer and Peter Howard the baker. They were probably the two most willing jurors and the least likely to present an excuse for why they couldn't attend. "Please look at this stream beside us and tell me if you think it looks to have been freshly disturbed or if it looks to have followed this course this past half century." She cast a sideways glance at Beck, who shifted from one foot to the other.

"Looks like it's been dug over, doesn't it?" said Howard. "Flows too straight for one thing. It doesn't look natural."

"And there's nothing growing on the banks," said Hale.

"It ain't natural," cut in Crowder, who'd made his way to the opposite bank. "It's been dug up and shifted over so he can steal my land." He tilted his chin toward Beck. "Bold as brass!"

"So the jurors agree that this river has been moved by the work of men?" asked Ela.

"I'd say so," said Howard.

"Me too," said Hale. "And it looks recently done as well."

Ela stared at Beck. "Isn't it lucky you have hired men standing right here ready to move it back for you?" She glanced at the arrogant Wheeler and his ne'er-do-well cohorts.

"You never said nothing about digging." Wheeler sat in his saddle. "I'm not doing any digging."

"So these aren't the men who dug it for you?" asked Ela. She half expected him to protest that no one had dug it but the hand of God.

But luckily for him he wasn't that stupid. "Nay, I have two lads that work for me. They're moving the sheep."

"Then get them down here and start them to moving the river back to where it belongs." She looked at Crowder. "Farmer Crowder, please mark out the correct course of the river so it can be moved back to its former location."

"Yes, my lady. I'll mark it with stones." Crowder shuffled off to look for stones.

"He could put it wherever he pleases," protested Beck.

"Indeed he could. And I don't think any man here would argue with him. And I'd advise you not to, either. I'm bringing a charge against you for harassment of Farmer Crowder. I believe you've taken strips of his land and paid men to march across his fields to irk him. I don't know why you've done it, but you shall pay for it."

"Pay how?" Beck looked alarmed. "I'm not a rich man."

"A jury of twelve men shall decide." She looked down on him from her horse. "And perhaps they'll decide to give him part of your property instead of a monetary payment."

"No! I can find the money," he protested. "I could buy the land."

"He knows full well that I'll never sell it." Crowder looked up from laying a stone. "He'll only get his hands on it over my dead body."

"Since we already have one dead body to worry about, perhaps that's not the ideal suggestion." What was keeping Giles Haughton up there so long? She stared at Bertram Beck, bright as a rooster in his red tunic. "You must immediately cease harassing Farmer Crowder by chiseling away at his borders and also by sending men across his fields. I don't care if there's an ancient right of way there. At the present moment you and anyone in your employ or your family are *forbidden* from using it." She allowed a hint of menace to creep into her voice during the last part.

Beck looked petulant. He opened his mouth as if to protest, then—once again—thought better of it.

ELA ASKED John Dacus to stay and keep an eye on Beck and his henchmen while she and the jurors headed up the hill to find Haughton. She rode up on her side of the river, and the jurors rode up the opposite bank. As they climbed higher, the stream narrowed to a trickle as it disappeared into the hillside as a spring.

Haughton stood near the place where they'd found the body and had set two soldiers to digging out the area.

"Did you find any further evidence to help us identify the dead man?" asked Ela. She jumped down from her horse and handed Freya to an attendant.

"The other items we've found date to an earlier time." He indicated a small pile of grubby shards of pottery and other items. "The patterns of the vessels are different from what we use today."

Ela approached the heap and picked up a broken piece of molded clay with a band of chevrons circling it. It looked to be the top of a jug of some kind. "The design is somewhat cruder and the vessel heavier than something I'd have at the castle, but is it so different to a rude vessel that a farmer would use?"

"People back then weren't so different than we are now," said Haughton.

She picked up another item. This time it was a piece of tarnished metal small enough to hold in the palm of her hand. A clasp or buckle, perhaps. "Do you think these are from before the time of our savior?"

Haughton looked up. "I couldn't say, my lady. This hilltop may have been inhabited over a long period of time. I'm sure you're aware that the mound your castle stands on was built in a much earlier time and probably bore wooden fortifications defending a long-ago chieftain."

"Yes." If she and Haughton were alone she'd have taken a moment to bemoan the dismantling of her beloved cathedral —which until recently had stood within the castle's outer walls—and her fears that the castle would one day follow suit. But that wouldn't be appropriate in front of the jurors. "I wonder how many men and women lived and died on this hilltop that now stands quietly cloaked in forest."

"Even if we dug down far enough to find their burials, they'd most likely have returned to dust by now."

Ela shivered slightly at the thought that the very earth she stood on might be made from the dust of those bones. If those ancient men and women weren't baptized, did their unshriven souls still wander the sun-dappled naves and aisles of the forest?

She chastised herself for such fancies and looked at Haughton. "Are you digging for signs of other recent bodies?"

"Indeed I am. But so far there are no more."

"I wonder what became of his clothes."

"We may find them yet."

Ela asked Haughton to go over the details with the jurors,

and walked around the site while he did it. Beck's wattle fence was gone and a rudimentary fence of branches and stones now divided Crowder's property from Beck's. No doubt old Farmer Crowder had strained himself lugging stones and hauling branches to build it. In many ways it would make more sense for him to sell his land to the younger man and retire in comfort.

But he was clearly too stubborn for that.

Juror Peter Howard asked about the position of the body —which had been laid in the hole unceremoniously, with the limbs tumbled about. Stephen Hale inquired after the murder weapon, which had been found buried a short distance away.

"And several witnesses have identified the knife as belonging to Oddo the Bald, the previous owner of this land," said Ela. "Which is why we thought it might be his body, but Sir Giles assures me that the dead man's build is too dissimilar."

"Our corpse is a shorter and slighter man than old Oddo. I'm sure you both remember him as a broad-shouldered man of about my height."

"Could he not shrink once under the soil?" asked Hale.

"Not the bones. Those never change," said Haughton.

"And with no knowledge of who the dead man is, it's hard to find a suspect," mused Howard.

"How long has he been dead?" asked Hale.

"Eight years or thereabouts. Maybe longer, but not too much longer."

"Eight years is a long time."

Ela could see where this was going. "Eight years or no, we have a murder victim and his killer must be brought to justice. If we find Oddo alive we'll be able to eliminate him as the victim."

"And likely accuse him of murder," suggested Howard. "A

dead man right on his own land and buried with his knife would point the figure of accusation squarely at him, wouldn't it?"

"It might indeed," said Ela. "But let's not jump to conclusions. Someone could have stolen his knife and used it." She felt Giles Haughton's skeptical gaze on her. "Or perhaps he was the killer. We must wait until we've gathered all the evidence and had time to sift through it."

BACK AT THE CASTLE, Hilda sat up in her bed, taking visitors like a splendid Madonna showing off her precious newborn babe. Ela's children made faces and sang songs for the tiny baby, who mostly slept and fed through all the fuss.

One person was notably absent. "Where's Ida?" Ela hadn't seen her eldest daughter all day. Her other children shrugged. No one else had seen her either.

Frowning, Ela set off to look for her in her borrowed chamber. Sure enough she was there, sprawled across the bed, reading a bound volume.

"What are you doing holed up in here, my love?"

"Reading."

"Reading what?"

"The romance of Tristan and Isolde." She slapped the book closed. "It's a foolish story. He should stop trying to blame a love potion for his sinful urges and find himself a princess who isn't already married." She paused, frowning. "My husband thinks it's my fault that I can't get pregnant. He told me to visit the herb-woman."

Ela moved into the room and sat down on the bed next to Ida. "Men always blame the woman. I can't tell you how many childless widows have remarried and then borne children with their new husband, so that's clearly not always the case."

"I hoped you could help me find the right herbs." Her daughter sat up on the bed. "Now I come here and find the entire castle alive with delight over the birth of some servant girl's bastard."

"Ida! I'm shocked at you."

"Well, he is a little bastard, isn't he? She wasn't married to the father."

"Poor Hilda is but an innocent child who was led astray and left to carry the burden. That she's able to find joy in it—and the rest of us as well—is one of God's blessings." Ela frowned. "And before you throw around such cruel words you should recall that your father's father was not married to his mother."

Ida blinked. "It's different if the father is the King of England."

"Is it? You're named after dear William's mother. I wonder how poor Ida de Tosny, a young innocent girl new at court, felt about being seduced or cajoled or intimidated into King Henry II's bed?"

Ida blinked, clearly scandalized.

"You must look with pity and kindness on young girls who are taken advantage of, and I hope never to hear such foul words from your mouth again."

"Ida's son—my father—went on to be a great man, loved and respected by all." Tears sprang to Ida's eyes. "I miss him so, Mama. I hadn't seen him for such a long time before he died, because I was married and living far away."

"Well, in his memory do a kindness to another girl who's found herself in the same position as that earlier Ida and bestow your blessings upon Hilda."

Ida pulled an embroidered handkerchief from her sleeve and swiped at her tears. "But the sight of her holding her baby is like a knife to my gut. I want one so badly, Mama. And so does Liam. In our first year of marriage he talked so fondly of having a son, or even a daughter." The tears started flowing again. "And now when he brings up the subject I feel scolded for not having given him one yet."

"It's not your fault. It's not his fault. The Lord himself knows when the time is right for you to bear a child."

"But you know some herbs I can take that will make it easier?"

"We can look through my medical books for advice, but not now. I have affairs to attend to, and your brothers and sisters would enjoy your company. It's been a long time since you came to visit."

"I know. I'm still getting used to running my own household. If I don't visit the kitchen morning and night and scold the cleaning girls I swear they'd all just sit around eating and nothing would get done."

"Maybe you'll be surprised by how well they'll manage without you."

"I doubt it." Ida stood up and brushed wrinkles from the front of her gown. "And then my absence will give my husband another thing to complain about."

"Don't fret about your husband, my angel. He'll miss you and your ministrations and be overjoyed to see you when you return. Mark my words, a little absence truly does make the heart grow fonder."

"Perhaps." She adjusted her fillet in the looking glass. "I miss him." She looked around at Ela. "I love him terribly, Mama."

Ela's heart swelled. "I'm so glad to hear it. Love makes the trials of a marriage easier to bear and the joys speak for themselves."

"I try so hard to make him happy, but I'm worried that he'll take a mistress."

Ela pressed her lips together. He would probably take a mistress anyway. Nearly all men did. Powerful men, anyway. They traveled with the king and went on crusades and pilgrimages and adventures of various kinds that took them away from their wives and into temptation.

"You can't worry about things you can't control. Love him with all your heart and do your best to be a good wife to him. But in the meantime, practice being a mother with your littlest brother and sister."

"And with Hilda's baby?" Ida looked skeptical.

"Why not? They say that when a woman is around babies it can cause her womb to open."

"Which won't do me much good if my husband isn't here," said Ida ruefully. "But I suppose it's worth a try."

"My lady!" a voice outside the door made them both turn.

"Come in," Ela commanded.

Albert the porter stood panting outside. "The guards have returned from Winchester with a prisoner in tow. His name is Oddo."

CHAPTER 8

"Why was Oddo the Bald arrested?" Ela followed Albert down the stairs and along the passage that led to the hall.

"He wouldn't come quietly, my lady. That's what they said. He's in the hall now."

Ela left Ida to decide whether to stay in her room sulking and reading stories or rejoin the world of the living. She could give her daughter advice, but she couldn't live her life for her.

Ela saw Oddo across the hall as she entered. At least she assumed it was him. A big, broad-chested man in a dusty green-colored tunic with his presumably bald pate covered by a brown linen cap. Flanked by guards, his arms behind his back, he stared sullenly at her as she entered.

John Dacus hurried over to her. "They aren't sure whether to put him in the dungeon. I told them to wait until you gave the assent."

"Thank you." She walked to her chair on its dais and took her seat, then summoned to the guards to bring him over. "Please join me, Sir John."

Oddo moved with a shuffling gait, but that could be the awkwardness of having his big arms bound behind his back. "Do you know why you've been brought here?"

"Something about my farm that I sold. What do I care about that? I sold it nigh on eight years ago." He sounded almost belligerent.

"Mind your tone," said Sir John. "You are speaking to your Countess."

Ela silently thanked John for his intervention. It preserved her authority not to scold people herself. "A man has been found dead on your farm." She watched his expression. Which did not reveal surprise.

Was that because the guards had already told him about the body?

"At first we thought it was your body we'd found," she continued. "Because a knife recognized as yours was found nearby, and no one had seen or heard of you for so many years."

Finally his coarse, weather-beaten face began to show signs of alarm.

Ela stared at him. "The coroner, who remembered your sturdy build, realized that the skeleton couldn't have been yours. This notion is confirmed by your living presence before us." She narrowed her eyes slightly. "Which presents the question—whose body lay buried where your farm meets Farmer Crowder's?"

"How would I know? Like I said, I've been gone these many years."

"Yet your knife remained there, buried a scant few feet from a dead man's corpse."

"Who says it's my knife?"

"Wilf Crowder, for one."

"He resents me not selling my land to him. He'd be happy to see me locked up for a crime I didn't commit."

"Why didn't you sell your land to him?" She couldn't understand personal resentments getting in the way of business. Money was money.

"He was never serious about buying it. I sold it to Beck for nearly four times what Wilf Crowder could have paid me. If he even has any money at all. He's never been much of a farmer."

Ela couldn't argue with that. Though it wasn't fair to judge his past performance on the efforts of his old age. "So he was never a serious buyer, in your opinion?"

"No." Ela saw no reason not to believe him, since Crowder could barely manage the farm he had. "And not only that," he continued. "I told Beck old Crowder was on his last legs and he might well be able to buy his farm from him as well. I was glad to be rid of the place with my hands and feet getting arthritic." That explained his shuffling movements. "I was ready to go put my feet up at my daughter's fireside in Winchester. She's kind enough to look after her old man."

So he had a reason to sell and a reason to sell to Beck. But what of the knife?

"Shall I summon Giles Haughton and ask him to bring the knife?" asked John Dacus.

"Please do." Sir John endeared himself to her more every moment. "In the meantime, Farmer Oddo, please ask yourself who the dead man might be."

"How would I know?"

"Can you think of anyone else who disappeared around the time you sold the farm?"

"It was a long time ago."

"Was there anyone else living there with you?"

"The two lads that worked for me. I took them on when my son, Simon, left to join the Crusades."

"When did your son come back?"

76

"He didn't. I dare say he started a new life somewhere else with the riches he plundered. Or perhaps he was killed in battle." Oddo showed no emotion at either of these possibilities.

Something prickled in Ela's gut. "So you never heard from him again? Not a letter or any word from a friend or fellow soldier?"

"Not a peep. He wasn't the type to worry about others and their feelings."

Ela suspected he inherited that trait from his father. "Is the boy's mother still alive?" No one had breathed a word of Oddo having a wife.

"Nay. Sadly she died almost twenty years ago of the scarlet fever."

"May God rest her soul," said Ela.

"And one day I'll be lucky enough to join her, but the Lord sees fit to keep me here, limping through yet another winter."

"I'm sure your daughter is glad of it."

Oddo let out a harsh laugh. "She's got enough mouths to feed already and that layabout of a husband to wait on hand and foot. She tolerates a crabbed old man, though, and I'm grateful for that."

They were getting off topic. "So your son never wrote to his sister, either."

"Not a peep. Not that I know of, anyway."

"And he left before you moved away to Winchester."

"More than a year before."

Ela wished Giles Haughton was here. Or at least a juror. Even John Dacus was now absent. Because she had a very strong suspicion about whose dusty bones lay spread out on the table in the armory.

"Do you have any other children?"

"Two daughters. One married a horse trader who took

her to Dorset. The other was carried off by a baker who set up near Chichester. I haven't laid eyes on either of them in years."

"I can see how there was nothing to keep you here in Salisbury, though you've missed watching our new cathedral rise up toward the heavens."

"Aye. Perhaps I'll visit it now that I find myself back here."

"The work of the stonemasons has no equal in England." Ela didn't know if this was true as she'd hardly visited every cathedral in England. She was stalling for time before she pointed the finger of accusation at Oddo the Bald. She wanted to be sure there were witnesses to his reaction.

AT LAST JOHN DACUS returned with Giles Haughton and two jurors: Thomas Price the old thatcher and Hugh Clifford the wine seller. The latter was a dapper man in his thirties with poker-straight brown hair and embossed leather boots. Ela summoned them toward the dais and asked them to listen closely.

"This man here is Oddo the Bald, former owner of the farm now managed by Bertram Beck. He sold the land to Beck some eight years ago. He tells me he sold it because his only son joined the king's army and went away to fight." She turned to Oddo. "How long ago did you say he left?"

"Nine years this spring, my lady," he replied, looking quite calm.

"So he'd been gone one year when you sold. And you didn't hear from him in all that time."

"Not a word, my lady. Not a scrap of a letter or a word passed to another."

"And based on that you assumed he wasn't ever coming

back and you sold the land that would have been his inheritance?"

Oddo had taken off his linen cap, revealing his shiny pate, and now wrung it in his hands. "Aye, that I did, my lady. It's a sad day when a man realizes he has no son to pass his hard work down to."

"But a year is not a long time," continued Ela. She allowed a slightly menacing tone to creep into her voice. "My husband went missing for months. He was wounded in a shipwreck and saved by monks on the Isle of Ré who nursed him back to health. People did start to whisper that he was dead but I never gave up hope. Never." She peered at him, waiting for a reaction. "And he came back to me just over a year ago."

Then was cruelly killed a scant few weeks later.

Oddo's expression had changed. If anything he looked confused. Wondering what this had to do with him.

"A year is not a long time at all," she said slowly. "Unless you knew for sure that your son was dead."

She said the last word a little louder than the others and let it resonate in the air, vibrating off the stone walls and the high timber ceiling.

"I don't know if he's dead. But I did know he wasn't coming back."

"What made you so sure?" Ela tilted her head sideways, as if deeply curious.

"He never wanted to farm in the first place," said Oddo gruffly. "Always more interested in drinking in the tavern and flirting with the ladies."

"So even if he was here he wouldn't have taken over the farm?" This seemed unlikely. What man would turn down the opportunity to manage a good piece of productive property that could support his family for a lifetime and beyond?

"He'd probably have sold it."

"Could you not have granted it to one of your daughters and her husband?"

Oddo looked at her like she'd lost her mind. "None of them is a farmer. You can't run a farm like it's a bakery."

"What about the horse trader?"

He snorted. "He doesn't even breed them. He buys and sells them. He'll buy a broken nag, fatten it for a week or two and sell it as a good carthorse. He's nothing more than a swindler."

"You seem to be surrounded by disappointing people, Oddo the Bald," said Ela coolly. "But I suggest that perhaps you knew your son wasn't coming back because you killed him yourself with your own knife, which we found buried not six feet away from him."

Oddo gasped. "Never!" He blinked and swayed and looked like he was about to fall over. "I never laid a hand on him."

This was not quite the reaction she'd expected. She glanced at the jurors. Price was open-mouthed in astonishment, and Clifford stared wide-eyed. Even Dacus blinked rapidly, looking from one face to another. Giles Haughton was the only one who looked unimpressed by her bold accusation.

"Why would I kill my only son?" Oddo's voice cracked. "The flesh of my flesh and my hope for the future?"

Ela felt a twinge of misgiving. Stunned by her accusation —to all appearances—he now looked like a fragile old man, not a hardened killer who'd been flushed out of hiding.

Still she knew better than to be taken in easily. "Perhaps you were disappointed because your son wasn't the man you hoped he'd be? You've admitted as much."

"But I'd never kill him for that. What would I gain from it?" He swayed again, and the guard standing next to him grabbed his arm and steadied him. "Are you sure it's him?"

Ela turned to Giles Haughton.

"We're sure of very little right now," said Haughton. "Could you describe the physical appearance of your son?"

Oddo blinked at him. "Blond hair and blue eyes. Never a stout lad. Took more after his mother, who was a slender slip of a girl when I met her."

"Would you say his build was both slighter and shorter than yours?"

"I'd say that, yes." Oddo's face crumpled oddly. "Is he really dead?"

Haughton frowned. "Did he have any distinguishing features? A limp or deformity of any kind? We have only the bones remaining, and it's hard to be sure of their identity."

Oddo shook his head. He stared around the great hall, bewildered, as if he couldn't quite believe he was here.

Either this was a performance worthy of a skilled mummer or Oddo was genuinely shocked and saddened that his son's body had been found.

If it was his son.

"There would be records of your son joining the king's army, even some years ago," said Ela. "With the king's garrison here we can request access to those records. Though it may take some time to retrieve them."

"If he's dead then he never joined the army," said Haughton. "Did he tell you that he intended to?"

Oddo, still looking rather befuddled, looked from Haughton to Ela to the jurors. "Did he?" he scratched his bald head. "I don't remember now. It was a long time ago."

Ela found herself growing impatient. Perhaps he thought that pretending to be an old man losing his wits would keep him out of the dungeon. "Nine years is not so long. If he didn't tell you he was joining the king's army, then how did you get that idea?"

Oddo frowned. He stared at her for a moment, then his

gaze rose, roaming over the painted plaster of the fireplace wall and toward the beamed ceiling. "Someone told me. Someone other than him."

"Who?" asked Ela impatiently. "One of your daughters?"

"Nay." He blinked again, as if searching his mind. "But it was a woman."

"Was he married?"

"Never."

"Was there a girl he courted?"

"Every girl in the village," said Oddo, his expression growing more focused. "But he never settled on one that he wanted to marry. Not that any of them would have had him, reckless as he was. He never wanted to be a farmer."

"He told you he wanted to be a soldier?"

"He wanted to see the world and make his fortune. He did say that. He may have even mentioned turning soldier, but I can't be sure now after all these years. Many a lad has dreams of fighting for king and country, after all, doesn't he?"

"Indeed he does, and a worthy ambition," said Ela. Her own sons were certainly being raised into men trained and willing to raise a sword for their king, should he call on them. "But you didn't encourage him in this aspiration?"

"I never took it seriously," said Oddo. "Boys will talk. I didn't believe it until after he was gone."

"But you believed it then?" Ela peered at him.

"Why wouldn't I? He was gone. I didn't know where he was. It made sense, didn't it?"

Ela ignored his rhetorical question. "Jurors, do you have questions for Oddo the Bald?"

Thomas Price's thick white eyebrows knitted together. "It seems odd that you never looked into where your son might have traveled to."

"He was a grown man. I couldn't stop him doing what he chose."

"How old was he?" asked Price.

"Four and twenty, not a lad at all. Still living off my bread and draining my ale to the dregs."

"He lived at the farm with you?"

"He slept in a shepherd's hut up by the woods at the top of the hill."

"The same hill where we found the body?" Ela looked at Haughton.

"I don't know where you found the body," said Oddo. "Or if the hut is still there. It was a flimsy construction since he built it himself. I don't even think it was still standing when I sold the place."

"We found the body up in the knot of woods on top of the hill, hard by the old hillfort that lies up there."

"Aye, that's the spot. He slept in the hut at night, watching the sheep or so he said, then he'd come down to eat in the daytime. Whether he was really there at night or in some merry widow's bed I couldn't say."

Oddo didn't show much fatherly love for his errant son. But he still didn't have much motivation to kill him.

"What of Farmer Crowder? Did your son get along with him?"

Oddo snorted. "Hardly. Simon was a great one for letting the sheep run onto Crowder's land. Sometimes I thought he did it just to spite him."

"Did you scold him for it?" asked Ela.

"Of course! Though I half thought Crowder deserved it."

"Why?"

"If you've met old Crowder, you'll know why."

Ela disliked his familiar tone. "I'll thank you not to make assumptions about my thoughts. And I've found Farmer Crowder to be a reasonable man. Please explain yourself," she said coldly.

"He always acted like he was better than everyone else

because his land was in his family for three generations. My old father bought my land. Doesn't that give me every bit as much right to it as he had to his?"

Ela thought it odd that either man—not noble by any stretch of the imagination—owned so much land free and clear with no liege lord over them, but they'd been through strange unsettled times when men could rise far and fall just as hard.

"All these years you believed that your son left to become a soldier without even saying goodbye to you?"

"Yes."

"That seems odd to me, especially since he lived on your farm."

Oddo cleared his throat. "We'd had words many times over one thing or another. At the time that he left we weren't wasting any more of them."

Ela watched him. He did look uncomfortable. Because he was embarrassed to reveal the poor relationship he had with his son? Or because he'd killed the lad and buried him in the woods?

She turned to Giles Haughton. "Is there some way that we can determine, without doubt, whether this is the body of Simon of Oddo or not?"

Haughton drew in a long breath. "Without distinguishing marks there might always be a question." He looked at Oddo. "Did your son have a piece missing from one of his teeth?"

Oddo frowned. "He did."

"Which one?"

"One of the front ones. He tripped and fell and chipped it on a stone when he was a lad of eleven or so."

Haughton's eyes narrowed. "Can you recall which tooth it was, exactly?"

Oddo looked up to the beamed ceiling, then back at

Haughton. "The right hand side." He shoved a thick finger into his own mouth. "This one."

Haughton nodded slowly, then looked at Ela. "It appears that we can indeed confirm that the body on the hilltop belongs to Simon of Oddo. The skull is missing a piece of the right front tooth."

Ela watched Oddo for his reaction to this news. Would he show the grief of a bereaved father or the anxiety of an accused killer? She was surprised to see him look relieved.

Giles Haughton took a step toward him. "Who do you think killed your son?"

"I couldn't say."

"You might well be blamed for killing him yourself. You've already admitted that the relationship between you was broken beyond repair. Perhaps he challenged you one time too many and you snapped and used your knife on him."

"You think an old man like me slayed a lad half my age?"

"You're taller and heavier than he was. I doubt you'd have had trouble overpowering him if you were angry enough."

"I'm not a hot-tempered man. Never was. I was disappointed in him, sometimes even embarrassed by his laddish foolery, but I never wished him dead. Certainly not by my own hand. Do you think I wish to burn in hell for all eternity?"

Haughton unwrapped an object he'd been holding in his hands from folds of grayish cloth. "Is this your knife?"

He brought it toward Oddo, who grew very still. "I believe it is."

"It has a unique construction, doesn't it? The carved finger grips are unusual."

"I made it myself to suit my needs."

"Have you ever made another like it?"

"Indeed I have. I made another just like it after I lost that one."

"How did you lose it?" Haughton held the knife up and turned it. If it was polished it would have glinted in the light through the high windows. But it was rusted and dull.

"I couldn't say. I carried it on me all the time, and one day it just wasn't there."

"How did you carry it?"

"In a sheath on my belt." He indicated the sheath on his belt, which held a much shorter knife.

"You have a different knife now?"

"I have a different life now. I need a knife only for cutting cheese and cleaning my nails, not castrating rams or stripping bark from a willow."

"Did you believe your knife was stolen, or did you think you lost it somewhere?"

Oddo looked around. "I don't know. I used to leave it in the kitchen after I cut my meat for supper. One morning it wasn't there."

"Did your son take it?"

"He swore he didn't."

Ela wasn't sure she believed any of this business about the knife going missing. It just seemed so much more likely that he'd used it himself to end the life of his errant son. "It's going to be hard to prove that you didn't kill him," she said slowly. "He was found dead in the woods on your land, killed by your knife. What do you expect the jury to think?"

Oddo's lips thinned as he stretched them over his teeth. "Perhaps he was killed by one of the girls he used so ill? I know he got at least one of them with child because I overheard her screaming at him."

"He refused to marry her?"

"Yes. He was bedding another one by then."

Ela frowned. "Excuse the question, but what made him so

attractive to a girl that she'd risk her reputation for him? He doesn't sound like much of a catch?"

"I can't say."

If he says that one more time…

"If I may interject," said Hugh Clifford, the wine merchant. "Simon was only a little older than me so I knew him as one of the local lads around my age. He had looks that the weaker-minded girls found appealing—golden hair and blue eyes and the like. He carried himself with confidence he didn't deserve and had a way of looking at them and talking to them that made them weak in the knees. Us fellows around his age all found it most perplexing and frustrating."

Ela looked at Clifford. "Do you know if any of these men grew angry enough with him and his misdeeds to end his life?"

Clifford shrugged. "If I were to mention any names it would amount to an accusation of murder, and I can barely remember who was making eyes at whom back then. I can think of one, though."

CHAPTER 9

"You can think of a man who grew angry enough with Simon to want to kill him?" Ela hoped this wasn't idle gossip. Any accusation made in front of the jury could send a man to the gallows.

"I do remember one time when Peter Hardwick, then the butcher's son and now the butcher, punched him in the face for talking to a girl he was carrying a torch for." Clifford paused and looked at Ela. "I don't fear to mention his name because a more honest and God-fearing man never took breath. I'm sure you all know him."

"Indeed I do," she replied, heaving a silent sigh of relief. Peter Hardwick had the skills to fillet a man, but they all knew he'd never commit such a foul crime. "And your example does illustrate how young Simon might have made himself enemies. His neighbor for one. We must interview Crowder and press him about his dealings with Simon. And we must learn which women Simon had entanglements with. They may have some insight into who killed him."

"Should I lock up this suspect, my lady?" asked the guard at Oddo's left shoulder.

Ela inhaled. Oddo was clearly a suspect in his son's death and she couldn't be seen to be too soft-hearted or people would gossip about the lady sheriff being easy on criminals. "Let him be kept under lock and key in the closet by the East Gate." There was a small room there for the watchmen to take shifts sleeping. "Make sure he has a pallet to sleep on and a chair." The guard frowned, clearly thinking this an odd request. "I don't want him catching his death in the cold, damp dungeon. We'll know more in a day or two." At least he didn't have flocks or herds that needed tending in his absence. That was a worse problem to deal with. "And someone must tell his daughter that he's here."

"She knows," said Oddo. "She was at home when they came to get me."

"And she didn't come with you?" Ela found that odd.

"She has the little ones to tend to. She can't leave them alone for long with that silly servant girl. One of my grand-sons drowned in the millrace behind the house four years ago."

"I see. My condolences. I trust that you'll be kept dry and fed in the castle while we pursue other suspects."

"I thank you for that, my lady." His gracious reply surprised her. It wasn't what she'd expect from a man being deprived of his liberty.

She waited while he was escorted away, then turned to Haughton and the jurors. "Do you think Oddo killed the lad himself?"

"It's possible," said Haughton. "It would explain him selling up not long after the boy disappeared. And he'd have a reason to be up on that hilltop and to bury him there."

"And his story about losing his knife was a tad too conve-nient," said Thomas Price.

"Everything does indeed point to him," said Ela. "Which to my thinking is a little too convenient. Almost like

89

someone wanted to kill Simon and point the finger of blame squarely at his father. But who?"

"Crowder might have hoped that Oddo would finally sell his land to him if his son was dead and he was accused of murder," suggested Price.

"But then why hide the body where it wouldn't be found for nine years? If he knew it was there he could have pretended to find it himself, but he never said a word, even when Oddo sold the land away from under him."

"Crowder could have killed Simon in a fit of anger," said Clifford. "After the boy let the sheep run over his land for the one hundredth time then cursed him out as well. He's a big man, and I've seen him in a temper. It's not pretty. He could have then stolen Oddo's knife to cover his tracks and try to trap his old enemy."

Ela looked from one man to the next. She could hardly imagine old Crowder killing the much younger man in a rage, but it wasn't worse than any other explanation they had. "We shall see what Crowder has to say for himself. Send out a messenger to summon him here after Tierce tomorrow morning, and we'll meet again to speak with him."

Thomas Price muttered that he needed to finish thatching the ridge on a cottage and could another juror come in his place? Ela told him to find one or more other jurors to stand in for him and to fill them in on the facts thus far.

THE NEXT MORNING, Ela was glad to see three jurors, Hugh Clifford again, but also Stephen Hale the cordwainer—who lived next door to Giles Haughton—and Hal Price, the old thatcher's son. It was often difficult to convince the most hardworking villagers to leave their labors early in the workday, but the pursuit of justice depended on their participation.

She sat on her dais, and two guards brought an angry Wilf Crowder forward.

"How's a man supposed to manage his farm if he can be dragged away from it in the middle of feeding his animals?"

"The morning is more than halfway over, Farmer Crowder. You've had plenty of time to see to your flocks." She leveled a stern gaze at him. "Do you realize you're a suspect in the murder of Simon of Oddo?"

"They did say it was his body. The teeth or something."

"Yes, his teeth have confirmed the identification. And his father has told us that you and Simon were often at odds because the lad would let the sheep he was tending run onto your land."

"He was a ne'er-do-well, that one. Lazy and insolent. Not cut out for farming or much of anything else. But if you think I'd lift even one finger to cut his useless throat, you're much mistaken."

"Perhaps you hoped that without a son to take over his land, Oddo would finally sell it to you."

Crowder snorted. "He'd rather die. And old Oddo knew that sniveling nitwit would never farm his land in any decent fashion. Would have let it go to rack and ruin if he'd had the chance."

Ela disliked his tone but didn't want to waste words on it. "Who else had access to that hilltop to kill him and bury his body?"

"His own father," said Crowder flatly. "Though I can't say I see him as a killer."

Ela looked around the hall as if a more likely suspect might materialize. "What about Beck?" She looked at the jurors. "When did he first appear in Salisbury and grow interested in the land?"

91

No one knew.

"He hardly rose from the River Avon in the morning mist," she said. "I need the jurors to ask their fellow townsmen when Beck first showed his face in this shire. He had the most to gain from Oddo giving up on his farm."

"Should I arrest Bertram Beck and bring him in for questioning?" asked John Dacus.

"Yes." It was time to act. "Any news of the women who… uh…knew Simon of Oddo?"

"Unfortunately the three girls we sought are all respectable married women now and seem to have lost their memories about the matter."

Ela sighed. Of course. And no doubt Hilda would do the same when she was married at last to a suitable husband. No girl wanted to revisit the foolish indiscretions of her youth.

"Someone must know the gossip, which is really what we need. Is there a source other than the girls themselves who'd tell us the truth about what happened with any of them and Simon of Oddo?"

Stephen Hale cleared his throat. "Una the alewife has an ear for gossip. The girls come to sit in her shop sometimes to chew the fat. She's been set up in town for at least ten years."

"I shall call on her," said Ela.

Dacus leaned in. "Should we arrest Crowder?"

"No," she said. His motive—if it could be called that—was flimsy enough. He had a hard enough time managing on his own, and she didn't think he was guilty of the murder. He was the type to gripe and make curmudgeonly remarks but not one to steal a man's knife and use it on his son. "He can go back to his farm."

"It's a good long walk for an old man," he grumbled. "And uphill, too."

"Give him a ride in the hay cart," she commanded to the

soldiers with him. Then she turned to Crowder again. "But don't leave the area as I'll need to talk to you again."

"Where would I go?"

Ela ignored his question but was glad he wouldn't have to walk all the way back in the March cold. The roads were still slippery, especially on the hills.

~

ELA COULDN'T RESIST VISITING Hilda and her baby. The little lad was so sweet and tiny, his pink fists curled against his sleepy face.

"Can we come down to the hall?" asked Hilda.

"Not yet. It's important to keep him away from too many people."

"Why? Everyone wants to meet him." Hilda pouted.

"I know, but new babes are fragile and need to be protected. Too much excitement can see them sicken and die."

"But look how strong he is!" She squeezed his thigh, which was barely larger than a chicken's.

"He's a big, beautiful boy, but he's still a newborn babe so best to keep him sheltered for now. Surely you remember your mother lying-in when she had your brothers and sisters?"

"On a farm?" Hilda laughed. "The cows want to be milked and don't care if you've just had a baby. Though me and the other older ones took over when she was having the last one."

"Well, it's better for you and your babe to rest in bed for some days. If you get up and walk about too soon you can start to bleed again." She gave her a stern look. Then she smiled. "I managed it after all my births, and you know as well as anyone that I'm not one to lie in bed all day."

"That's certainly true," said Hilda. She kissed her baby's head. He already had a patch of thick blond hair. "And I shouldn't complain about lying around all day like a countess while servants bring me food and drink, should I?"

"You should give prayerful thanks for your good fortune and the safe delivery of your baby."

"When will you find me a husband?"

Ela wanted to laugh. The girl was incorrigible. Still, she enjoyed Hilda's feisty spirit. "When I find a sturdy and sensible young man who will make you a good husband."

"Will he be handsome?" Hilda's eyes brightened.

"Oh, dear me, no." Ela leveled a serious gaze at her. "Handsome men are nothing but trouble, as you already know. I think a nice, stout man with two or three chins and perhaps a wart on one of them."

Hilda's eyes widened with alarm. "But then I shan't love him."

"Love grows in the heart, my dear, not the eyes. As you mature you'll realize that." She had trouble keeping a straight face. "But maybe not the wart."

"He will be taller than me, though, won't he?"

Ela pretended to look thoughtful. "I'm not sure. You're a great tall girl, almost my height."

"But your husband was tall as an oak. Everyone says so."

"I was born to be Countess of Salisbury, so I had a forest of oaks cultivated for me from birth. And I wasn't foolish enough to get pregnant by a twisted elm tree I wasn't even supposed to talk to."

Hilda's smile faded. "I suppose his being tall isn't so important. Drogo wasn't tall. He was very strong, though."

It wouldn't be easy to find the right man. Ela's own circle was all aristocrats, knights and others of high social status who couldn't possibly marry a young peasant girl, even one with a manor. Even a newly minted doctor or lawyer would consider Hilda Biggs beneath him. What she really needed was a younger son of a yeoman farmer like Crowder or Oddo. Someone who wasn't quite a peasant but wasn't a member of the gentry, either. A merchant or tradesman's son might do, if he didn't mind learning to farm. But who?

It was a tricky problem, and she'd not yet spotted the perfect candidate. Now Hilda was busy with her baby—and imprisoned in the castle—but Ela knew she'd better find a likely suitor soon before the silly girl had her head turned by another unsuitable swain.

An odd idea occurred to her. "Is there anyone you think would be a kind husband to you and a good father to your baby?"

Hilda cradled her baby in her arms and studied his peaceful face. "I don't know. I'm not very good at telling who's good and who isn't. I don't have enough experience of the world. I spent my whole life in my family's cottage until I came to the castle to work for you."

Ela felt this showed wisdom beyond Hilda's tender years. She also sensed that she was holding back something. "But just for an example, is there a lad from the town or from the surrounding area who seems like the right type of person?"

"Well..." Hilda looked up shyly. "Dunstan Miller seems kind, and he looks strong and healthy."

Ela racked her mind trying to picture the lad. "Is he the miller's oldest son?

"Yes."

He was a big, raw-boned lad of about three and twenty with a shock of dirty-blond hair. Likely enough, she supposed, if he wasn't already promised to someone else. But —"As the oldest son I've no doubt he's being schooled to take over his father's trade. His father wouldn't be happy to lose him to running a manor."

"See? I'm not a good person to ask. I didn't even think

about him planning to become a miller." She looked down at her baby. Then she looked up again at Ela, big gray eyes wide. "But you might be surprised. The miller might like the idea of his son being a lord of the manor. And he has other sons who can carry on his trade."

Ela considered this. "You're right, of course. See? Don't think I have all the good ideas. I'll make inquiries about the boy and see if we can find out what he's made of. Where did you meet him?"

"I've seen him at market. My family would bring chickens and eggs to sell. And I saw him one time at the horse fair two summers ago. I went to look at the horses and so did he, and we exchanged a few words."

Ela wondered how many other pretty girls young Dunstan Miller had exchanged a few words with. The last thing Hilda needed was to be saddled with a flirt and a ladies' man who'd be spending his nights away "on business." Still, that kind of thing wasn't hard to find out. She could ask the same alewife whom she intended to quiz about Simon of Oddo. Alewives knew everyone's business.

She decided to visit the woman that very afternoon.

CHAPTER 10

*U*na Thornhill's shop leaned right up against the inside of the castle wall. Its location just steps from the busiest gate made it popular with farmers and merchants from around the region as well as residents of the town.

Ela rode there herself with an attendant, who waited outside with her horse when she went in.

A short, stout woman, Una stood bent over a vat of ale as she entered, but she straightened up when she saw Ela. "My lady! God be with you. What can I get for you?"

"God's blessings upon you, Mistress Thornhill." Ela didn't really like ale—she found it bitter—but it seemed churlish to ask this good woman's advice without making a purchase. "I seek your knowledge on two local matters, and I'd be glad of a cup of your best ale."

Una Thornhill wiped her chapped hands on her apron and hurried to a cupboard in the back of the shop. She withdrew a green glass cup, rubbed it with a linen rag, then carried it to the row of kegs. Each of the five wooden kegs sat on a sort of stool that lifted it high enough for her to put a cup under a wooden spigot near the bottom. She opened a stream of ale and poured it into the cup slowly enough to prevent it forming a big frothy head.

She brought it to Ela, once again wiping the cup with the rag, which Ela noticed with relief was quite clean. Ela took it. The liquid was cool and the glass cold in her hand, which wasn't entirely pleasant given the chill in the fireless room. She lifted the glass. "To your health, Mistress Thornhill. Would you do me the favor of taking a seat for a moment to speak with me?"

The woman's round face crumpled with consternation. "I'd be happy to." She looked anything but happy, but she led the way to a cluster of scuffed wooden stools around a battered table and gestured for Ela to sit down. "What can I help you with?"

"I know you're privy to a lot of…." She didn't want to say the word *gossip* and get the alewife feeling defensive. "Conversation between the womenfolk in the town."

"I can't argue with that. The girls do love to come here for a bit of a chat as they drink some refreshment after their work is done."

"I'd appreciate if you could cast your mind back a while. Nine years, in fact. I'm wondering if you know which girls might have been enamored of a certain Simon of Oddo who used to live in these parts and had—if I'm informed correctly —a fondness for the ladies."

"Oh, that's a very bad business." Una still held the rag in her hands and she twisted it as if wringing it out. "I heard they found his body up high in the woods on his father's farm."

Ela's breath quickened. Word got around quickly. They'd only established the dead man's identity without a doubt on the previous day. "Indeed. We're trying to stitch together a tapestry of what was going on in his life at that time."

"So you can find out who killed him?" Una peered at her with curious brown eyes.

"Yes. Not that we suspect one of the girls, but knowing who he was involved with, or who he made advances to, will help us understand who might have motivation to kill him."

"A jealous husband, like?"

"Yes. Or a rival suitor. Or an angry father. There are a lot of possibilities."

"But wasn't he found with his father's knife?" She leaned forward, which drew her faded red gown tight over her large bosom. "If you ask me, that points the finger of blame squarely at his old man."

"But what motivation could he have?"

Her forehead scrunched under her white headscarf. "Lost his temper with the foolish boy? Everyone said young Simon was insolent as well as a lazy wastrel."

"I find Oddo the Bald to be a phlegmatic sort of man," said Ela. "I don't see him being quick to anger or rash in his actions. I questioned him about the death this morning. He seemed sure his son had gone away to fight."

"I can't say I know old Oddo. I don't think he's ever been in my shop and he's a man of few words at the market."

"He seems well respected. As does his neighbor Wilf Crowder. Those two should be the prime suspects, given the location of the body, but they're both sensible older men who have no strong motivation to knife the lad to death. That's why we're looking around to find out who else was involved in young Simon's life at the time."

Una sighed and scrunched her linen rag between her meaty hands.

She knows something.

Ela realized she hadn't yet sipped her ale so she raised the cup to her lips. The bitter amber liquid stung her tongue, but she hoped she managed not to show it on her face. "Very refreshing."

The aftertaste could probably wake the dead. But Ela knew her taste buds were spoiled by the finest Burgundy wine—and that other people praised Una Thornhill's ale to the skies.

"I thank you, my lady. Trade's been a bit off lately with so many of the townspeople picking up sticks and moving to the new town down by the cathedral. Sometimes I wonder if I'll have to move my whole business down there. It wouldn't be easy even for two strong men to heave these big kegs up onto a cart and I could hardly drain them all or I'd have no business since brewing ale takes time."

"I think we'll all be here for a while yet." Ela hated to watch the town around the castle lose its population, but there were advantages. The village inside the walls had been overcrowded to the point where the moat reeked of filth in the summer. "Do think back nine years and help me solve this mystery which vexes us all. I'd hate to see the wrong man hang for the crime, and there's always a risk of that if we don't find the right one."

As sheriff, Ela presided over trials involving stolen hens or unfaithful wives or flour cut with chalk, but a murder would have to be tried at the assizes by the traveling justice. It was her duty to produce the suspects and a jury of local men who understood the situation and had opinions about it, but it was the justice's responsibility to pronounce the final verdict regardless of whether or not she agreed with it.

Una Thornhill huffed. "I do hate to bring up the past when it could spoil the present. And dear Poppy is well settled with her husband now." She peered up at Ela.

"Poppy who?"

Una pressed her lips together and drew in a deep breath. "Poppy Allen. She was Poppy Brightwell back then, of course. They say Simon of Oddo got her with child. They also said she wasn't willing and that he took her by force, but I don't know if that's true or not."

"Oh, dear." Ela swallowed. "I could quite see why she wouldn't want to dredge that up. Did the child survive?"

"Aye. She married Will Allen, who was her sweetheart, and had the child seven months later. Everyone is supposed to believe it's Will Allen's child, but there was a lot of talk at the time that it was Simon's."

"How did people know this? Whom did she tell?" Ela couldn't imagine broadcasting such news throughout the town.

"I truly don't know. All you have to do is tell one person in this town and the news spreads like a fire. They muttered about it when the baby had blonde hair and light eyes like Simon, not brown like Will and Poppy."

"My children have hair and eyes of all colors, though my husband and I have similar coloring." She regretted the statement the moment it came out of her mouth. Why give the village gossip fodder for rumors about herself? People had commented on her sons Richard and Stephen both being dark when she and William had light brown to blondish hair. She knew he was the only man she'd ever lain with so God could choose any color from his palette to paint his creations. "Do you think she told her husband about what happened?"

"I doubt it. Would you?" The alewife realized what she'd said and clapped her hand to her mouth. "Begging your pardon, my lady. I quite forgot myself."

"Don't trouble yourself, mistress. I appreciate your candor. And, no, I probably wouldn't tell anyone, but I realize that not everyone is made of the same stern stuff as myself. I wouldn't blame a girl for wanting to spill her tears and seek comfort from a friend or relative over an unexpected pregnancy, whether the incident leading to it was wanted or not."

"You are good-hearted, my lady. Many would see nothing but blame. But you can see why things could be difficult for Poppy and her husband if the flames of gossip started licking around their door again."

"Indeed. If Will Allen believed that Simon of Oddo had raped his betrothed, he'd be well motivated to kill him. On the other hand, a jury would likely side with him and set him free."

"Even if they weren't married? And he used another man's knife?" The alewife's frank questions gave Ela pause. Using another man's knife—presumably to deflect blame—was a heinous crime and spoke of malice aforethought. And it was true that if the couple weren't married it would fit social convention more neatly if the girl's father forced her rapist to marry the girl, rather than letting her marry her innocent betrothed.

The whole situation seethed like a snake pit that could release serpents in all directions and ruin several lives.

"Was she the only girl known to have associated with Simon of Oddo?" Ela already knew there were more.

"Nay. He chased Anna Temple for months and wore her down, they say."

"That name sounds familiar." Ela couldn't think where she'd heard it.

"She was a dairymaid. Only been in town a few months. An orphan, I think. Lived above the milking shed with the other girls. When she got pregnant she drowned herself in the well. It took three men to pull her body out."

Ela crossed herself. "A sad business. I remember it now. The jurors and the coroner were called out, and no one knew why she'd done it. It was determined to be an accident."

"No one wanted to spill out the poor girl's shame when she was already dead, but they knew the truth."

"It seems that a man can take advantage of a girl easily if she's forced to hide his crimes in order to protect her own reputation."

"'Tis a sad truth. And a girl knows that if she tells her father or her brother what happened, they'll be compelled to hunt down the sinner and slice his balls off."

Ela flinched at the crude language, and her ale almost jumped over the side of her glass cup. "Then they'll end up in court facing a murder charge," she added. "A girl who's ill-used finds herself between a rock and a hard place."

"And if someone like this Simon of Oddo chased girls all over Salisbury for five years or more, he might have angered enough people to have a crowd chasing him to his grave with pitchforks." The alewife leaned back and pressed her lips together.

"So half the men of Salisbury might have wanted him dead. But why use old Oddo's knife?"

Una Thornhill shrugged and looked at Ela's cup. Ela realized she wasn't drinking it fast enough to be polite. She took a sip and managed not to grimace at the taste. "I didn't only come here to ask about Simon. There's another matter, and a much happier one."

"Oh, yes?"

"There's a young girl in my care called Hilda Biggs, a niece of my treasured former maid, Sibel."

"I've heard of the girl."

Ela froze. "What have you heard?"

The alewife's eyes widened. "Um, that she's a very pretty thing and found herself in the family way."

"Her betrothed was a knight and a friend of my husband's who was tragically murdered." Ela decided to get to work on reconfiguring the story of Hilda's relationship with Drogo.

"He intended to marry her and give her child his name, but he's now sadly dead and I find myself looking for a suitable husband for the girl."

Una Thornhill's curiosity lit up her face. "I heard the babe was born. Is it a boy or a girl?"

"It's a boy, and he's to be called Thomas Blount, after his father, whose family estate he'll inherit. So the girl and her babe will come with property that can provide a good income. I need to find her a sensible man who'll help her manage the property until the boy comes of age and who won't try to exploit her or ill use her and the child."

"Goodness. I'd think men would be lining up at the castle gates. Hilda's a beauty from what I've heard."

"Too lovely for her own good, I'm afraid. And she's spirited as well. As far as I can tell she has no head for business, though she's yet young and has time to learn."

"So what you need is a man of at least five and twenty—or more—experienced in the ways of the world and who can make a go of the property as a farming concern."

"Exactly." Ela felt a sense of relief that she'd made herself understood. "But not someone so grand as to feel that a peasant girl was beneath him."

Una Thornhill scrunched up her brow. Ela took another bracing sip of her ale. If only there was a way she could discreetly pour it out. But there wasn't, so she took another. "What do you know of Dunstan Miller?"

"Oh!" The alewife's face creased into a smile. "If I had a penny for every time I hear his name."

"It's on everyone's lips?" That wasn't good.

"The girls do talk about him. He'd have his pick of them if he wanted. Which he doesn't. At least not yet."

"Why do you think that is? Too busy sowing his wild oats?"

"I don't know the boy except to wish him a good day, but

I haven't seen a girl crying because of him. Sighing is more like it."

"So he's considered a catch?"

"He stands to inherit the mill. And his father's pleased as punch about it to hear his wife talk. The boy's mother thinks he's the finest prince to ever walk the earth."

Ela wondered if she'd ever idly bragged about the virtues of her own sons. Yes. She definitely had. But wasn't that one of the joys of being a mother? She could hardly begrudge Mistress Miller's pride in her own son. "Is her opinion shared by others?"

"I've heard nothing to contradict it."

Ela took yet another bracing swig of her ale. She needed to make more of a dent in it. "He sounds promising. But will his family be furious if he's presented with an opportunity that could make him forgo working for the family mill?"

Una Thornhill's weathered brow wrinkled a little. "I can't say they'd be happy about it. But you say this girl comes with a fortune?"

"Not a fortune, exactly. A property. It has a lot of potential but will need to be skillfully managed."

"And what does a miller know about managing a manor?"

Ela's heart sank. "A farmer would probably be better."

"But a sharp lad can learn a new trade easily. Would there be anyone to guide him?"

"Hilda herself grew up on a farm so she understands the management of animals and how to grow a garden in the course of a year. It's the planning and the marketing that needs a good and thrifty mind. For the first three years or so they'll be trying to spin gold from straw."

"The boy does seem to have a good head on his shoulders."

"I must meet with Dunstan and his parents." This was an awkward situation to be sure. It was bad enough trying to dream and scheme marriages for your own children. At least with marriages involving titles and fortunes she knew the rules of the game. This was different. But she didn't want to place the burden on Sibel, now busy with her own new marriage. "So you know of nothing against the boy?"

"Nay indeed." Una wiped up an imaginary spill with her rag. "You might say he's the most eligible bachelor in Salisbury. Hilda would be the envy of every girl in the shire."

Perhaps Dunstan Miller won't want Hilda. She is cradling another man's babe.

But Ela didn't want to sow doubt in the alewife's ear as it might ferment in her vats and get drunk up by the townspeople. "I thank you for your time and the opportunity to slake my thirst."

"Will you not finish it?" Una looked at the half-full glass with disappointment. "I can give it to you in a clay cup for your journey."

"I fear I would spill it while riding my horse." Ela handed her the green glass cup. "But I thank you for the offer and for your wise counsel. God go with you, Mistress Thornhill."

Ela exited the ale shop with her head spinning from all the information she'd acquired and from the unaccustomed ale. Her attendant helped her mount and she sat in the saddle for a moment, pondering where to ride next.

If she spoke to Poppy it must be subtle. There would be nothing discreet about the sheriff riding up to the unfortunate girl's house, so she'd have to come up with a more cunning ruse to spend time alone with the girl. In truth she preferred to leave her alone. And poor Anna Temple was no longer alive to question.

But calling on the miller's family would answer some questions now burning in her mind and would hopefully bestow on them glory rather than shame.

She turned to her attendant. "We're riding to the mill."

CHAPTER 11

The mill sat hard by the River Avon and used the stream's power to grind grains into flour for the people of Salisbury. Ela could hear the water sluicing through the mill wheel and the scraping of the grindstones as they approached.

Built partly of stone and partly of wattle-and-daub, the mill had a thatched roof in good repair. A fine coat of flour lay like new snow on parts of the path and courtyard. The miller and his family lived in a newish cottage next to the mill, the thatch still bright and trim. Smoke rising from the roof spoke of warmth and comfort within.

A saddled horse stood tied to a post, patiently awaiting its master's need. It barely blinked at the arrival of their two horses. The entire scene was one of prosperity and industry and warmed Ela's heart to her quest.

Except that no one was to be seen.

Ela asked her attendant to dismount and knock on the door of the house. The knock roused a woman to the door, wiping her hands on her apron.

"Ela, Countess of Salisbury, wishes to speak with you."

The woman looked past him and her eyes grew round. "Good morrow, my lady." She wiped her hands with increased vigor. "Do you seek my husband? I know he's been very busy and hasn't attended the juries as often as he might—"

"That's not why I'm here." Ela didn't want to waste time getting off on the wrong foot. "I'm here on a personal matter. Something that might bring great joy to your family."

She'd considered her words carefully. If she'd started with, "It concerns your son Dunstan," or similar, they might have worried that he was accused of a crime and being summoned before the sheriff.

Mistress Miller looked confused. As well she might.

Ela dismounted and handed her horse to the attendant. "Might I speak with you in private?"

Alarm crossed the woman's face. "Um, my children are within." She gestured into the house.

"Perhaps we could walk to the other side of the mill?" As she said the words light drizzle began to drift down from the white sky.

A barn constructed of rough timbers sheltered the sacks of ground flour until their owners came to pick them up. Ela could see a pile of sacks within. "Could we stand in here, out of the rain?"

"To be sure, my lady." Mistress Miller seemed more alarmed than curious. "What might I help you with?"

"My visit concerns the marriage prospects of your eldest son, Dunstan." The Miller's name was Paul Dunstan, so the son was named after both his father and his father's profession. It might be hard to pry him away from them both.

"What of them?" Her answer came fast, as if she couldn't control her anxiety. "He's not yet betrothed, though not for want of trying."

"He's asked a girl to marry him?"

"Oh, no," she shook her head, which flapped her clean, white kerchief. "I've suggested one after another and he just says he's not ready yet."

"How old is he?"

"Three and twenty! And with a fine future ahead of him. He's well ready to settle down."

"Why do you think he hesitates?" It occurred to Ela that he might not be interested in girls. While that didn't usually prevent a man from marrying—out of sheer social necessity —it would certainly make the marriage less joyful for the girl.

"Can't say I know. He's bent over books in the evening, reading by candlelight. Waste of good tallow if you ask me."

"Reading?" Ela couldn't conceal her surprise. "Where did he learn to read?"

"Bishop Poore's school for the boys of the parish. The bishop lends him books from his library. He reads about all sorts, medicine, farming, and the Bible, of course. Drives his pa and me half mad asking us fool questions about things that are none of our business."

Ela's heart beat faster. And warmer toward her sometime adversary Bishop Poore. "He's a curious lad, then?"

"Oh, yes. And keeps a stack of parchment covered in sketches of things he wants to try. He's drawn a dovecote and a henhouse with built-in roosts. Not that we need them. We've got a perfectly good barn." She sighed. "He probably knows a wife won't let him burn up all their good candles poring over bits of parchment when he should be getting a good night's sleep."

Ela could barely conceal her excitement. He sounded ideal. But what would his parents make of Hilda? What would he make of Hilda?

"I have a young lady in my care." She hesitated. "She's lately…widowed—" Perhaps that rumor would get around.

"And in possession of an estate that's lain neglected for some time. I seek an enterprising husband who can manage the estate for her."

And manage her, while he's at it. Young and impetuous, Hilda needed the guidance of a cooler and wiser head.

"And you think...our Dunstan?" Poor Mistress Miller looked more confused than ever. "He's just a miller's lad, not a fine lord."

"And this girl grew up in a farm cottage near Salisbury and has never lived on a manor in her life. She's the niece of my beloved maid, Sibel."

"Oh." Her face darkened. "It's Hilda Biggs you're talking about."

"Yes." Ela felt like she'd been slapped. "Do you know her?"

"I know of her. She's the talk of the town. Got pregnant by an old poacher who got his throat slit." She shook her head. Then seemed to remember she was addressing a countess. "Begging your pardon, my lady."

"The man was a brave knight named Thomas Blount, not a poacher." Well, he was once caught poaching but was never actually convicted of it. "He was a great friend to my family and once saved my husband's life on the battlefield. And Hilda has borne his son and will soon take possession of Fernlees, his manor near the London road."

"Will she now?" Mistress Miller looked heartily disapproving. Then her expression shifted. "And you're thinking that Hilda Biggs should marry my Dunstan?"

Suddenly it seemed a terrible idea. Hilda was wayward and spirited and foolish as a young colt. Their precious son was clearly the apple of his parents' eye, and Ela could jolt his life off course in her efforts to see Hilda settled.

"Yes."

Mistress Miller seemed to mull this over. Which was a

start. "She's a very pretty girl. Too pretty for her own good, if you ask me."

"Her beauty's not just on the outside. She has a warm and generous heart and is already proving to be a caring and attentive mother."

"How old is her babe?"

"But a few days. Her new husband could raise it as if it were his own, and it would know no other father. And she could give him many more sons and daughters." A girl who'd borne another man's child at least had the advantage of a proven womb.

"My husband's been shaping Dunstan to take over the running of the mill. Dunstan has ideas for improvements to the mill wheel."

"Has he implemented any of his ideas?"

"Oh, no. My husband doesn't like change. He prefers the old ways that have supported us for years."

"So Dunstan's inventive nature is thwarted."

Mistress Miller blinked. "I suppose it is a bit."

"But with a manor in his possession he might find a field of engagement for his plans."

"What if his ideas turn out to be cloud castles and he leads them both into ruin?"

Ela couldn't tell if she was joking or not. There was a gleam of...something in her eyes. "Somehow I doubt that." If they thought their son feckless they wouldn't be grooming him to take over the mill. "Do you have another son who could take over the mill in Dunstan's absence?"

"We have four lads." Her expression was inscrutable. But she wasn't protesting the idea. "But you can't make our Dunstan do anything he doesn't want to do. The Lord knows I've tried. He'll have an opinion on the matter. He'll have to meet her and see what he thinks."

"I think that's quite sensible. And Hilda says they've met."

"What?" She looked shocked. "When? He never said a word."

"I think they've exchanged a few words at one fair or another, nothing serious. But perhaps he'll know who she is. Is he here right now?"

"No, he took the cart into town to fetch bread. He'll be back in a while if you want to wait."

Ela didn't fancy standing around the mill yard tapping her foot. She had too much to do. "Perhaps you could present the idea to him, and if all goes well he shall see the estate with his own eyes as well as the girl. And we'll see whether he's agreeable."

And whether I am. Ela certainly wasn't going to agree to Hilda marrying him unless she approved of the boy. If Hilda's past taste for men was anything to go on, he might prove to be a scoundrel or a wastrel. She hadn't spent money on legal efforts to secure Fernlees for the girl and her child to watch it get squandered away in wagers or sloppy management.

"I shall tell him then."

Ela thought the miller's wife very self-possessed. She didn't seem intimidated by Ela's rank or her rather surprising request, but stood there, flanked by bags of fresh-milled flour, as if she dealt with such business every day.

"May God's blessings be upon you and your family," said Ela. "I know every mother wants the best for her son, and I thank you for taking this matter into consideration."

They walked back through the rain to where Freya pawed the ground impatiently while her attendant held the mare's reins.

"Farmer Crowder is dead." The words greeted Ela as she rode up the castle mound. John Dacus rode up to her. "I was coming to look for you. The hue and cry has been raised, and Giles Haughton has gone to see the body."

Crowder dead?

Ela had harbored thoughts of a small meal and perhaps a few quiet moments in prayer. Now she watched those plans evaporate. "How is he dead? He was at the castle this morning."

"He was found drowned in the stream at the very place where he accused Beck of moving it."

"Found by whom?"

"By Beck himself. He came to the castle to raise the hue and cry."

"Where is Beck now?"

"He went back there with Haughton to show him the spot."

"Is he trying to hide his own guilt?" She turned her horse around and they started riding—once again—toward Crowder's farm. "What more obvious suspect could there be?"

"But then why would he come to the castle?" Dacus wore a fine gray cloak that billowed in the wind. "Surely that speaks of innocence?"

"Or the desire to trick others into thinking you're innocent." Ela frowned at the white sky. "Beck is the kind of man who'll move a river to gain a few rods of land. Greed can be like a sickness for some men. They covet everything they see and can't help but try to pinch off a morsel when no one's looking."

"But what does he gain from killing his neighbor?"

Ela sighed. "His land? Crowder has no son to inherit. No doubt he hopes to buy it cheap from whatever heir can be found."

"If there's no heir, then who is to sell it to him? You can claim it for yourself or for the crown."

"True. Under the circumstances it would be tempting." The ability to seize land or goods was a known perk of being a sheriff. Ela did not wish to develop a reputation for the abuse of her powers, but keeping a property out of the hands of a man who'd kill for it was a good reason to claim it. "How does Beck claim he died?"

"He says he found him face-down in the stream."

"That stream is barely a trickle. I can't believe a man could drown there."

"It does seem suspicious."

THEY RODE across Crowder's land—happily without running into any hirelings riding over it to assert Beck's right to cross it—and down through the woods to where the stream trickled out of the hillside.

Haughton's bay palfrey stood asleep, its reins tied around its neck, but woke and whinnied to their horses as they approached. Since no jurors had arrived, Dacus offered to leave her with Haughton and return to Salisbury to chase them up.

Ela spotted Haughton a little farther down the stream. He crouched over the water, his green cloak swept behind him to keep it out of the water. Ela's stomach clenched when she saw the crumpled form of Wilf Crowder at his feet, brown homespun tunic clinging to his broad back and water sloshing around him as it made its way down the hillside.

I'll never get used to the sight of a dead body.

She crossed herself. "Has a priest been summoned to give him last rites?"

Haughton looked surprised. "It's a bit late for that."

114

"I suppose it is." She said a quick prayer for the passage of his immortal soul. She had no quarrel with Wilf Crowder, except that he was too proud to accept the help he badly needed.

Bertram Beck stood nearby, mousy hair being tossed by the wind and an odd expression on his face. "Don't you need to call jurors to witness the scene?" he asked.

"They're coming," said Haughton. "It's not always easy to pry them from their work."

"Can you tell how he died?" Ela asked Haughton as she drew closer, picking her way past the stones Crowder had arranged to redraw the border between his land and Beck's.

"There's a wound on the side of his head."

"From a blow?" She glanced at Beck.

Who immediately protested. "From a fall, surely. He must have slipped in the mud and hit his head on one of these rocks he was moving." Crowder had created a line of large stones, pulled from the woods, to mark the boundary. One lay almost under his body. Likely he held it in his arms as he fell.

Ela glanced at the ground and saw footsteps in the mud near him. "Did you make these?" she asked Haughton.

"No. I was careful to approach without disturbing the ground." He gestured to a neat line of footsteps that circled in from behind him.

"Then whose footsteps are these?" She pointed to the sizable male footprints around him.

"They're mine," said Beck "I saw him lying here and hurried over to help him."

Frustration surged in Ela's chest. "You've left your marks all around a dead body."

"Would you have me leave him face-down in a stream? I didn't know he was already dead. I thought maybe he'd just fallen."

"Did you see him fall?"

"No."

"When you checked him, was he still alive?"

"No. He wasn't breathing."

Ela looked at Haughton. "Can you tell how long he's been dead?"

"Not long at all. Rigor Mortis is only just setting in."

"So Farmer Beck here must have conveniently come upon him just moments after he died."

Haughton pried Crowder's hair away from the wound. "From the look of it he fell and hit his head hard enough to knock himself out, then because his face was in the water, he inhaled water and drowned."

"Do you view it as an accidental death?" She looked at him hard, wanting him to know he could communicate a coded response if he needed to.

He didn't look up at her. "I don't like to jump to conclusions."

"He was an old man," called Beck. "And he'd been laboring over these fool rocks since yesterday. Slipped and fell. Plain as the nose on my face."

"Farmer Beck, you are to return to your house at once and not leave it until you are given permission." Ela spoke in her sternest tone.

"What?"

"You heard me. You're the only witness and also the prime suspect. If you argue with me further you'll sleep in the dungeon tonight."

His mouth opened, then closed again, and he stumped off into the woods, heading toward his house.

"What are you thinking?" asked Ela of Haughton, once Beck was safely out of earshot.

"Seems a bit convenient that Beck turns up right after he falls to his death," he mumbled. He lifted the dead man's clothes and examined the body for marks.

"Perhaps Crowder fell and instead of helping him up, Beck seized the opportunity to hold his nose and mouth under water."

"Or perhaps he pushed him down in the first place. Then confounded any investigation by treading all around him so we'll never know what happened.

Ela looked into the woods after Beck's retreating form. "But by reporting the murder he surely put himself in the mind of everyone as number one suspect?"

"No doubt he thought that rushing in to raise the hue and cry would make him seen innocent."

"Why would he want jurors here?" Ela found the whole situation perplexing.

"Perhaps he hopes to have the death firmly established as an accident, with witnesses, so he can go on his merry way firmly above suspicion," said Haughton.

Ela sighed. "It would have been easy enough for Crowder to slip in the stream and hit his head."

"Indeed it would. And with no witnesses it will be hard to prove he didn't."

"If only we could quiz the squirrels and wrens. But why would Beck be here in the first place?"

"He could make the claim that he wanted to be sure Crowder didn't move the boundary too far back onto his land," said Haughton.

"Arranging his death is one sure way to interfere with his work."

Voices heralded the arrival of three jurors riding up the hill from the direction of Beck's house. Their horses' breath steamed in the cool afternoon air. Haughton explained the situation and guided them around the body, then asked for any insights they might have.

"Looks like he fell, don't it?" said Matthew Hart, one of the oldest jurors.

"Slipped in the stream," offered Thomas Pryce. "And banged his head."

"We must consider the possibility of foul play," said Ela. "He was in the middle of a boundary dispute with his neighbor Bertram Beck. The dispute was found in Crowder's favor so his neighbor might have reason to want—" What did Beck want?

"Revenge." Thomas Price uttered the word with some relish.

"But for what?" asked Matthew Hart. "He didn't even get a fine for taking the land."

"Only because the case hasn't been judged yet. He'll most certainly forfeit either money or goods to pay for his transgression." Ela had no intention of allowing the greedy and lawless among them to gain advantage over their neighbors while she was sheriff. "But this isn't the first body to be found on this hilltop, as you know. We must determine if this death is somehow linked to the death of Simon of Oddo, not a full furlong from this spot."

"But Simon died nine years ago."

"Crowder was here nine years ago," said Ela. "And Beck came here around that time. Perhaps Beck killed Crowder because he knew too much about the death of Simon of Oddo?" She was grasping at straws, but she could see that it would be too easy to dismiss this death as a sad accident—exactly as Beck would hope if he was the killer.

Then another thought occurred to her. "Oddo…the father. He was in these parts nine years ago, and returned to them yesterday. I asked the guards to hold him in a room at the East Gate." She looked at her nearest attendant. "Was he still there this morning?"

"As far as I know, my lady."

"A man who's killed once is more likely to do it again," muttered Haughton. "Especially if he has reason to cover his tracks for the first killing."

"But why would Oddo kill his old neighbor? He'd quit this neighborhood and left his old life behind."

"Crowder came right out and accused him of killing his son in front of witnesses yesterday."

"True. He did." Ela struggled to remember his exact words. He'd prevaricated somehow, not wanting to see his neighbor as a killer. "But Crowder had said all he had to say on the subject already. So why kill him now?"

Giles Haughton shrugged. "Perhaps Oddo thought Crowder might remember some forgotten detail or uncover some clue—buried on this land—that would see him hang?"

Ela shook her head. This was most perplexing. "But how could he kill him from within the walls of the tower? They're ten feet thick. He's under guard. It's impossible"

"It's a mystery, to be sure," said Haughton. "Let's get this body back to the mortuary so I can take a look at his lungs and see if he died before or after his face met the water."

Two more men had arrived from the castle, along with a donkey cart to transport the body back to the castle. The cart waited at the bottom of the hill. Haughton summoned them to come get the body. They heaved it out of the shallow water with little ceremony and carried it between them like a dripping sack of wet grain.

Ela crossed herself again at the sight, and muttered another quick prayer for the immortal soul of old Wilf Crowder. "We must make arrangements for his animals. They must be fed and tended tonight as he had no one to help him. I'll take possession of his farm for now, to keep it safe from the depredations of his greedy neighbor." The jurors muttered in agreement.

She rode back down the hill and across Crowder's fields,

where new grass blades peeped through the soil. "Who are his heirs, I wonder?" she asked.

"Perhaps he has a will drawn up," said Haughton. "It would be rare for a farmer not to."

"True." She frowned. "I'll have to consult with the clerk who keeps property records. And we must keep a close eye on Beck. He's still high on my list of suspects."

"As well he should be."

They rode back to the castle through a persistent drizzle, arriving as darkness fell. She parted ways with Giles Haughton at the castle gates and rode back into the court-yard with her attendants. Once inside she shed her damp cloak and greeted her children. Ela couldn't wait to sit down with a cup of warmed wine. But first she needed to make a quick visit to the small guard room to check on her prisoner.

There, she made an unexpected and startling discovery.

CHAPTER 12

"How long has he been like this?" Ela quizzed the guard standing outside the door.

"I don't know." The boy was too flustered to remember his manners. His blond hair stuck out sideways and gave him a startled look. "I gave him his supper a few hours ago and haven't heard a peep since."

"Because he's dead." Ela looked at the slumped form of Oddo the Bald on a low pallet on the floor with only a thin mattress over it. He was curled up on the mattress but as if he'd fallen asleep sitting and slowly keeled over.

She'd already checked for a pulse. There wasn't one.

"Call for Giles Haughton immediately."

Did they really have to raise the hue and cry again? The poor jurors had only just left for their homes and their hearths and their suppers. On the other hand she didn't want to be accused of concealing foul play inside her own castle. "And raise a jury."

Guards hurried away to execute her orders. Ela felt very tired. Couldn't she have enjoyed just one cup of wine and a small bowl of Lenten pottage before another body fell at her feet?

She chastised herself for complaining. Old Oddo would never complain again. But how was he dead, locked in here by himself?

"Has anyone been in to visit him?" she asked the guard.

"Not a soul, my lady." He straightened his back. He was very young. "I've been here all day guarding the door."

"Did you fall asleep at any time?" As if she could expect an honest answer to that question.

"Heavens, no, my lady. I've been standing up the whole time."

"And you never went away to use the garderobe?"

He hesitated. "Well, I did do that once or twice. But Matthew stood in for me."

Another man, considerably older, with gray at his temples and a square, weathered face, stepped forward. "No one went in the room while I stood guard."

"And what about Oddo leaving the room? Did he go to the garderobe as well?"

"Oh no, my lady," said Matthew. "There's a chamber pot in there for him to use."

Ela looked around. She couldn't smell a chamber pot. "Where is it?"

Matthew came into the room. "It was in that corner."

"And now it's gone." Ela peered at him. "Who came in to fetch it? One of the boys or a maid?"

Matthew blinked and scratched his head. He looked at the blond boy. "Billy, who took the pot?"

The boy blinked, confused. "A lass, I think."

"Which one?"

"One of them girls from the kitchen. The same one who brought him food."

"What did she look like? Brown or blonde hair?"

"Brownish-blondish maybe. I don't remember her face."

Ela wasn't even sure he was telling the truth. He likely didn't remember. Perhaps he'd wandered from his post.

"Where's the bowl for his food?" she asked. Oddo could have been poisoned.

Billy looked around. "That's gone, too. She must have taken it."

Ela sighed. All evidence gone. Oddo slumped over, breath gone from his body and limbs rigid. He'd been dead for some hours and no one had noticed.

ELA LEFT Oddo's body under guard—with different guards—and hurried to the kitchen, where she quizzed cook about Oddo's bowl.

"I never gave him anything. No one ever asked me to send food to him."

"And none of your girls retrieved a bowl?"

"Why would they? They didn't know he was there, let alone that he had a bowl." The cook could be blunt. As well she might be with such a vast household to cook for. "Will you be eating?"

"Not yet, Cook. I must find out where this food came and went from."

"Well, it weren't from my kitchen. Not without passing through someone else's hands anyway."

When Ela reentered the hall, Giles Haughton was handing his cloak and gloves to an attendant. "I hear Oddo is dead?"

"Slumped over in his room. Now both of the old neighbors are dead, and I can't make a whit of sense of it."

She led Giles to the small chamber by the gate, where he

studied the oddly hunched body, then crouched down to examine it.

"No sign of foul play—no bruises or cuts or ligature marks on his neck."

"He must have been poisoned. The cook said she never sent food for him, but someone brought him food, then spirited the bowl away along with his chamber pot. I have no idea who."

Haughton frowned at her. "How did they get past the guards?"

"I don't know. Though these young lads don't always take their work seriously enough. Guarding an old man probably didn't seem much of a challenge. And I suppose they were more concerned about stopping him from leaving than preventing another from entering."

Haughton waited for the jurors to arrive before doing a detailed examination of the body. Ela left them to it and retreated to her chamber.

ELSIE BRICE, Ela's maid, was in her room lighting the fire and jumped when she entered.

"It's only me. Has the death made you anxious?"

"What death?"

Ela sighed. Where to start? "Can you unpin my veil and take off my barbette and fillet?" Her head ached. She sat on her grooming stool and tilted her head back. "How's Hilda doing?"

"She's fine." Elsie moved behind Ela and started unpinning her headwear.

"And her baby?"

"Fine too."

Ela fought the urge to sigh again. Elsie could be taciturn

to the point of rudeness. But the poor girl had been through a lot, first being orphaned in an unusually cruel way, then sold to child-slavers. It might take some time—or all the time in the world—for her to lay down the burdens she carried with her.

"What did you get up to today, Elsie?" She asked as warmly as possible. "While I was running around like a chicken with its head cut off."

"I fetched your clean linens from the washerwoman and folded them in the trunk."

"Excellent."

"I polished your belt buckles."

"Good girl."

"I bound some fresh lavender to hang from your bedposts."

"I can smell it. Aren't you clever. Anything else?"

"And I took some food to that old man in the tower. I don't think anyone else remembered him. Yesterday I heard you saying that you wanted him to be taken care of, which is why he isn't in the dungeon."

Ela froze. "What food did you take him?"

"My own food. I wasn't hungry anyway."

Ela turned to stare at the girl. Who looked strangely hopeful as if expecting to be praised for her generous gesture. "That was thoughtful of you. And did you collect the bowl after he was finished?"

"Yes. And his chamber pot because it was stinking up the room."

"Where did you put them."

"I washed them outside in the yard. I took the clean bowl back to the kitchen, but when I went to put the chamber pot back there was a crowd so I left it in the hallway nearby."

That was about the longest sentence to ever come out of

Elsie Brice's mouth. She seemed so proud of her accomplishments.

But still. "Did you know the old man is now dead?"

"What?" Elsie's mouth dropped, and her eyes opened wide.

Ela felt her shock as a stab to her own heart. "Aye. He lay dead when I went in to visit him. Was there a guard at the door when you went in?"

"Yes. I think his name is Billy. I said hello to him and told him why I was there."

"He didn't remember you."

"No one ever does." Elsie's lip quivered. "I'm cursed. Only bad things happen around me."

Ela rose quickly and put her arms on the girl's shoulders. "That's not true at all. And it was so kind of you to think of old Oddo and bring him food. Was he alert when you went in to get the bowl?"

"No, he was asleep but sitting up, like. He's really dead?" Tears streamed down Elsie's face. Probably more for herself and her own cursed fate than for an old man she'd barely laid eyes on.

"He is. Giles Haughton is with him now. And the jurors."

"Will I hang for it?" She sounded strangely calm.

Her mother had been hanged for the murder of her father.

"Never, dear Elsie. I know you didn't kill him."

But who did? And how?

THE NEXT MORNING, the bells for Tierce had barely sounded when shouting rent the air of the great hall.

"You've killed him!" A woman rushed in, eyes wide, gray

shawl thrown back over her shoulders. "You've killed him for nothing."

Ela rose from her chair on her dais, where she'd been settling a dispute over a pair of ill-made shoes. "Silence! Guards, hold her until I am ready to meet her."

The guards who'd chased the strange woman into the room grabbed hold of her arms and wrestled her back away from Ela. Ela knew she had to maintain authority and not let people think they could come in here and browbeat her. Her heart beat faster, though.

She settled the minor dispute between the cordwainer and his disgruntled customer by insisting that the shoe be remade, and drew in a deep breath.

"You may approach." She kept her chin high and her tone cool. "What is your name and what brings you here?"

"You know what brings me here!" hissed the woman. "My father's dead."

"Your father is Oddo the Bald?" Ela spoke more softly.

"Was Oddo the Bald." The woman's eyes spit fire. "And he was alive and well when he left my house to come here to answer fool questions about some land he sold eight years ago."

"We put him in a quiet room here in the castle, with provisions and comforts."

"Then how did he die?"

Ela swallowed. "We're not certain. It seems likely that his heart stopped." Haughton could find no signs of violence, and his corpse displayed no telltale signs of poisoning.

"Well, wouldn't that be convenient?" Her voice pealed through the air. "Comes here to answer a few questions and drops dead all by himself."

"He was an old man," said Ela softly.

"Not that old! And you called him here because my brother's body was found up on that hilltop? He had nothing to do with that."

Did she know something? Ela's senses pricked like a hound that's spotted a hare. "Do you know who did kill your brother?"

She blew out. "Could have been half the people in Salisbury. My brother, Simon, wronged near all of them at one time or another." She seemed to calm down a bit. "But not my father. The old man loved his son even though he was a thorn in his side."

"Did your father know Simon was dead when he sold the farm?"

"I suppose he did, though he thought Simon had gone abroad and got himself killed fighting. Or whoring with another man's wife. That would have been more like Simon." Her eyes narrowed. "But Simon's not the reason I rode here at dawn this morning from Winchester without stopping on the way." She paused for a moment and a worried look came over her face. "Can I see his body?"

"Yes. It's in the castle mortuary. The coroner took him there to examine the body for signs of foul play. But he found none."

"Of course he didn't." She looked angry.

"We have nothing to hide. Why would anyone at the castle want to kill your father?"

"I don't even understand why he had to come here about something that's long said and done. Water under the bridge."

"A murder is never water under the bridge," said Ela. "A killer must be tried for his crime even if three score years have passed.

Ela glanced around the hall. A handful of people waited to talk to her about various local matters, but nothing seemed urgent. And she wanted to press Oddo's daughter further about Simon. She might know more details about who he spent time with around the time of his death. "I'll walk to the mortuary with you."

THE MORTUARY WAS a small wooden building inside the castle compound, erected to keep the odor of death out of the main rooms of the castle. With Ela's large household and the royal garrison, not to mention all the people living in the town inside the walls, questionable deaths—usually accidents of one kind or another, but also fights between the soldiers— were a not infrequent occurrence. Bodies were laid out there and examined before being prepared for burial.

Ela, trailed by two guards, led Oddo's daughter—Emma was her name—through the castle courtyards and into the mortuary. Another guard stationed at the door opened it for her. She held her breath for a moment, anticipating the unpleasant smell, before entering. Oddo's body lay on the table, covered in a length of linen.

Emma was a sturdy woman of near forty with a white scarf knotted over her mousy hair, which escaped at the temples. The wind had reddened her skin during her long ride. She approached the draped form with some trepidation.

Ela moved forward and lifted the corner nearest his head. "You can see his face if you like. He'll look like he's sleeping."

"I've seen a dead body before," she snapped.

She's just nervous. Ela held her tongue. Emma lifted the cloth and took a long, hard look at the face. He didn't really look like he was sleeping. His skin had turned gray and clung to his bones, and he seemed to have shrunk.

"He had many years more life left in him."

Ela didn't want to argue with her, though he looked at least sixty and possibly closer to seventy.

129

"He might have died from the shock of being called up here and then locked up in a cell."

"Quite possibly," Ela admitted. At least Emma seemed to be accepting that no foul play had occurred.

"There should be compensation." Emma looked up and her gray eyes met Ela's. "For his family's pain and suffering."

"He was brought here for questioning in relation to a murder." Ela didn't intend to be a pushover. "And kept here because there was reasonable suspicion that he might be the murderer."

"He never killed anyone in his life."

"Unfortunately your opinion is not solid evidence." Oddo's daughter could stir up considerable trouble if she made a fuss in the town. There could certainly be no question of compensation. An old man dying while in custody was unfortunate but sadly not unusual. "And he was put in a quiet dry room in the castle, not down in the dungeon, because I wanted to guard his health. I'm very sorry for your loss, but it seems most likely that God called him to be by his side. Perhaps we could pray together for the safe passage of his immortal soul."

Emma pulled the sheet back over his face. "What prayers could save him now when he died unshriven in this God-forsaken place? An old man dragged from his home and the bosom of his family?" She stared at Ela.

"The Lord is merciful."

"Not to my father, he wasn't."

"Don't speak to the Countess of Salisbury like that or you'll be clapped in irons." A male voice came through the door. Followed by the hearty form of John Dacus.

"Good day, Sir John." Ela greeted him, secretly glad of the uninvited chastisement. "There's no need for that. She's distressed by the loss of her father." She turned to Emma. "We'll make arrangements to return his body to Winchester with you in a cart." That would save her the expense and worry of finding transport.

"I thank you for that at least." Emma face showed no signs of grief. Perhaps she was still in shock.

"And there remains the matter of who killed your brother."

"I don't know who killed him."

"It was a long time ago, but we're trying to paint a picture of who he associated with at that time."

"I was already living in Winchester by then with my husband, Tom Acre."

"You didn't make visits home?"

"I came back at least once a month to visit my father and try to convince him to sell up and move."

"You wanted him to come live with you?"

"Yes. And my husband wanted him to invest in a new dyeing shed and new vats."

"Your husband is a dyer?"

"Aye." Ela's breath slowed. So Emma and her husband had a vested interest in seeing the farm sold. And thus would not want it passed on to her brother.

Did Emma Acre realize she'd just revealed a motive?

"What did your brother think about your father selling the farm?"

"He was dead against it, as you'd expect. Even if Pa didn't leave it to him to be squandered or gambled away, he still had a free place to live on it. He'd have just stayed up there, with his whore, until Judgment Day if he could have."

Ela glanced at John Dacus, then back at Emma Acre. "What do you mean, with his whore?"

"He was living in sin with a woman."

"A woman from the village?" Ela cast her mind back through the names she'd heard mentioned. They were all ordinary village girls who'd been seduced—or forced—into a

131

quick fondle, but no one had said a word about their living with him.

"Nay. From somewhere else. They said she ran away from her husband."

"Did you meet her?"

"Meet a woman who'd live in a man's house and share his bed with nary a thought for her marriage?" Her voice rose. "I'm a respectable woman and a Christian." She pressed a hand to her chest. For the first time Ela noticed the discoloration of her cuticles and nails that spoke of her husband's profession.

"What was her name?"

"I don't know. And she'd hardly have used her real name. It's against the law for a woman to run off and leave her husband." Ela glanced at John Dacus again. "Your lot would have rounded her up and sent her back home."

"Did he say why she left her husband?"

"I don't know. I didn't speak to him. Only knew about her because Pa complained about them living in sin on his property."

Ela wondered why Oddo hadn't mentioned this particular woman when he was alive. Perhaps he'd been embarrassed to have such flagrantly sinful and illegal behavior taking place on his land and involving his own son.

"Can you think of anyone who might know who she was?"

Emma's brow furrowed for a moment, then she pursed her lips and shook her head. "I've told you all I know. My father might have known more, but he's dead now and you'll never hear another word from his lips, more's the pity."

And Crowder, too. If anyone else would have seen this mystery woman it would be their nearby neighbor searching the woods for his stray sheep.

So Simon of Oddo had a mysterious woman living with

him at the time of his death…. Where was she now? And what happened to the hut they'd lived in? If they could determine the location of it, perhaps—

"Sir John, would you accompany me on another ride to Bertram Beck's farm?"

CHAPTER 13

To reach the hilltop they rode up through Beck's farmyard instead of crossing over Crowder's land as they'd become accustomed. If Bertram Beck had any objections to their presence that might be further indication of guilt in the murder of either Oddo or Crowder.

Ela wasn't surprised to see Beck emerge from his barn as their party approached, bells jingling and hooves thudding. He watched them ride into his yard and waited silently until they stopped.

He thinks we're here to arrest him.

The thought intrigued Ela. Was revenge on Crowder for taking back his own land enough of a motive for murder? Maybe it was if you could get away with it by making it look like an accident.

"Did you ever meet Simon of Oddo?"

"No. I bought the land from his father."

"We've learned that he lived here with a woman."

"In my house?" He indicated the thatched house with his thumb.

"No. Up in a shepherd's hut on the hillside. We'd like to see it."

"I don't know what you're talking about."

"Perhaps it was pulled down."

"Or fell down." Beck said. "Things rot away in the woods. All the wet leaves falling on the thatch and that."

"Quite." Ela decided this was enough of a preamble. She turned her horse and rode through the farmyard. Beck, less arrogant than previously, watched without protest.

His sheep-studded fields sloped up toward the wooded hilltop, his farm almost a mirror image of Crowder's. They rode into the woods and circled through them a few times looking for any traces of a hut. There were none.

"Odd that even the posts are gone," said Ela. "Almost like someone was trying to hide it."

"Farmers often repurpose the wood for another building," said John Dacus. "And a small hut might not have had corner posts. The thatch and wattle-and-daub—if a rustic hut even had such features—would quickly rot down to nothing."

"True. And eight seasons of leaves have woven their tapestry over it."

"And the pigs have rooted through these woods as well."

"But if you were a farmer—" Ela looked around. "Where would you build a hut up on this hill?"

Sir John turned his horse and rode to the edge of the woods. "Right here at the tree line where you can watch the sheep and look out for thieves, either human or animal."

Ela climbed down from her horse and handed Freya to an attendant. She walked slowly around, looking at the ground, where green shoots poked through the leaf litter in places among the trees. She kicked at the leaves with her shoe, disturbing worms in the rich earth.

"If Bertram Beck never saw the hut, then Oddo the Bald must have dismantled it before he sold the place."

"He'd be well motivated to if he hoped to stop his ne'er-do-well son moving back into it if he turned up again," said John.

"True. But Simon didn't go away. He's dead and was lying some yards from here the whole time. Killed with Oddo's knife."

Ela inhaled deeply of the cold March air. "Perhaps Oddo couldn't stand to have his son living defiantly in sin on his land. He could have killed him, then destroyed the shed to erase his memory."

"Or to keep people from looking around up here for him."

"I wonder if the woman was here when he died."

"She could be the killer for all we know," offered John.

"But what would her motive be? If he gave her shelter she'd be out on her own again."

"Maybe she went back to her husband. We must find her and question her."

"Indeed, but no one knows who she is." Ela frowned. "No one in the town even seemed to know of her, or that Simon of Oddo had a woman living up here with him. Only his family knew."

"And now Oddo is dead and his sister doesn't know who she is."

"Or she won't say?"

"She can be compelled," he suggested.

"With thumbscrews?" Ela peered at him.

"Perhaps not." He looked chastened. "And why wouldn't she say, if she did know?"

Ela walked a few steps in one direction and then in another. The hem of her gown brushed over the leaves and stirred up dust motes in the midday sun. "If we found a body buried underground, and a knife, we can find the hut."

"And what then?" John sighed. "We're not going to find her seal with her name graven around the edge. The local people rarely own anything but the clothes on their backs and a pot to cook in." He shifted in his saddle. "Besides, we weren't looking for a body when we found one. We sought traces of the ancient earthworks."

"Indeed." Ela pondered as she looked around the woods. "But we'll come back here with rakes and brooms and shovels and men with strong backs and see what else we can find."

~

THE NEXT FEW days passed in a flurry of day-to-day business about the castle. Ela dealt with minor local matters and managed her household and fussed over Hilda, who grew impatient to leave the confines of her room.

"I think you've lain quietly long enough," said Ela at last.

Hilda was already up and pacing about the room, holding her baby and cooing to him. "I can finally get dressed and go downstairs?"

"Yes. Your baby is healthy and sturdy, and you've healed well from his birth." She hesitated, hardly able to keep herself from smiling. "And I have a surprise for you."

"What?" Hilda spun around.

"I've arranged for us to meet with Dunstan Miller and his parents at Fernlees."

"What?" The girl stared as if her brain was addled. "When?"

"This afternoon."

Hilda gasped. "But I can't! My hair…" Her hand flew to it. "It needs to be brushed a hundred times to make it look half decent."

Admittedly her scalp looked rather oily and her hair straggled over her shoulders. "Elsie shall brush it for you and oil your scalp with lavender. But since you're already a mother I think you should wear a fillet and barbette like a matron.

"Like a real lady?"

"Yes. I shall give them to Elsie who shall dress you in them."

Hilda's eyes sparkled. "And a veil?"

Hilda was not a girl who knew when to stop. "I think a fillet and barbette will be quite adequate."

"I can wear my blue gown." It was one Ela had given her. An old one of Ida's that fit her nicely and had a pretty trim. "You met with him?"

"I haven't laid eyes on him. I spoke with his mother."

"And she liked the idea of him marrying me?"

"She didn't slam the door in my face." Now Ela did smile. "I think the prospect grew on her. She wants to see the manor and evaluate its potential. And she wants her son to meet you. She said she'd never force him to marry against his will. And she made it clear that he has quite a strong will."

Hilda's smile grew broad enough to reach her dimples. "Dunstan Miller." She tested the name on her tongue. "I'd be Mistress Miller."

Ela wasn't overly excited by that idea. "I think we should leave that name to those of the family that grind our flour."

"You think he should change his name to Blount, like my son?"

Ela tried not to laugh. "I feel quite certain he won't wish to do that. But perhaps a name after his father, who's known to the jury as Paul Dunstan. He could be Dunstan Paulson."

"Or maybe Dunstan Fernlees, since we shall live there." She kissed her baby's face.

"If he's agreeable—to the living part—of course. I like that idea. It cements the idea of your ownership as a family." Since Hilda was only acquiring the estate through her baby's father, there was always the grim possibility she could be forced to quit it, in favor of a distant biological heir, if her son were to die.

But if the family grew closely associated with the place they might more successfully sue to keep it. Lawsuits could overturn even ancient rights in this contentious age.

"When are we meeting him?" Hilda put her baby down in his cradle, and her hands fluttered to her face in agitation. "I must wash myself and dress."

"I told them we'd set out after Sext services." The church bells could be heard across the plain so it made sense to plan meetings around them. "You and I shall attend services to pray for the success of your marriage—whether it be this one or another."

"I shall start praying right now. Dunstan Miller is very handsome."

"But is he clever and kind? When looks fade you'll appreciate those other qualities far more."

Hilda sighed. "You're always so wise. Far more so than my own mother." Her pretty face fell. "She hasn't come to see me."

"Give her time, my sweet."

"She probably says my child is a bastard and wants nothing to do with me."

This was likely true. And they didn't think too well of Ela, either, for allowing the fornication to happen under her roof. Hopefully in time they'd soften and at least be civil to their daughter. Or perhaps they wouldn't. "It's their loss and my gain."

Ela leaned over the cradle and admired the baby's sweet chubby cheeks. Little Thomas had long lashes like his mother and a sweet pink mouth. So far he'd been quiet and easygoing, with none of the bouts of colic that made people decide their new infant must be a changeling.

~

HILDA ARRIVED at the castle chapel in time for Sext with a smile on her face. Elsie had brushed Hilda's hair until it shone, then pulled it back into a tight knot at her nape. Ela's snow-white fillet and barbette framed her lovely face and complimented her roses-and-cream complexion.

She and Ela listened to the psalms, then prayed silently. After the service they hurried out to the courtyard—Hilda anxious not to be late. "Why are the psalms always so angry?" asked Hilda as they hustled down the passage.

"What do you mean?"

"In the first one they're angry with their enemies, in the second God is angry with the people, and in the third they're all angry with God!" Ela was so accustomed to the familiar words of the Sext psalms that she barely registered their meaning any more. But Hilda rarely attended the Sext service—or any service—as she was usually busy with her duties.

"Life is hard," said Ela after a moment's thought, lifting her skirt to step up into the next corridor. "And filled with suffering." Poor Hilda had suffered enough in the past year for two or three lifetimes.

Hilda looked incredulous. "Your life isn't hard."

Ela laughed. They turned down the passage toward the courtyard. "I enjoy the luxuries that God has blessed me with, but don't think I'm not angry with other people and even with God at times."

"Why?"

"He took my husband to his bosom, leaving me a widow."

"True."

She wished she could blurt out the truth about the man who'd taken her husband's life to further his own ends. Fury at his murderous act of revenge still tore up her insides. But she must carry that secret to her grave or blight her children's futures.

They emerged out into the bright midday light of the courtyard.

"Where's the cart?" Usually Hilda and Elsie and any other female attendants rode behind the guards in a small cart.

"There's no need. You shall ride."

Hilda's eyes grew wide and moved to a fine black palfrey that Ela had ordered to be tacked up for her. "But I don't know how."

"All you have to do is climb up and sit there. You'll be led by the guard."

Hilda stared at the horse as if it might turn into a fire-breathing dragon. The groom stood waiting to help her up.

"Put your left foot in his hand," Ela suggested. "Then grab the saddle with both hands and hoist yourself up."

After some scrambling and huffing and puffing, Hilda sat awkwardly on the horse, in the chair-like sidesaddle, looking rather terrified. "I'm so high up."

"You'll be fine. He's a very quiet gelding and you don't have to steer him. Just relax. Horses don't like it if we're tense. It makes our bones feel hard on their back."

Hilda gripped the front of the saddle with both hands as they lurched into action. Ela couldn't even remember the first time she rode. She'd probably been a toddler propped on the front of her father's saddle. She could sit astride and steer her own mount before she turned seven.

The journey to Fernlees passed quickly and they arrived to find the miller's family already assembled in front of the house, their horses standing under some nearby trees. Ela wondered if they'd arrived early to nose around the property. If they did they'd have discovered they weren't alone there since there was a lad in the woods behind the house, bundling dead wood into faggots to use for fuel after Hilda moved in.

"Someone said there was a body found here," said the miller, after they'd made the introductions.

"That is true, sadly," said Ela. "One of the former occupants was found dead. His killer also left this earth to be judged for his sins." It was a long story and she hoped they wouldn't ask her to explain it. "But the house has been blessed and aired and is ready to hum with life again."

"It's a big house," said Mistress Miller. "It'll be a challenge to keep the chill out."

"It has two chimneys," said Ela. She didn't remember seeing a chimney on the miller's house. Only the grander houses had them. "And a thick thatch to keep the warmth in. The thatch has been repaired and the walls whitewashed."

Why did she feel like she was trying to sell them a pig in a poke? She should let the situation speak for itself. "If you've had a chance to walk around you'll see there's a nice mix of good pasture, some arable fields and productive woods. The lad is cleaning up the woods now and making good use of the fallen branches."

Ela turned to Dunstan Miller, eager to see what he was made of. "Do you have any thoughts about how such a property should be managed?"

"I suspect it would be best to start with a cow for milk, chickens for eggs and a small flock of sheep for wool to sell." The lad was indeed comely: tall, with a broad forehead and expressive brown eyes. "I'd sow barley in autumn and wheat in spring, and if it grew well in this soil I'd grow enough to grind into flour for sale." He smiled at his father.

Who smiled back. It was a good sign when a son admired his father and the father liked his son.

"That sounds quite sensible," said Ela. She looked at Hilda, who gazed starry eyed at young Dunstan. Her baby had been left at home with the wet nurse. "Hilda, do you have any particular thoughts about the management of Fernlees?"

Hilda looked at her in surprise. "I know little of such matters. I'd leave the planning to my husband. I'd do my best to keep things just how he liked them."

Good answer. Even as Ela felt a stab of disappointment that Hilda seemed so ready to turn over authority to another, it was the right thing to say to warm her prospective husband and his parents to her. And Hilda, garrulous and curious as she was, would never sit idly by while a man ran the place to ruin.

The miller's wife looked pleased by her answer. Ela decided to tackle the most awkward issue head on. "As you know, dear Hilda is newly widowed and has just given birth to a babe. If your son is to marry her he must take on the responsibilities and joys of being a father to this boy and raising him to be a man.

The miller and his wife both looked at their son. Who looked earnestly at Hilda. "I'm sad for the loss of your... husband. And if we do marry I pledge to be the best father I can be to your son and the best husband to you."

This was going far too well. Ela began to worry that there was something she didn't know about the miller's family. Why were they so quick to warm to her rather outrageous proposal that their firstborn son—and the heir to their prosperous mill—marry an unchaste servant girl? She hoped she wasn't thrusting poor Hilda into danger. Lord knows the poor girl had suffered enough in her short life. "Hilda, do you have anything to say to Dunstan? Or questions you'd like to ask him?"

Hilda looked thoughtful for a moment. "I'd like to ask him to marry me."

She said it calmly and clearly as if it was the most natural statement in the world. It fell into a stunned silence, as they all stared back at her.

"I think that you and Dunstan should take a little time to become acquainted with each other," said Ela quickly. "Marriage is a lifetime commitment and not to be entered into lightly."

Unless there are vast properties and great sums of money involved. Her own older children's marriages had each been a foregone conclusion since before they could talk. The character of their betrotheds was hardly a consideration. Why did she want more for Hilda?

"Perhaps Hilda and I could walk about the house and grounds," suggested Dunstan.

"If Mistress Miller agrees to accompany you as a chaperone, I'm in full agreement." Ela had already proven herself to be an inadequate chaperone to Hilda, as evidenced by the girl becoming pregnant out of wedlock in her household.

"I'd be content to do so," said his mother, who did look rather pleased by the turn of events. And why shouldn't she? All the thatching and weeding and mending of rotted wood and rusted iron had made Fernlees inviting and picturesque in its lush setting. The ungrazed pastures glowed rich and green, and the tree branches bristled with tight buds. Promise for future prosperity and happiness surged around them like the sap in the trees.

Ela made conversation with the miller, who happily didn't ask any probing questions about the dead body they'd found moldering in a chest, its putrid fluids leaking through to the floor below. Or the other dead body found crushed by a cartwheel in the courtyard. Everyone seemed to have forgotten about that one. The miller spoke of his son's bright mind and good head for figures.

"Would you be sorry to lose him at the mill?" asked Ela.

She didn't want to leave this question unaddressed and find later that all parties had regrets.

"Of course, but I have other sons and this seems a promising opportunity. If he grows corn for me to grind into flour, we can both profit from his labors."

After a short while Hilda and Dunstan appeared around the side of the house, with his mother in tow. Dunstan looked nervous, his eyes casting about from Hilda to Ela to the packed earth of the courtyard at their feet. Hilda looked pale as a ghost except for two bright spots of color high on her cheeks.

What's amiss?

Did the two young people manage to have a falling-out in the short time they'd spent with each other? Had Hilda waxed on about her lost love or Dunstan lorded it over her in some way?

Ela couldn't stand the suspense a moment longer. "What's the verdict?"

CHAPTER 14

"I'd be most pleased to have Hilda as my wife if she'll do me the honor," said Dunstan, looking at Hilda, so nervous he could barely get the words out.

Hilda's face brightened instantly. "I'm happy to accept," she said, in a clear, confident tone that took Ela by surprise. "I promise to be a good wife to you and a good mother to our children." She looked at Ela. "If it pleases my lady."

"It does indeed." Relief flooded Ela. For a moment she thought this promising match had run aground on some rocks hidden in the long grass of Fernlees. "We must plan the wedding. It can take place as soon as Lent is over."

Hilda's face fell. "But that's ages away!"

"Hardly. It will give us time to make arrangements." Ela turned to the miller. "Which church would you prefer?" Most local people had a favorite, usually the one nearest to their home, where they'd been baptized and married and where their ancestors lay buried, going back a hundred years or more, for some.

"Wherever it pleases my lady," said the miller.

Cunning, thought Ela. Perhaps they hoped she'd hold the

ceremony in the castle or at the cathedral and she'd be stuck paying for the festivities. "If you have no preference, Hilda and I will plan it together, and the celebration afterwards shall take place here at Fernlees."

Hilda smiled and Dunstan Miller looked happy enough. He kissed Hilda's hand, then the miller's family mounted their horses and rode away.

"That went smoothly," said Ela, with relief, as they disappeared out of earshot.

"Did you think he wouldn't want me?" Hilda looked amused.

Ela sighed. She certainly didn't want to compliment the girl on her beauty and make her grow vain. "A manor with good grazing and a sturdy house won't wrinkle and freckle with time." She shot Hilda an arch smile.

"So you think he wants Fernlees and not me?" Hilda seemed to contemplate this as a possibility.

Ela regretted her comment. Hilda had been through enough, and—abandoned by her own parents—did not need to have her confidence knocked. "I feel sure that your charms are at least as much of an enticement as the woods and fields of Fernlees. He can hardly have missed your spirited character, and you've already proven yourself as a mother of his future children. I'm sure he feels doubly blessed to gain you and Fernlees at the same time."

Hilda looked relieved. "I do hope so. And it will be a big relief to be a married lady. I think foolish boys will finally stop tormenting me."

"Who?" Ela hoped it wasn't one of her sons.

"Oh, no one in particular. You know how men are."

"Not really. A countess isn't subject to insults from ordinary men. And I was a countess from a very young age."

"Oh, yes. I forgot about that."

THEY MOUNTED their horses and rode back to the castle, where they shared the happy news. Ela's oldest daughter, Ida, sat in a chair by the fire in the great hall, holding Hilda's baby. She stood and held the chubby little boy, wrapped in swaddling, out to Hilda with the longest face Ela had ever seen. "He's a lovely baby," she said flatly.

"Doesn't he smell just like fresh-baked bread?" said Hilda with a dimpled grin, taking him into her arms.

"Yes." Ida looked like she was about to cry.

Ela's heart pinched. "Thank you for taking care of Hilda's baby, my sweet."

"Oh, the wet nurse did that. I have no milk, you see." Her voice quavered. "I just held him when he wasn't feeding."

The bells for Vespers sounded. Ela grabbed Ida's arm. "Let's go to the chapel and pray."

"For the success of Hilda's marriage," said Ida with a wan smile.

"And that you may be blessed with a baby of your own to love," said Ela.

"All in the Lord's good time," said Ida woodenly, as they turned toward the chapel. "Perhaps the Lord doesn't wish me to know the joys of motherhood. I might have offended him in some way, and he's chosen to punish me thus."

They entered the doors to the chapel, and Ela took in a deep draught of the incense smoking in the burner. The fading evening light shone through the colored glass of the small stained glass window high behind the altar.

"Nonsense, my pet. I'm sure it's nothing of the sort. But prayer can only help."

ELA SENT John Dacus ahead with a crew of men to dig around the site of the old shepherd's hut. She told them to mark out any features they discovered, whether they related to the events of eight years ago or eight hundred years ago. And they were instructed to tell Sir John where any objects or implements were found.

If nothing else she could commission a good map of the site that would record the legal boundary between the two properties and provide a record of the ancient inhabitation of the site. She found herself intrigued by the people who trod this land before her ancestors arrived here from France.

This castle she'd inherited from her father was built upon a great mound constructed by men from another age, defending their hilltop from different enemies. They'd built the great stone circles nearby and buried their dead in massive barrows that rose from the fields. All of their efforts wasted and their souls now barred from the gates of Heaven because they didn't know of the one true God.

People said they'd worshipped the lightning and rain and trees and that the stone circles had something to do with the rise and set of the sun. They must have been very simple people. Ela didn't like to dwell on their misguided beliefs too much as it seemed unholy to think of such things.

She spent the morning in the great hall, overseeing her children's lessons and looking over documents and hearing arguments related to a disputed will. She also set her daughters Ida and Petronella to work on embroidering some good but plain linens she'd bought for Hilda's surprise trousseau. If Hilda saw them at it, they were to say it was for themselves. By midday she was ready to quit the bustle and smoke of the great hall and take a ride to get some air.

With two attendants in tow, Ela headed—yet again—up into the disputed woods.

Bertram Beck stood off to one side, glowering at the men

turning up the soil and digging holes on both sides of the marked boundary.

"Ah, my lady." John Dacus strode toward her, stepping over a gaping hole in the earth. "We've found a wondrous multitude of things."

"Like what?"

"Broken clay jars, mostly, but also some iron implements." He pointed to an odd piece of metal so rusted it looked like it might crumble to dust.

"What is that?"

"A tripod, I think. Made to hold a pot over a fire."

"It looks like the ones people use now. Do you think it's ancient?"

"I doubt it. Probably would have rusted to nothing by now. It could be from when Simon lived here."

"So you've found the location of the old shepherd's hut?"

"It seems to have been right"—he turned and strode a few paces to his left—"here." He pointed to a freshly dug area of the ground. "You can see one of the old corner posts here. It's been snapped off."

Ela looked up at Bertram Beck, who stood in easy earshot. "Was there a structure here when you bought the place?"

He stared at her with what felt like unfettered hatred. "I don't believe there was." His lips settled flat across his teeth. "Must have been gone by then."

She wasn't sure whether to believe him or not. He'd lied about the boundary so what else was he capable of? Yet he was the one person they hadn't found a solid motive for. What would he have to gain by killing Simon of Oddo? And if he'd buried the body up here, why would he summon the attention of the sheriff by causing a disturbance over the boundary?

A shard of light bounced up from the ground and caught her eye. "What's that?"

"What?" John Dacus followed her gaze.

They both walked closer, and Ela peered at the shiny object catching a ray of sunlight even here in the woods.

"It's a ring." She crouched down and picked it up from freshly dug earth. "Did you find this already?"

"No. It's so small it must have escaped our eyes."

The ring was very tiny indeed. Small enough to fit only on the littlest finger of a woman. A braided gold band set around a tiny blue gem that was probably glass. The glass had trapped the light for an instant.

"A woman was here," said Ela. "But when? Is this recent or ancient?"

She handed the ring to Dacus, who wiped it off on the hem of his cloak and held it up to the light. "It's a pretty thing, isn't it? Hard to say. There are scratches on the gold, but that could be from the soil." He handed the ring back to Ela.

Who stared at it. "I suspect that if we can find the owner of this ring, we'll know who lived up here with Simon of Oddo."

"That ring was found on my land," piped up Beck suddenly. "It's mine by right."

"This ring is a clue in the murder investigation," said Ela sharply. "Would you like me to charge you with hindering our efforts to solve it?"

"No, but—"

"Silence."

Beck glowered. Ela had a feeling she hadn't heard the last of his claim to the ring.

～

"Oh, it's pretty." Hilda exclaimed over the ring. "Is it an emerald?"

"Emeralds are green, silly," said Petronella. "Sapphires are blue."

They sat around the fire as the night grew long. Hilda cradled her baby at her breast. Ela could swear the little lad grew so fast she could almost see it. Ida's needles poked in and out of the linen shift on her lap, leaving a trail of blue and gold flowers around the hem.

"I need to find the owner," said Ela. "What's the best way to do that?"

"You must ask people," said Petronella. "And the one who owns the ring will know it."

Hilda scoffed. "If only. Half the people of Salisbury would say it's theirs just to keep it."

"God sees everything," said Petronella snippily.

"If that stopped people from committing crimes, we wouldn't need a sheriff, now, would we?" Hilda paused from stroking her baby's hair to defend her point.

Petronella opened her mouth to retort, then apparently thought better of it.

"Don't argue about it, girls," said Ida, without looking up from her needlework. "Mama will know how to find the right person."

Ela, silently stitching away at the edge of a handkerchief, wished she did. She did have an idea, though. "We can send a crier through the town to announce that the ring has been found. Whoever can come to the castle and describe it gets to keep it."

"Ah, that is clever," said Ida. "Only the person who lost it will know what it looks like."

"Someone might guess," said Hilda. "Would you give it to anyone who said they'd lost a gold ring with a blue stone?"

Ela hesitated. "They'd have to say where they lost it."

"Under the circumstances they might decide to let it go," said Ida, glancing up from her sewing. "Especially if the stone is glass."

"Gold is gold. It can be melted down. Someone will come forward."

"Unless they're dead," said Hilda, in a matter-of-fact tone. "Everyone keeps winding up dead."

"Hilda!" Ela scolded her. "That's a terrible thing to say."

"It's the truth, though." Hilda unlatched her sleeping baby off her nipple with a now-expert finger and pulled her dress back into place. "First one farmer, then the other. And one of them's son was dead. Maybe the ring is bewitched."

"Hilda! You know there are no such things as witches." Ela spoke sharply again. Hilda had somehow turned into a regular member of the family—outspoken and quarrelsome as any sibling—rather than a docile servant. Ela admired her spirit even as it annoyed her. "And Oddo's death seems to be a natural one. Crowder's may well be too."

"He slipped and drowned in three-finger-deep water?" Ida looked up. "Unlikely."

"He was an older man. Three score years at least. He had a bad hip and he'd been lifting heavy boulders to mark the boundary of his property. The weight of a stone could have unbalanced him or made him fall harder."

"You think two men—enemies while they were alive—died of entirely natural deaths on the same day?" asked Ida.

"I don't know what to think," said Ela. "But tomorrow I shall invite people to come forward if they know anything about this ring."

THE NEXT MORNING a young man with a bugle went forth into the village around the castle, then down to the new town, to proclaim that a valuable ring had been found and anyone with information as to its appearance and whereabouts should come to the palace to describe and claim it.

A trickle of people came almost immediately, then turned into a steady stream that flowed all day.

"It was gold, with two clasped hands."

"Three rubies, there were, all set in filigree gold."

"A small green stone set in a band carved with spirals."

They took a rest to eat a quiet meal of pottage and soft white bread with gooseberry preserves. Ela sighed. "You'd think every man and woman in Salisbury had lost a ring. The woods and fields must be littered with them. If only pigs could sniff them out! I'd put the money toward the monastery to be built in my husband's name."

"They're greedy. They're hoping to guess it," said Hilda. "Some of them will come again for another try, you mark my words."

"Speaking of greedy, you've eaten all the nutmeats," said Petronella. "I wanted a morsel for my cat."

"She's eating for herself and her baby," said Ela, with a frown at Petronella.

"Her baby's outside her belly now," said Petronella, her neck stiffening.

"But it can't feed itself and gets all its sustenance from her milk."

"I'll never breastfeed a baby," said Petronella with disdain. "I'd hate to have milk dripping down me."

Hilda glanced at the front of her gown, where a dark circle had formed where her nipple lay underneath. She reached into her sleeve for a handkerchief and mopped at the stain.

"The Lord may have plans for you that catch you unawares," said Ela to Petronella.

"Like marrying me off to some baron or count for money?"

"A life has different stages," said Ela. "You can always become a nun and dedicate your life to Christ later on."

"I'll starve myself to death before I'll marry a man," Petronella spat, before storming off out of the hall.

"Pride is a grave sin," muttered Ela in her wake. She'd need to have a stern private conversation with her defiant daughter.

"What's the bee in her bonnet?" asked Ida.

"She's been agitating to take the veil immediately. She won't even wait until Lacock Abbey is built."

"So why not let her?" said Ida, sewing her flowers. "She's so pious and persnickety. She'll be better off there marching around the cloisters chanting prayers than she will here with her long, sour face curdling the milk."

"It's such a grave decision," said Ela. "She's still so young. She needs time to grow up more before choosing to forgo the joys of marriage and children to become a bride of Christ."

"Petronella's wanted to be a nun since she could say her first words," said Ida. "I hardly think she's going to change her mind now."

Ela didn't think she would either, but sometimes womanly desires could take a young lady by storm. Look at the trouble they'd got Hilda into. And last year Ela had helped a young man and woman who were outcasts in the village because they'd abandoned their religious vows and left their cloisters to marry.

"Petronella has the liberty to attend every Mass here in the castle. She has time for reflection and prayer. And she's a great help with Ellie and Nicky."

The two little ones hadn't even looked up at their conversation. They sat at the end of the table, eating and chattering away with their tutor, who schooled them in letters and numbers, and the nursemaid who kept them out of Ela's hair while she was busy with her duties.

"You don't want to lose her to the convent," said Ida.

"You're right," said Ela with a sigh. "It's bad enough to give a daughter to a loving husband. At least she can come visit. Once she takes her vows Petronella might not leave the cloister again."

"There are nuns who come to market," said Hilda. "They sell wool and butter."

"Some nuns attend to the business of the order, but that's at the discretion of the abbess. Many never leave the walls of their convent. No doubt they're glad to be quit of the secular world and its troubles, but it's hard on their families." She dabbed her mouth with her napkin and rose from the table. "I must go hear about more lost rings. If we could make a chain of all the lost rings of Salisbury I suspect it would reach right up to Heaven."

THE PROCESSION of claimants went on all afternoon, interrupting the more important business of settling local disputes and the unending tasks associated with managing her manors and the castle household. And there were the two monasteries in the planning stages—one in her husband's memory and one in her name.

A draughtsman had instructions to make drawings and her stewards pored over the lists of required materials and tried to assess the feasibility and cost of acquiring all the goods and labor required. Ela insisted that both monasteries should be erected and completed as quickly as possible—and there was so much to be done before the first cornerstones could be laid.

She hoped to look over their notes after she'd finished listening to descriptions of rings.

"There's one more visitor today, my lady." Albert the porter seemed apologetic. As well he might. It had been dark for some time, and she longed to relax by the fire with a cup of spiced wine. "A woman named Margery Willoughby."

"Send her in." The name didn't sound familiar. Which mostly meant that she hadn't been accused of any crimes or involved in any altercations. It was surprising how many of the ring seekers were already familiar to Ela because they'd appeared before a jury for one reason or another.

Margery Willoughby was a short, plump woman of thirty or so, with a clean white scarf covering most of her dark hair. She bowed her head respectfully as she approached Ela.

"Good day, mistress," said Ela. "What brings you here?" As if she didn't know.

"It's about the ring," said Margery. She spoke so softly that Ela could hardly hear her. "I've come about the ring."

"You and everyone else here today." Ela couldn't hide the ennui in her voice. "What did your ring look like and where did you lose it?"

Margery swallowed. "It was a gold ring, braided gold, with a...with a..."

Ela grew impatient. "Speak up, I can barely hear you."

Margery took a step closer. "With a blue glass stone." Again, she barely whispered the words, as if they held some deadly secret.

And it was the first accurate description Ela had heard all day. "Why are you speaking so low?" Ela now spoke softly herself. Clearly something worried this woman.

"I don't want anyone to know," she whispered. "That the ring was mine."

"Surely they'll know that if you claim it and take it home."

157

"I don't want to take it home." she hissed, alarm in her eyes.

Ela's curiosity was getting the better of her. But they still hadn't established Margery Willoughby as the true owner of the ring. "Where was it lost?"

"I'm not sure exactly." Her eyes darted around.

She's lying. Ela had dealt with enough liars in her life to know the signs. "Where were you living at the time that you lost it?" Could Margery Willoughby be the mystery woman who lived in in sin in the shepherd's hut on Oddo's farm?

Margery swallowed. Her hands knotted together, and Ela noticed that under her thick gray wool cloak she wore a gown of good green wool, with embroidered cuffs. The toes of her neat leather boots peeked out beneath her hem, unscuffed by wear. She looked like the wife of a prosperous merchant, not a strumpet who'd leave her husband for the bed of a known rascal.

"I'd rather not say."

"You can't have the ring if you can't describe the location where it was found. It's a rather specific spot."

"I don't want the ring." Her eyes pleaded. For a moment Ela thought she was going to cry.

"Then why did you come here?" This made no sense.

"I don't want anyone else to see it." Margery's eyes darted around the room, as if she might be arrested by the guards at any moment.

"Why not?"

"I don't like to say."

Ela rose to her feet, her frustration getting the better of her. "Would you feel able to talk more freely in a quiet chamber, away from the great hall?"

Margery nodded.

"Follow me."

CHAPTER 15

*E*la led Margery out of the hall and down a hallway to a small chamber used for garrison business—reprimanding wayward soldiers, conveying private orders, etc. If Deschamps, the garrison commander, wasn't there, she could use it to speak to the woman in private. She opened the door and was relieved to see it empty. The room held a table and chairs and very little else.

Ela went in and motioned to her attendant to wait outside the door. Then she ushered Margery in and closed it.

As the door clunked against its frame a thought occurred to her.

This woman could be Simon of Oddo's murderer.

Ela gestured for her to sit in a chair, and Margery did so with some hesitation, gathering her skirt neatly around her legs.

"Your description of the ring is accurate," said Ela. "Where were you living when it was lost?"

Margery's mouth worked. "It was a difficult time in my life."

Ela waited. She could see the woman didn't want to tell

159

her anything. But then why risk exposure by coming here at all? Why not just let someone else claim the ring?

"The ring was given to me by my first husband. I took it off and buried it in the woods. I didn't want to see it or him ever again."

"You left your husband while he was still alive?"

She nodded. "He used to hit me. One time he punched me so hard that I lost the child I was carrying. I've never conceived another child since. He must have broken something inside me."

"I'm sorry to hear that. Did you go home to your parents when you left your husband?"

"My parents were both dead. I had nowhere to go, but I couldn't stay. I feared he would kill me. I left the house and started walking and after a long time walking on the road I met a kind man who offered me a place to hide."

"Simon of Oddo?"

Margery's look of shock—and terror—let her know she'd guessed correctly. "You found the ring up on that hilltop, by the hut?"

"The hut is gone now, but yes. You hid it there while Simon was still alive?"

She nodded. "I stayed there some weeks with him. Maybe months. He gave me food and shelter."

In exchange for sharing his bed, no doubt.

"Were you still there when he died?"

Margery stared at her. "He died?" Her brown eyes searched Ela's as if she felt her fate rested in Ela's hands.

Ela didn't respond. She wasn't sure she believed Simon's death was news to this woman. "You were still living there at the hut at the time he disappeared?"

She hesitated. "Yes."

"But even if you weren't there when he died, you must

have seen a disturbance in the soil from where he was buried. He was killed and buried right on top of that hill."

Ela watched Margery's throat move as she swallowed. She peered at her, increasingly suspicious. "Did you have good reason to want Simon of Oddo dead?"

"No!" Margery jerked so violently that her chair scraped on the floor. "He was good to me. Most of the time anyway."

"Did he tell you he was going away?"

"He talked about making his fortune, maybe even going on a Crusade. I thought it was idle chatter but then one day he was gone."

"What did you do then?"

"I stayed up there for a while. I didn't know what else to do."

"How did you eat?"

Margery hesitated, clearly embarrassed. "I went to the cookshops and bakeries and asked if they had any spoiled wares I could have. People were kind, and I managed to hold body and soul together."

"Did old Oddo know you were in the hut?"

"I suppose he might have. He came up one time looking for his son, then called me a—a bad word. But he left me unmolested either way."

"When did you leave the hilltop?"

"I was offered a—a position in a cookshop."

"Which one?" Ela knew them all to look at even if she hadn't been inside.

"The one with the red-painted doorway."

"Willoughby's pies and—" The woman's last name sank in. "You married the owner."

Margery swallowed. "I did. Hugh Willoughby. He was very kind to me. He's a good husband."

Ela couldn't even picture him. "I don't know him."

"He's been an invalid these many years. He rarely leaves his bed now."

"Was he an invalid when you met him?"

She nodded. "He's older than me. But he takes good care of me."

Ela tried to process the entire unsavory situation. "But what of your first husband? Did you ever divorce him?" She wasn't even sure a woman of Margery's class could get a divorce or annulment. She'd certainly never heard of it.

Margery's face crumpled below her mouth. "No. And he doesn't know I'm here. I had a different name then. No one here knows me as the same person. My first husband lives twenty miles away in Devizes and by now he must think I'm dead. But if word of the ring got back to him he'd know that I came to Salisbury and he might come here looking for me and—" She broke out sobbing.

Ela bit her lip. She felt bad for the woman, but marrying another man without divorcing the first was bigamy and a crime in the eyes of man and God. "So you heard everyone talking about the ring and knew the news was spreading throughout the shire. You came here to put the news to rest."

Margery nodded, wiping at her tears with a sleeve. Her good-quality clothing suggested that she'd had a soft landing from her previous hard life. Though still quite young, she had a round, owlish face with a small hard mouth that wouldn't attract hordes of suitors. Her invalid husband who couldn't leave his bed must be an improvement over one with the energy to raise his hand to her.

"What was your name before?"

The woman hesitated. "I don't like to say. I'd rather forget the past."

Ela struggled with her impatience. "I'm afraid the law doesn't allow you to forget a marriage."

Tears welled in the woman's eyes. "You're going to tell him, aren't you?"

"I don't know what I'm going to do, but right now you're a suspect in Simon of Oddo's murder and I'm going to need you to be completely truthful with me."

It occurred to Ela again that if this woman was the killer, it might not be safe to stay alone with her. She hoped the guard outside the door was paying close attention.

"My name was Grizeldis," rasped the woman. "My husband was—" She broke off as if a hand suddenly tightened around her throat. "Ebbo Fuller."

"Does he still live in Devizes?"

"I don't know. I've made sure never to go that way for any reason." Margery—or Grizeldis—started trembling. "I've been so scared that he'd find me, and beat the life out of me to punish me for running away."

"In truth, the law would be on his side," said Ela. "You should have reported your husband's violence to the sheriff."

Margery stared at her, her round owlish eyes blinking. "And what would he have done? Most men think their wives are their property, like a stool or a spindle, to treat as they please."

This was largely true. Ela had hoped that the Magna Carta would offer more protection for women but had tried to be satisfied with the small gains made for the independence of widows.

"I had no father to speak up for me, and no mother or brothers or sisters. I was all alone and had no recourse but to close my eyes as his fists rained down on me." Her voice grew steadier. "Everyone knew he beat me—I had bruises on me, didn't I?—and no one said a word. No one cared." Tears now streamed down her face, but she held her chin high. "After the midwife delivered my dead baby she said some kind words to me but then she left me with him and he beat me for losing the baby. If I hadn't run away I'm sure I'd be dead right now."

Ela felt her heart clench as Margery recounted her grim ordeal. "You have my fullest sympathies. Did Simon ever treat you thus?"

Margery blinked. "He never hit me. If he did I might have killed him." Her lip quivered. "And I say that because I can see I've walked into a pit of vipers and I'm never going back to my life. You're going to have me sent back to Devizes, aren't you?"

"No, I'm not." Ela made that decision as she said it. But what to do? This woman was undoubtedly a suspect in Simon of Oddo's death, despite her protestations. On the other hand she had a lot to lose here in Salisbury: her comfortable life at the pie shop with an indulgent husband; her carefully kept secrets. She had little motivation or opportunity to run away to evade capture.

"Can you promise me that you won't leave Salisbury for any reason while this investigation is under way?"

Margery nodded, her eyes red with weeping. "What will you do with the ring?"

"I'll keep it locked up for now. And I'll send out word that its owner was found so people will stop coming here to claim it."

"But you won't tell them it was me?"

Ela couldn't shake the feeling that she was being roped into something. "No. But you may well be called here to testify before a jury."

"About the ring?" Her eyes widened with terror.

"About the death of Simon of Oddo. You could be the last person who saw him alive."

"The killer was the last person who saw him alive," she said slowly. "And I swear I didn't kill him."

Ela couldn't entirely imagine the rather petite and plump

Margery wielding Oddo's knife to kill Simon, but with only the skeleton left they had no way of knowing how skillful or violent the killer was. One quick stick in the right place could fell a man as big as a tree if it severed an artery.

And Margery could have gained access to Oddo's knife. Living on his farm she could have crept into his house or barn and stolen it while he lay asleep.

Misgivings sent prickles along Ela's arms. But she couldn't bring herself to arrest Margery for murder and bring the full weight of the law down on her for adultery. It would destroy her life, and even if she didn't hang it might send her back into the violent hands of her abusive husband.

Why would Margery kill the man who'd given her shelter and safety?

But if she didn't kill him, who did?

"Did Simon have enemies that you know of?" She wondered if Margery, or Grizeldis, knew about his other lovers.

"He wasn't well-liked," she admitted. "He said as much. One time a man came up the hill looking for him, swearing and saying that he wanted to tan his hide."

Ela's interest pricked up. "Did he say why?"

Margery looked down at the floor. "He said he'd been... interfering with his daughter."

So she did know.

"Was Simon there?"

"He was out. When I told him later he just told me to be quiet and that it was none of my business."

Maybe the girl's father killed him in a jealous rage? A father could hardly be faulted for wanting to protect his daughter's honor. "Do you know who the father was?"

Margery shook her head.

"How did you feel about Simon chasing other women?"

Margery looked at her for a moment with her round eyes,

then blinked and looked down again. "Who was I to expect him to be faithful to me when I was already married to another man?" Her voice was flat.

"You never thought to try to get your marriage dissolved?"

"I thought of it, but I knew he'd refuse. And he'd have dragged me home and taken out his anger on me." She looked up at Ela again, something steely glinting in her gaze. "I'd die before I'd go back to him."

So Margery found herself between a rock and a hard place, desperate to avoid her cruel husband and forced to share the bed of a man who lay with other women. She had plenty of motivation to kill someone.

"Is your husband still alive?"

"I've heard no word of his death."

"You haven't tried to find out?"

"Who would I ask? I don't want anyone to guess who I was. I was very thin back then and now I'm quite fat, but my face is the same. Someone might recognize me. I haven't been within ten miles of Devizes since I left it all those years ago."

"Well, I shall investigate whether your first husband is alive or dead. If he's dead then you'd be freed from that yoke, at least."

"And my current marriage would be legal?"

Ela frowned. "I'm not sure. I've never seen a case quite like this. If he died before your marriage, it would be legal, yes. If you married while he was still alive, then I suppose it wouldn't. You'd have to marry again, but there would be no impediment." An odd thought occurred to her. "Does your new husband know you were married before?'"

Margery's gaze fell to the floor again. "Yes. But he's a kind man. He took pity on my sorrows and married me anyway."

Her husband must be a forgiving man indeed.

"Did he know about Simon?"

She nodded yes, looking shamefaced. "But he never blamed me for taking shelter with him. He saw that I had no choice and that I would have starved otherwise."

Ela wondered about this invalid husband who was so willing to overlook his young wife's moral failings. "Does he know you're here?"

"Nay. I didn't want to trouble him with the news of the ring. He's so frail now and hardly keeping body and soul together. I don't want him to be dragged into anything." She wiped her hands on the front of her gown. "He's a good Christian and has a fine reputation in the town and wouldn't want word of my past to get out."

"Or people might refuse to buy the pies at your shop," said Ela. It wasn't a question. Scandal had a way of drying up business. She'd seen it more than once.

Margery nodded. "I've built a new life for myself, and I'm happy now. I'd hate for this discovery of the ring to bring it all down around me."

"Unfortunately we have a dead body whose murder must be solved, so I can't let the matter of Simon of Oddo's death rest. And now there are the deaths of Simon's father and his closest neighbor."

"I had nothing to do with them," Margery said, a little too fast.

"But do you have any idea who might want them all dead?"

She shook her head, mouth pursed like an owl's beak. Ela couldn't shake a feeling of unease. "That hilltop is cursed, though," said Margery. "That's what they say. All the dead souls of the people who lived there long ago."

Ela peered at her, startled. "What makes you say that?"

"Well, it's creepy, isn't it? To think that was a place where hundreds of people lived and died and then it all just grew over with woods. And all their bodies moldered away and grew up into the trees."

Ela shivered involuntarily, but it was a very small shudder so hopefully Margery didn't see it. That hilltop did have an eerie feel to it. Though that could be explained by the ghoulish discovery of the murdered body of Simon of Oddo.

"What do you know of the history of the spot?"

She shrugged. "Nothing really, but you could see the ditch around an old mound. I dug a garden in the spring and found old bits of pottery. Nothing worth keeping though."

"Unlike your ring. Weren't you tempted to sell it? The gold is worth something."

"At first I just wanted to hide it. Later when I was desperate for money I tried to find it, but I couldn't remember where I'd buried it." An odd expression came over her face. "Perhaps I could have it now. I could sell it quietly."

"Unlikely, with everyone in Salisbury trying to claim it as theirs."

"But they don't know what it looks like." Again that owlish stare. "You didn't tell anyone."

"True."

"Can I have it?" The sudden eagerness in Margery's eyes gave Ela pause.

"It's put safely away for now." She wasn't sure why, but she didn't want to give it back yet. "It's still evidence in a murder."

"Not now that you know it was mine, and I didn't kill him." Margery's confidence had soared. "It would pay for a fine new painted sign for the pie shop."

"Indeed it would." Ela felt a sudden cooling of her feelings toward Margery. "And in time you shall likely have it. But there are still inquiries to be made. It's evidence of your marriage to another man."

"He only gave the ring to me because he had it already. It

belonged to his mother. She died and he gave it to me then. He told me the stone was only glass. If it was worth anything very much he'd have sold it instead."

Ela wondered if she could really just forget about this woman's first marriage. Could she allow an adulteress to go merrily about her business in their midst? Surely that was a dereliction of her duty to the people of Salisbury.

Ela drew in a steadying breath. "I shall need to speak with your husband—your second husband."

"About what?" Margery's face tightened with alarm. "He's very frail. He can't leave his bed."

Ela wasn't entirely sure what she wanted to ask him. Mostly she wanted a sense of whether Margery could be trusted—or not. "I shall call on him at your home."

CHAPTER 16

The next morning Giles Haughton came early to the castle to break his fast with her.

"Three dead bodies and not a single murderer in the jail," said Haughton almost as soon as he sat down. Idle pleasantries were not his style. Ela liked that about him.

"Better that than an innocent man should lose his freedom."

The kitchen maid had laid out a modest feast of pastries made with dried fruit and almond paste. Ela helped herself to a portion appropriate to the Lenten season.

"Oddo's body went back to Winchester with his daughter," said Haughton. "What am I to do with the body of Wilf Crowder in the mortuary? He has no heir to claim it."

"I'm more concerned with discovering his killer."

"If there is one." Haughton lifted a brow and took a sip of spiced wine. "The jurors might conclude that Crowder slipped and fell to his death, banging his head on a stone. Therefore his own land—the slippery mud and the hard boulders together—could be accused of claiming his life."

"We can hardly arrest his land and lock it up in the dungeon," Ela said drily. She bit into her pastry.

"Nay, but as the murder weapon—if you will—the land could be claimed as deodand for the crown. Especially in the absence of an heir. As coroner—or crowner as they used to say—it's my duty to make sure the king gets his due."

Ela blinked. "In the absence of a legitimate heir that may be the best course." Her voice sounded flat. In truth she didn't like the idea much. The king could give the land to whomever he chose—either local or distant—and the new owner or tenant might turn out to be a thorn in her side. Especially if the king's closest confidant—and her mortal enemy—Hubert de Burgh had any say in the matter.

But, new in her role of sheriff, she didn't want to flout convention or contradict the king's coroner unnecessarily. A good working relationship with Haughton was essential to her success. "Is that what you'd recommend?"

Haughton shrugged. "It's just an option. What has been done for Crowder's livestock?"

"I sent a man there to tend to them."

"Since you're providing feed and care for the beasts you could claim them yourself in recompense."

Ela took pains to avoid the appearance of profiting from her role as sheriff. But she didn't want to be seen as a fool, either. The pursuit of justice did bite into her own purse more often than she cared to admit. "Perhaps I shall. But first we must determine if there's a murderer among us—who should be seized and tried at the assizes—or if it truly was an accident."

"The only real suspect is Bertram Beck, his neighbor, who stirred up this dispute about the boundary. He might have seen an opportunity to end his rivalry with his neighbor in a way that would be interpreted as an accident." Haughton took a bite of pastry and chewed.

"But with no witnesses or evidence an accusation would be pure speculation."

"He might have counted on that," said Haughton, patting his mouth with his napkin. "It's the perfect crime in many ways." He picked up a nutmeat and surveyed it. "Except that —despite his greater age—Crowder was the bigger and stronger man and I'm not sure that Beck could have overpowered him easily enough to execute such a plan with confidence. Crowder himself might have proved the victor, and Bertram Beck have drowned in the stream."

"Beck doesn't strike me as a man of physical courage," said Ela. "He's a sneak, moving boundaries when no one is looking and hoping that no one notices."

"The kind of man who wins his battles in the law courts, not the battlefield."

"Is there any other kind of man these days?" asked Ela with a raised brow. "Sometimes I feel like my dear husband was the last of his kind."

"William Longespée was a great man, brave and true, and his loss is felt keenly by all of Salisbury. We're blessed to have his good wife to lead us in his stead."

"Daily, I ask God for the wisdom and courage to do his will in Salisbury. And I'm grateful for your guidance as I learn my new role." She paused and drew in a breath. "Do you think we should arrest Bertram Beck?"

"For the murder of Crowder?"

"He could hardly have murdered Oddo, who died inside the castle, could he?" asked Ela.

Haughton shrugged. "Poison could have been slipped into his food by a messenger. But I agree that seems unlikely. Circumstances suggest that Oddo's advanced age, combined with the shock and discomfort of being detained in custody, caused his heart to stop."

"And Beck wasn't here when Simon of Oddo died all

those years ago. The property didn't change hands until a year later."

"Yet it fell into the hands of a stranger from up north," said Haughton. "Which is odd in itself. If you're asking me whether he should be arrested, I say yes. Press him and see what squeezes out."

"He must be punished for his efforts to steal his neighbor's land. An imprisonment could be justified on those grounds alone. I shall take your advice and have him arrested today."

"If you like, I shall arrest him myself, with a phalanx of jurors to witness the event," said Haughton.

"And I shall make arrangements to safeguard his livestock. The same man who's managing Crowder's farm can oversee it for as long as needed."

"My lady." Albert the porter's voice drew Ela's attention. "Master Bertram Beck wishes an audience with you."

"Well, speak of the devil," muttered Haughton, looking past Ela toward the entrance to the hall. Ela turned to see Beck, dressed in a bright red cloak, staring right at her.

"This should be interesting," said Ela under her breath. "Give me a moment to take my seat, then send him to me." She didn't want to entertain him at her dining table. She wiped her hands on her napkin, then walked to the dais and climbed into the chair she used for her official business.

Haughton had a quiet word with two of the hall attendants—perhaps summoning jurors to be witness to events—then walked over to join her as Beck strode purposefully across the hall.

A small knot of people already waited there for Ela to take up her seat, but she beckoned for Beck to come to her first and he swept past them with a supercilious glance. "Good morrow, my lady. Perhaps you can guess why I've come?"

To surrender yourself to the mercy of the courts? "I do not play guessing games."

"I seek the ring. It was discovered on my land and from what I hear no one has come to claim it, so I claim it as mine to keep. Surely anything found on my land—whether it be a tree, a shed, a sheep or an ancient valuable—is mine, bought part and parcel along with the very soil I grow my crops in."

Ela wondered if he'd practiced his speech. It had a studied air. "What makes you think no one has claimed it?"

"I heard in the market that a dozen people have made an attempt, but none could prove themselves the owner."

"You heard wrong."

"Who owns it?"

Ela had no intention of revealing Margery Willoughby's identity to Beck. "That is no business of yours."

"But the ring is mine! If it has sentimental value, they may buy it from me."

"I'm afraid not." Ela began to relish the opportunity to knock Beck off his high horse. "Since you will be unable to buy and sell goods from the castle dungeon."

"What?" He stared at her, uncomprehending. Ela looked at Giles Haughton.

The coroner cleared his throat. "You are being arrested for the murder of your neighbor Wilf Crowder. It's well known that you were in conflict with him over the boundaries to your land, and it's my belief that you pushed him to his death."

"But I didn't! He fell. I just found him, that's all."

"Very convenient your being there at exactly the right moment," said Haughton.

"I wasn't. If I'd been there at the right moment I could have helped him out of the water and he wouldn't have died." Beck's face tightened. "What do I have to gain from his death?"

"His land, which you clearly covet."

"I admit it was foolish of me to divert the course of the stream, and I regret it."

"If you hadn't dug a new course, Crowder wouldn't have needed to mark the boundary with stones and put himself in danger. Even if he did slip and fall to an accidental death you are still culpable and can be charged with manslaughter."

"So you don't think I pushed him?" Beck looked from Ela to Haughton.

"That will be determined by a jury of your peers. In the meantime you'll be confined to the jail here at the castle."

"But my animals—"

"Will be tended to on your farm in your absence."

"But what if I perish of cold and hunger in the dungeon?" Beck began to shake.

"You shan't perish of hunger," said Haughton. "And in that fine wool cloak you won't suffer much with the cold."

"And you shall have time to contemplate the iniquity of trying to steal your neighbor's land," said Ela. She signaled for the guards to remove him, and Haughton gave them the direction to put him in the dungeon.

After Beck had been taken away, gesticulating and protesting, Haughton turned to Ela. "I feel I'm playing the role of your co-sheriff today. Where is John the Dane?"

"He went to visit his mother in the north of the shire. She's ill with an ague. I thank you for doing his dirty work in his stead."

"I'm most glad to be of assistance." He bowed his head before leaving to attend to other matters. Ela thought it rather odd that he mentioned John Dacus, who people called The Dane for no reason she could fathom. She suspected he was curious about this new man in their midst and for an instant she wondered if he was even jealous.

Not like a jealous husband, but like a...

Like a what?

Ela shook her head slightly—purportedly to free her veil but really to dislodge this nonsense from inside her mind— and lifted her hand to invite the next petitioner of the morning.

≈

THE NEXT DAY, Ela set out to visit the pie shop kept by the Willoughby family. She brought Bill Talbot along with her as an escort. She'd spent little time alone with him lately. He'd kept busy teaching Richard and Stephen the manly arts of war now that young William was married and gone. She wasn't sure if she imagined it, but lately he'd been rather distant.

"How are things with you, Bill?" she asked, as they walked out of the castle and into the town that surrounded it.

"Good. Stephen is a fine horseman, and Richard is already showing considerable accuracy as an archer."

Ela peered at him. "I didn't ask about my sons. I asked about you."

"What is there to say about myself? I live to serve your family." He didn't look at her.

"You're angry." She couldn't hide the surprise in her voice. "Why?"

"I would be ungrateful indeed to bite the hand that feeds me." He glanced at her mildly. "What have I done to offend you?"

"You're offending me right now with this manner that is both officious and obsequious. I thought we were friends. I find friends in very short supply and can't afford to lose one."

"Oh. You seem to be well supplied. John Dacus hovers around you like a jovial shadow, and Giles Haughton is never far from your elbow."

Bill Talbot was jealous. Ela wanted to laugh. Why did men have to compete for everything? "Bill, your words pain me. You've been my closest confidant—apart from my beloved husband—since you rescued me from my confinement in Normandy when I was a girl. You've listened to my woes and dried my tears and even put your life in danger for me. You stand apart from all other men, where I'm concerned."

Bill made an odd mumbling, grumbling noise.

"John Dacus was installed—against my will, I might add—to make sure I don't disgrace the role of sheriff by my very womanhood, and he's doing a marvelously self-effacing job of it. I have nothing but good things to say about him. Giles Haughton has the skill and experience I need at my right hand. But neither of them can shine a light on the feelings I have for you."

Such words might sound odd coming from a widow to an unmarried man. But their different stations in life ensured that there could never be even a whiff of romance between them. And she was almost certain that Bill Talbot had always preferred the male form to the female one, though she'd never be imprudent enough to say it.

"I'm most gratified by the favor you show me." Bill looked a bit sheepish. "And I'm mortified that I seem to be fishing for compliments. Perhaps I was worried that you no longer need your old friend Bill Talbot now that you're High Sheriff of Wiltshire."

"Then let me reassure you that I need both your friendship and your guidance now more than ever. And don't think I undervalue the role you play in raising my sons to be men now their father is gone. That alone is worth a prince's ransom. But I need you at my side, a trusted ear and a steady support. If I seem dauntless and resolute it's only because I've managed to keep a brave face beneath my veil for one more dawn."

A smile creased Bill's kind and handsome face. "I've known you long enough to know that your dauntless streak goes right to your core."

~

THE SIGN outside the pie shop showed a picture of a pie with a slice cut out of it, against a red background. It hung from an iron bracket in the wall and gave the establishment, with its red painted doorframe, a look of permanence and respectability. On closer inspection the building itself was a ramshackle wooden structure leaning against its neighbor, its tiles seemingly repurposed from more than one roof.

Bill knocked on the door and a lad opened it—a boy of about twelve, with a shock of light brown hair. He stood in the doorway and stared at Ela.

"I'm here to see your master and mistress."

Margery appeared in the gloom behind him. "Bring them in, Phil." Ela stepped into the dark interior of the shop. A sole fly buzzed over a table of pies. An oven glowed in the back of the room, and the smell of cooked fish permeated the space. No doubt once Lent was over, the aromas of cooked ham and mutton would fill the air.

"A fine shop, mistress," said Ela.

"I thank you. Might I offer you a pie?"

Ela remembered her valiant effort to quaff a cup of ale. "No, thank you, I've just breakfasted. But perhaps Sir William—?" He refused as well. They stood for a moment in an awkward silence. "May we meet with your good husband?"

Margery blinked. Her hands fluttered around. She looked like she would rather take them anywhere than to her husband. No doubt she feared Ela would tell him she was already married to another man.

"Come with me." In her rasped whisper, Ela could hear a silent plea to keep her secret.

Margery led them out a door in the back of the shop and up a narrow flight of stairs to a room directly above. Heavy curtains covered the sole window, trapping the heavy aroma of baked pies. Ela could barely make out the bed in the half-light, but as her eyes adjusted she could see the slight form of a body beneath the layered covers. How could he bear such heavy coverings? The ovens below overheated the room, and Ela found her winter cloak burdensome in the oppressive atmosphere.

Bill announced her name, which hung in the fish-scented air.

"Hugh Willoughby?" She peered at the shriveled form in the bed.

"What you find left of him," said a small graveled voice. "I've barely left this bed in years."

A convenient alibi, should he feel the need for one. "How many years?"

"I've lost count now."

"Were you bedbound when you met your wife, Margery?"

"Not completely, though my use of my legs was limited. I could still operate the shop at that time."

"It must be a great relief to you that your good wife can run the business while you rest in bed."

"Indeed it is."

Ela could see the arrangement was mutually beneficial. In breaking it she'd ruin two lives. But did this man kill Simon of Oddo nine years ago? Margery had said that her husband knew of her sojourn with Simon. Perhaps he was jealous of his younger, more robust rival? Though Ela wasn't clear on whether Margery had met Willoughby only after Simon abandoned her—at which time he was likely already dead. That's how she'd described it.

"How did the two of you meet?" Ela wanted to know if their stories matched.

Hugh Willoughby shifted slightly under his bedclothes. "She came to the shop seeking a pie."

Ela glanced at Margery. Who twisted her fingers together inside her clean apron.

"Did she have money to pay for it?"

"She did not." His voice sounded clearer, as if use blew away some of the dust in his windpipe. "She'd fallen on hard times, with both of her parents dead and no place to go."

"Ah." Ela hesitated, wanting to probe further but not upset the applecart—or the pie table—altogether. "So you offered her shelter. Was she living locally?"

Ela knew the answer to this question, but his answer would be revealing. "She was, but she'd found herself in the clutches of a harsh and cruel man who made promises but refused to marry her. She had a terrible scar on her belly where he'd injured her."

Ela glanced at Margery, whose eyes fixed on the floor. Had she rolled the two men—Simon and her first husband—into one as she vied for a more promising prospect?

"And did she leave him for you?" asked Ela.

The silence that followed told her something was amiss. Margery started trembling and suddenly burst out with a cry that made Ela jump.

CHAPTER 17

"Simon left me!" cried Margery. "Or at least I thought he did. Now it seems he was dead in the ground just a stone's throw away from me."

"What does it matter?" said the man in the bed with some force. "He's dead and gone ten or more years now."

"Nine years," said Ela.

"You're upsetting my wife."

"Murder is generally upsetting," said Ela. Her eyes had adjusted to the light enough to get a better look at Hugh Willoughby. His thin skin stretched over sharp features, suggesting great age. "What did you think about Margery living with another man?"

"Every woman's got to live with a man, doesn't she? Don't have a choice. If they have no father, then they need a husband. I don't blame her for making do with what circumstances provided her."

"But you say he was cruel to her." Ela peered at him. He had sharp pale blue eyes that looked much younger than the rest of his face. "Did that give you reason to hate him?"

"I never met him, did I?" His pale eyes flashed with—something—that made Ela's gut twitch.

"How did you not meet him? Simon of Oddo lived near the town and by all accounts had some reputation as a troublemaker, at least where women were concerned. Surely he came into your pie shop?"

"I wouldn't know. I don't quiz people on their name and occupation. If they have money they get a pie." He shifted and shuffled in his bed, and Margery hurried forward to push pillows underneath him and raise his head and shoulders higher. "Are you trying to accuse my wife of murder? She's gentle as a lamb and wouldn't raise a finger to kill a fly."

Ela inhaled deeply. She couldn't easily imagine Margery killing anyone. She didn't seem wily enough for one thing. She'd let herself be buffeted by fate—and men—and made the best of her small lot. She stood there right now, kneading her fingers into her apron and looking like she wished the floor would swallow her.

On the other hand she had kept the secret of her first marriage—and her living husband—from everyone for nine long years. And she had a lot to gain by being rid of Simon of Oddo so she could take up with the far more respectable Hugh Willoughby and move into his warm pie shop, instead of living on promises with an unfaithful ne'er-do-well in a drafty hut in the woods.

Ela glanced at Bill, who, as usual, stood there in stolid silence.

She could build a case against Margery. Based on the information they had she was certainly a suspect. But should she? She wanted to talk to Margery alone. She had no wish to ruin the woman's life if she was indeed innocent of murder.

"We must get back to the castle. I'll send word if we need

more information." She gestured for Margery to lead them downstairs.

Once back on the ground floor, with its ovens and fresh-baked pies, Margery's colorless lips pressed together and she looked afraid of her own shadow. Ela half wanted to apologize for putting her in an awkward situation. She felt sorry for Margery and her difficult lot in life, but not if she'd killed a man in cold blood.

"I could have you arrested," she said quietly. The shop was empty, because Margery had barred the door before taking them upstairs. "Did you meet your current husband before Simon's death or after?"

Margery blinked her small round eyes. "I'm not sure. It was a long time ago."

"You don't remember if you left one man for another?" Ela kept her voice hushed but didn't hide her disbelief. "If Simon was alive—and a jealous man who threatened violence—you might have motive to kill him to free yourself to pursue Willoughby."

"I didn't do anything!" Margery's eyes bulged. "I swear it. I never wanted anything but a quiet life. I'd never kill anyone. Do you think I'd have come to the castle about the ring if I knew it was found near a dead body?"

She made a good point. Still, perhaps she was more afraid of her first husband than of being prosecuted for a nine-year-old murder.

"You truly don't know if your first husband is still alive?"

Margery trembled like someone with a fever. "I'm afraid to find out."

Ela found this odd. Surely any woman would seek intelligence about a monster she needed to avoid at all costs. She intended to find out herself if Margery's husband was alive, and if possible, to learn the true story of what had happened between them.

~

"I NEED you to locate a man called Ebbo Fuller." Ela sat in the great hall the next morning, issuing orders to Clerebold Rufus, a young clerk she'd charged with making sense of the records the previous sheriff had left behind. He'd proven himself quite able to track down information that had gone missing, so why not a person? "He might be in Devizes. He used to live there."

"Yes, my lady. Is he a fuller?"

Ela frowned. "I didn't think to ask. I suppose that's a fair assumption, though it could be his father's trade. He was married to a woman called Grizeldis." Ela hesitated for a moment. "She may have died."

May God forgive her for this small lie, but she didn't want to set Ebbo Fuller on the trail of his wife. She didn't need another murder on her hands—his taking revenge on the woman who betrayed him.

"I'd like you to find out where he lives—if he lives—and to find the details of their marriage: what year it happened, witnesses, that kind of thing. The local parish should have some records."

"I'd be happy to, my lady." He did look happy, his pale face beaming beneath his appropriately red hair. "Should I tell him to come here when I find him?"

"Oh, no." Ela's said quickly. "In fact, there's no need to interact with him at all. Rumors of him are not favorable. If you can find out if he lives or dies without him knowing, that would be best."

"I'll be as discreet as possible." He frowned. "But if anyone asks why I need information about Ebbo Fuller, what should I say?"

Ela hesitated. "It's a matter of…property. That should be vague enough to seem important without provoking too much interest. You can say you don't know further than that."

"Which would be the truth." His grin cheered her. But his innocence worried her.

"Take an armed escort. You can never be too careful when you're about on the sheriff's business."

"Certainly, my lady." If anything the prospect cheered him further.

~

WHEN RUFUS HAD GONE, Ela rose from her chair by the fire and approached her greyhound, Greyson, who loved having his nose rubbed, and who did a funny dance when she scratched near his tail. Bill stood nearby, armed with a wooden sword, instructing Stephen in the art of parrying a sword thrust.

She beckoned him toward her. He handed his sword to Richard and told her sons to practice killing each other.

Ela didn't feel like laughing. "What do you think, Bill, did Margery kill Simon?"

"Somebody killed Simon," he answered. "And buried him. She wouldn't be my first choice."

"Why not?"

"She's small. And plump."

"She wasn't always plump. That's the pies."

"Then she'd be even weaker. She's short, too. Simon wasn't exactly strapping, but he'd easily overpower her. I think he was killed by a man."

Ela settled back into her chair near the fire. Greyson followed and nudged at her softly with his long nose until she stroked his head. "No one seems to have strong enough reason to want Simon dead. His father was disappointed in him, he'd annoyed several fathers, brothers and young

185

suitors in the village and his neighbor disliked him, but killing a man with a knife takes a special sort of enmity."

Bill pulled up a chair. "Perhaps Margery's new husband wanted him out of the way so he could lay claim to her?"

"That thought occurred to me, but he's frail as an autumn leaf."

"Simon of Oddo died nine years ago. Surely Willoughby wasn't a wraith beneath the sheets at the time he wooed his bride."

"But even Margery says he wasn't in good health back then. As you've already observed, Simon of Oddo was killed and buried by someone hale and hearty."

Bill leaned back in his chair. "And his killer may be one of the men who've died in the last few days."

"And their deaths may be connected to us finding the body." Ela frowned. "Except I can't figure out how."

"Bertram Beck couldn't have bought Oddo's farm if the old man was keeping it for his son. He had something to gain by getting Simon out of the way."

"Except that by all accounts he didn't move to this area until Simon was dead." Ela rubbed Greyson's ears and he trembled with appreciation.

"Are we sure of that, though? If he'd been sniffing around he might have spotted the opportunity to buy the farm if Oddo could be persuaded to sell. Then he might have seized the opportunity to send young Simon away on an adventure."

"Except instead of the Holy Land he went straight into the arms of the holy family."

"Or the bowels of hell, more likely, based on his reputation."

Ela crossed herself. "He'd have died unshriven. Perhaps his soul haunts those woods."

"Perhaps his wicked soul stirred up the dispute between the neighbors."

Ela looked up at Bill and was relieved to see a sparkle of mischief in his eye. He laughed at her expression. "Did you think I'm about to start blaming crimes on troubled spirits?"

"I'm sure you wouldn't be the first." Ela drew in a deep breath. "And that wooded hilltop has certainly stirred up no end of trouble. Three men dead, one in prison. I wouldn't be surprised if rumors started about it being cursed."

"Perhaps it's haunted by the souls of the ancient people who created that ring fort."

"You may as well say that about this castle," said Ela. "For it's built on a far larger ring fort that's just as ancient."

"Would that the castle was haunted." His face saddened. "There are some old friends I wouldn't mind hovering at my bedside in the night."

"If I weren't so sure that my William is sitting at God's right hand, I'd say the same." Ela felt her heart pinch. How did she still feel his loss so keenly more than a year after his death? Would the pain never lessen? "Perhaps I should feel sorry for Simon of Oddo, since no one seems to grieve for him."

"You care enough to hunt his killer when most would be glad to let his bones quietly rot in their place."

"Do you think me mad to want justice for an nine-year-old crime?"

"Not mad, no. I know your principles drive you." Bill hesitated for a moment. "But whose life will be overturned in the process?"

"You're worried about Margery."

"I don't even know Margery." Bill attempted a placid expression.

"Apparently you know her well enough that you're worried I'm about to ruin her life."

"Our visit may have already caused a rift in her marriage. What woman wants her husband reminded about her former lover?"

Ela blinked. Bill was so blunt lately. Perhaps he felt more free to speak openly now that her husband was dead. She wasn't sure if she liked that or hated it. "Her husband already knew about Simon. And besides, what could such an old and infirm man do? He's hardly going to turn her out of the house. He couldn't lift a hand to make the pies if he wanted to."

"Mama! Mama! Richard killed me!" Ela's youngest son Nicky ran up to her, tears streaming from his eyes. He flung himself into her lap with such force that her greyhound skittered away.

Ela looked up for her older son, but he'd vanished along with Stephen. "Did he stab you with his sword?" She kissed her son's curly blond mop of hair.

"He killed me with it!" wailed Nicky.

"Where does it hurt?"

Nicky pointed to his head, then his stomach, then held up his hands, as if to let her examine them for stigmata.

"You still seem to be very much alive," she said softly. "Let me kiss your wounds." She kissed his flushed forehead and his little belly, and each of his soft hands. "A mother's love is the finest salve. That's what all the doctors say."

"That did help." His serious expression made her want to laugh.

"What a relief. We really can't have any more people dying this week." She smiled but also glanced at Bill. Of course her young son knew nothing of the deaths taking place around him. "We're far too busy getting ready to celebrate Easter."

Nicky's eyes lit up. "Will there be colored eggs?"

"It would hardly be Easter without them."

"And can I roll them down the hill?"

"Only if you're still alive by then." She stroked his cheek. "Do you think you'll manage?"

"Oh, yes. And I shall eat pork and lamb and—" He looked around the room. "Stephen! Easter's coming."

Stephen ambled over. He'd had the good sense to put the wooden sword away. "I hope the great hare doesn't hop away with you in his basket."

"There's no great hare," sneered little Nicky. "Everyone knows that. It's not real. Jesus died on the cross and rose again."

Ela realized Albert the porter was hovering nearby. Sometimes he hesitated to interrupt her when he considered a visitor unimportant or even undesirable.

"Yes, Albert?"

"There's a woman here with a pie for you."

Ela glanced at Bill.

"Can you ask her to leave it in the kitchen? And if there's a message for me, you can bring it to me. Tell her I'm engaged in sheriff's business." Was it Margery hoping to buy her secrecy with a pie? That might work better on someone who didn't have a castle kitchen at her disposal.

Ela chattered with her children about their plans for Easter. There would be a feast with guests, games for the children, tables piled high with sweetmeats…

Albert came back, mercifully without a pie. "She said to thank you for your kind visit yesterday, my lady."

Ela raised her brow. Her visit was hardly something requiring thanks. Most people considered an investigative visit something of an intrusion. "Thank you, Albert."

"I wouldn't eat that pie if I were you," said Bill.

"I don't plan to. Still, I hardly think she'd bring a poisoned pie by with her own hand."

"I suppose that wouldn't make sense, would it?"

"Why would she poison a pie?" asked Stephen.

"She wouldn't," said Ela, not wanting to stir up gossip among her children. "He's joking."

~

"Mama." Ela was deep in prayer, on her knees at her prie-dieu, when Ida appeared in the door of her solar, carrying Hilda's baby.

"It's almost bedtime, my love. I'm at prayer. Can it wait until morning?"

"Hilda's very ill. She can't keep anything down, and she's shaking so much she can't hold her baby."

Ela sprang to her feet. Ida's expression alarmed her, and Hilda's baby struggled in her arms. "Here, let me take the lad." She held out her arms and took the tiny boy, who was just finding the energy to kick and squirm. "When did she become ill?"

Ela rushed down the corridor, holding little Thomas firmly.

"After supper tonight. She was fine earlier. She was singing songs to Nicky and Ellie while she fed her baby."

Poor Hilda lay curled on her side on the bed, retching, the odor of yellow bile in the air. A kitchen maid scrubbed at the mess, and another arrived with a bowl of water and a fresh rag.

"Hilda, what did you eat for supper?"

Hilda barely seemed to hear her. She gagged and heaved, now on all fours on her mattress, giving Ela unpleasant flashbacks to her tortuous labor. Ela handed her baby back to Ida and approached her. She touched a hand to Hilda's forehead. "No fever. What did you eat?"

"Just some bread and jam," rasped Hilda.

A horrible thought occurred to Ela. "Did you eat any pie?"

CHAPTER 18

*H*ilda retched again, but her stomach was too empty to give her relief. Tears flowed from her eyes, and her body shook like she was in a snowdrift.

"Bring blankets to warm her," Ela called to the maids. "And tell Cook to boil water."

She stroked Hilda's back for a moment. "I'm going to make you a brew that should settle your stomach." She went downstairs to the tiny room where she kept her dried herbs and mixed a sachet of ginger, fennel and cloves. She folded the mix into linen and took it to the kitchen, where the cook had a pot of water heating over the fire. Ela scooped out some hot water with the dipper, strained it through her herbs and hurried back upstairs while it steeped in a wood cup.

"Mama!" Richard's cry stopped Ela in her tracks at the top of the stairs. "Nicky's been sick everywhere. All over our bed." Ela froze. Sickness in the home was a mother's worst fear. She turned to follow Richard to the room he shared with his brothers, careful not to spill the hot cup of brew in her hands. She found little Nicky sobbing, also surrounded by the contents of his stomach.

"What happened?" Ela asked of Stephen, who stood there looking helpless.

"He started coughing and now he's made a mess everywhere."

"Hilda's sick as well."

"Serves them right. I told them not to sneak that pie from the kitchen."

Ela's blood froze. "What pie?"

"The pie Cook had sitting on a shelf. She said no one was to touch it. Hilda dared Nicky to sneak it and they ate it. I told them not to as it's Lent and it smelled like meat—and it might be poisoned, even though you said it wasn't—but you know how Hilda is."

Indeed she did. Willful!

"Fetch a maid to clean up," she said to Richard. She thrust the brew in its wooden cup into Stephen's hands. "Bring that and follow me." Ela gathered Nicky in her arms—which she was only barely strong enough to do as he grew older—and carried him back to Hilda's room.

Hilda was now curled up in a ball shivering.

"How much of the pie did you eat?" asked Ela as she entered.

Hilda stared at her blankly, pale lips barely moving.

"We only ate a little, Mama," said Nicky, before his body convulsed in another series of empty retches. "It didn't taste good."

"Where's the pie now?" she asked.

Neither of them answered.

"Where's the pie? Tell me the truth at once." She stared at Hilda. After all she'd done for this girl now she'd endangered her own life and Nicky's with her mischief.

"I threw it in the garderobe," stammered Hilda weakly.

"Then it's sunk into the pit. Which is a shame since it might be evidence if you've been poisoned," snapped Ela. "What were you thinking taking a pie that doesn't belong to you?"

"Poisoned?" Hilda let out a howl. "Am I going to die?"

I'm tempted to kill you with my bare hands, thought Ela for a moment. Then she focused on giving Nicky a sip of the warm brew.

"Eww, it tastes bad," he whined.

"It'll settle your stomach." She forced him to take a few sips.

Then she brought the cup to Hilda. Hilda shook her head.

"Drink it before I force it down your throat."

Tears sprang to Hilda's eyes. "I'm sorry, my lady. The pie looked so tasty and I'm so hungry all the time from nursing little Thomas and I—"

"Never mind about that. Drink this." The maids returned with fresh sheets and more water, and Ela called for one to send for the doctor and for him to bring treatment for poison. She also called for guards to immediately arrest Margery and bring her right to this room so she could tell them what poison she'd used. Hopefully there would be time for the doctor to furnish an antidote, if one existed.

BY THE TIME the doctor arrived, both Hilda and Nicky had stopped convulsing, but they were now listless and quiet. That made Ela more nervous.

"Where are the guards with Margery Willoughby?" she called down the hallway. The doctor bent over little Nicky, who lay on the bed next to Hilda, his blond curls damp with perspiration.

"They're bringing her through the gates now," called back Bill. "I'll escort her up myself."

Ela mopped Nicky's face. "I don't feel well, Mama."

"How much of the pie did you eat?" she asked.

"Just a bite. Maybe two. I didn't like it."

"And you, Hilda?"

"Only a bite. Well, maybe three or four bites. I was very hungry." Ela could barely hear her. "But it was bitter."

The doctor took Hilda's pulse. "Heartbeat is rapid."

"What does that mean?" Ela clutched Nicky to her chest. For all the times he'd exasperated her by pinching his sisters or teasing the cats or hiding in a chest for hours, she'd give a rib to have him back to his usual antics.

The doctor opened Hilda's mouth and examined her tongue. Then he peered into her eyes.

"Could be belladonna poison—deadly nightshade. It works to overstimulate the heart and can stop it."

Ela let out a tiny cry. "Is there an antidote?"

"I'm afraid not. An emetic can be useful, but from the sounds of it they've both vomited all they can."

"I gave them a tea of ginger, fennel and cloves to stop the vomiting." Had she made a terrible mistake?

"I don't think you did any harm." He met her gaze. "If they were going to perish it would likely have happened already."

Ela shivered and held Nicky tight in her arms. "We must pray," she said to Petronella and Ida, who hovered nearby. Richard and Stephen had gone with Bill to look for the guards, and they all entered the room at once, with a disheveled Margery in their midst, her arms held by two guards.

"You brought a poisoned pie," said Ela, fury ringing in her voice. "Did you hope to kill me?"

"I never!" Margery's face was white. "I baked it special for you and when you didn't take it, then I thought to bring it."

"The pie sat untouched in the kitchen until this foolish girl and my youngest son thought to steal it and eat it. Now the doctor tells me they both show signs of belladonna poisoning."

"I'd never put poison in a pie," wailed Margery. "Why would I?"

"Because I know your secret?" spat Ela. "About your first husband." She didn't care whose secret she spilled right now. She'd like to get her hands around this woman's neck.

Margery blinked. "My husband is ill in bed." She shrank a little. "He told me not to bring the pie. He said to throw it away. But I didn't like to see a good pie go to waste."

Ela froze. "Why would he tell you not to bring it?"

"I don't know. But after he fell asleep, instead of throwing it away I brought it to the castle, to give you something tasty for your supper."

Was her invalid husband up to something that Margery didn't know about? "Who baked the pie?"

"I did. I do all the baking. My husband can't rise from his bed without help. Even then it's too hard to get him down the stairs these days. He hasn't been in the kitchen since before Epiphany."

Ela looked from Hilda, to Nicky and back. "Did you eat anything other than the pie?"

"No, my lady, I promise," said Hilda, through chapped lips. She was shivering again.

Nicky pushed his head into Ela's skirts, like he was a newborn puppy. Her heart ached with fear for him. Could his small body fend off the poison?

"If you've killed my son I'll see you hang for it."

"I didn't kill anyone, I swear!" Margery wailed.

"It may surprise you that all killers say that. And you'll remain here under arrest."

"But what about my husband and the pies?"

195

Ela could hardly believe her audacity. She'd half killed Hilda and Nicky—they weren't out of the woods yet by any means—and she was fretting over her pies? "You said there's a boy that helps you."

"Phil Dawson."

Ela peered at her. "Did Phil help you bake the pie you brought?"

She thought for a moment. "He rolled out the pastry. I assembled it and baked it."

"So Phil had a hand in this pie."

Margery swallowed. "Yes, he did."

"Did he know that you intended to bring it here?"

"No, he went to visit his mother out across the fields. She needed help fetching firewood."

"So it was entirely your decision to bring this pie here."

Margery's gaze fell to the floor. "I thought it would please you."

An odd feeling twisted Ela's stomach. Why would anyone bring a poisoned pie to the very place where everyone would instantly suspect her of poisoning it? It made no sense.

"Was this the same pie you offered myself and Bill at the shop yesterday?"

She looked shamefaced. "It is, but I heated it up special and they gain flavor with time."

"I don't care how fresh it is, I care when and why it was made. Did you make it especially for our visit?"

"Yes, my husband told me to be sure to welcome you with it and to use all the best ingredients."

"And some poison," said Ela.

"Never!"

"They ate some tarts as well," said Stephen, who was standing in the shadows, behind Margery and the guards. "Nicky hid them when I came in the room."

Poor Nicky lay almost limp in Ela's arms. "Nicky, I'm not angry with you. Where did you get the tarts?"

"Cook said I could have them." His poor little voice was so thin.

"Did you have a tart, too?" she asked Hilda.

"An apricot one, yes."

"See! It wasn't my pie," protested Margery.

"I'll have to speak to Cook about the tarts. But for now, you're under suspicion." She hesitated, unwilling to send her to the dungeon without at least trying to learn more about the poison in Nicky's and Hilda's bodies. "If you tell me which poison was in the pie it will go better for you at trial."

"I never used poison. Never!" Margery's voice rose to a shriek, and Ela could see her becoming hysterical. Ela needed to focus her energy and calm on nursing Nicky and Hilda and helping the doctor. "Take her to the jail."

Margery screamed and protested about her helpless invalid husband, but Ela barely heard her cries.

"Are any of the tarts left?" Ela asked Nicky softly. He shook his head. She looked up at Stephen and Richard. "Did you eat any?"

Richard mumbled that he had eaten a blackberry tart and it tasted fine.

"What flavor did you have, Nicky?"

"I had blackberry, too."

Ela frowned. So it likely wasn't the tarts. "I wish we had that pie."

"Their heart rates are growing steadier." The doctor pressed his fingers to the pulse in Nicky's plump wrist. "They might be past the worst of it. You must keep them hydrated and rested and watch them until morning."

Ela didn't want the doctor to leave, but he assured them there was nothing he could do. Ela cradled Nicky in her arms and sat next to Hilda, who soon started to babble about her wedding.

"You must be feeling better," said Ela. "If you can think about cakes and music."

Ida had been walking back and forth cradling Hilda's baby through all this. He became increasingly fractious and once the doctor left he began to wail. "The poor mite is hungry."

"Let me nurse him," said Hilda, already baring her breast.

"No!" said Ela, fear striking her heart. "If there's poison still in your blood and milk it could harm him. He's so tiny. Have someone call for a wet nurse."

She hadn't hired a fulltime wet nurse for Hilda, as she would have for one of her own babies, because despite all appearances to the contrary Hilda was supposedly a servant and expected to feed her own baby. Ela had fed hers too, but not all of the time and it was a relief to have an experienced nurse take over at night so she could tend to her husband's needs. But there was always a wet nurse, or a mother who could be pressed into service as one, somewhere in the castle or the town nearby.

Hilda fussed and wanted to hold her baby, but Ida held him fast and reassured her that he'd be fine and he'd just cry harder if he could smell her milk.

"I'm fit to burst," protested Hilda. "I need to be milked like a cow."

"That's probably not a bad idea," said Ela. "To rid yourself of the spoiled milk."

Hilda started crying, then Nicky started crying, and soon Ela was greatly relieved that their energy suggested they were both well on the mend.

THE NEXT MORNING Ela attended Prime before dawn to give thanks that Nicky and Hilda made it safely through the night. The color had returned to their cheeks, and Hilda had nursed her baby, who seemed healthy and content.

Clerebold Rufus arrived while Ela was breaking her fast with some fresh bread and honeycomb. He'd found Margery's husband alive and well and working in his name-sake trade in Devizes.

"I stayed the night at an inn last night, so I could hear any chatter about Ebbo Fuller from his neighbors."

"What did you learn?"

"They say his wife left him for another man and that he was furious enough to want to kill her."

Ela blinked. "Did he know where she went?"

"None of them seemed to know. One said he tried to track her down—years ago, when she first left—but they don't know if he found her or not."

"But he could have come here and killed Simon of Oddo in revenge." Ela tried to wrap her mind around this possibility. "But if he came and found her with Simon, why wouldn't he force her to go home with him?"

"It's not easy to force a woman to do something she's set her mind against," said Clerebold, with a sly grin. Then his expression vanished. "Begging your pardon, my lady. I forgot myself."

"No matter." She'd learned to take these lapses of judgment as reassurance that people felt they could speak to her as if she were a man. "According to her he tried to shape her behavior with his fists. I'd imagine that will only work on some women. With others it will drive them away for good."

"His wife is alive?"

Ela pressed her lips together. "You have no need of that knowledge. Is Ebbo Fuller well thought of?"

"As a fuller, yes. He even employs two girls to tread the

cloth when business is bustling." Clerebold hesitated. "I asked if his first wife is alive because it seems he's married again."

Saints preserve us. Ela tried not to react. "To whom?"

"A young girl, according to his neighbors. I didn't ask her name as I didn't want to seem too interested. I didn't meet with him or do anything to alert his attention to my visit, as you suggested."

"Good." What a mess. Now four people were committing bigamy on her watch as sheriff. Would God judge them harshly for breaking their vows or her more harshly for letting them get away with it?

If she let them get away with it.

She inhaled deeply. "Good work, Rufus. Please say nothing of your journey or its purpose to anyone."

He looked confused for a moment, then recovered himself. "Of course, my lady."

HILDA WAS VERY contrite all that day, offering to clean all their rooms and ferry dishes back and forth to the kitchen. She followed Ela into her solar after dusk, offering to scrub the corners of the room. "Hilda, you can't clean a room with a baby in one arm."

"Yes, I can. How do you think my mam did it?" Ela had to ponder this. And Hilda's customary insolence in asking the question. Hilda carried her baby expertly in the crook of her arm as if she'd been doing it all her life. Which, as the oldest of several siblings, she probably had.

"Clearly, your mama was a woman of great resources, but you need to focus on getting your strength back. And don't eat anything else you're not supposed to."

"Will she hang?"

"Who?"

"The woman who poisoned the pie."

Ela had half-forgotten Margery being dragged into the room last night. "If it was truly she that did it. She protests that it isn't."

"How can you find out if she was telling the truth?"

"Sometimes you can't find out. Sometimes you never know for sure. That's why we have jurors to offer their opinions and a judge to make the final decision."

"So someone innocent might hang just because everyone thought they did it?"

Ela inhaled deeply. "I work hard to make sure that doesn't happen."

"But it could?"

Ela nodded. "It can happen quite easily if a person is unpopular or poor and doesn't have anyone to defend them. That's why it's important to evaluate every case based on the facts."

"So the facts of the pie are that Margery brought it, and it made Nicky and me very sick—but didn't kill us." Hilda looked thoughtful. "Are there any more facts to consider?"

"Indeed there are." It amused Ela that Hilda wanted to act as a juror in this case. "Margery brought the pie, and even baked it, but it was her husband who told her to make it. He instructed her to give it to Bill and myself at their shop when we visited."

"But you didn't take it?"

"No. I know better than to eat food prepared by murder suspects. You'd be shocked if you realized how often people try to poison one another."

"But poison doesn't always work."

"No. The person must eat or drink a good deal of it, depending on what it is. You and Nicky are lucky that the pie didn't taste very good."

"I bet the poison made it bitter."

"Some are tasteless. Those are the dangerous ones." Ela sighed. She'd never know for sure what poison had killed her beloved husband, though the doctor suspected arsenic.

"It makes me half afraid to eat and drink."

"It was bad luck that you happened to eat that pie." Poor Hilda did seem to be cursed sometimes. "But you should never have taken it. You should pray for better judgment. What would your future husband think if he knew you stole a pie?"

Hilda looked chastened. "What if I'm not a good wife?"

Ela felt a flash of anxiety. What if she wasn't? It was a strong possibility. "It's your duty to be a good wife. Every woman is nervous about the responsibilities of marriage and raising children. If you try your hardest you shan't go far wrong."

Hilda already had experience raising her younger siblings. She also—rather unfortunately—had experience with sex. Learning to obey her husband and look up to him in all matters might prove to be more of a challenge.

"He's handsome, isn't he?" Hilda's eyes had taken on a faraway look.

"He is indeed. And you've had the unusual opportunity to choose your husband. So far I think you've made a fine choice, but don't think that gives you liberties in how to behave as his wife."

"But I shouldn't let him beat me, should I?"

Ela drew in a shaky breath. "A sensible man knows better than to beat his wife."

"Because then she might poison him."

"Hilda! I should hope not. Because then she'd hang."

"And they'd both be dead."

"How did we get started on this conversation? You're making me very nervous about your marriage. Your good husband is charged with running Fernlees manor, and you and he must work hard to make the most of your good fortune and create a good life for your children. It's your job to guide your children and shape their behavior and morals."

"I shall ask myself, 'What would Ela do?'" Hilda looked like she expected praise. Ela was more tempted to scold her for the overly familiar use of her given name.

"You might better ask yourself what our Lord and savior would do," she said primly. "And be sure to pray for guidance morning and night."

A knock on the door—which was open—made her start. Ela turned to see a panicked Elsie Brice standing in the door.

"What is it, Elsie?"

"There's someone in the hall to see you, my lady."

Ela made out the shadowy form of Bill Talbot standing at the top of the stairs, just behind Hilda.

"I shrink from disturbing you in your private chamber, my lady," he said, stepping forward, face taut. "But someone has confessed to the poisoning."

CHAPTER 19

$\mathcal{E}$la hurried down to the great hall, expecting to see Margery there, red eyed and contrite and flanked by guards. Instead she was confronted by a boy no taller than her armpit, with tousled hair and no cloak to protect him from the evening chill. He shivered uncontrollably. Ela recognized him as Phil, the boy from the pie shop.

"What's amiss here?" said Ela, her maternal instincts surfacing as she ushered him to the fire, where a good blaze was banked against the evening chill. The boy's teeth chattered, and he stammered out a rush of words that made almost no sense.

"You poisoned the pie?" Ela peered into his face. A sprinkle of freckles covered his nose. "Who made you?"

"No one made me," he sputtered. "I did it all by myself."

Ela's gut twisted. She didn't believe him. He'd been put up to this. Someone—Margery's husband most likely—had sent this tender lad to suffer a fate they were too cowardly to face. But she'd better work sideways to tease the information out of him. She knew from her own boys that a child sworn to an oath could be as trustworthy as a knight of the realm. "Why would you do such a thing?"

He stared at her with big brown eyes. "To kill you."

Ela startled at his bluntness. Out of the mouths of babes…. "What quarrel do you have with me?"

He shook his head. At least he'd stopped shivering. "You came to the pie shop to cause trouble for my master and mistress who always treated me kind."

"I'm trying to find a killer. Would you have me leave a criminal unpunished?" She ignored a bubble of sympathy for him. "You're telling me that you put poison into a pie to try to kill me, and in fact made two beloved members of my household very ill. My young son Nicky might have died."

The boy's lip quivered. "I'm sorry for that, ma'am. It was you I wanted to kill."

Ela blinked, torn between slapping his face—which she would never do—and wanting to laugh at his audacity—which was borne of bravery or foolishness or both. It was time to stop beating about the bush. "Your master put you up to this."

"He didn't. And now he's very ill. He's desperate that the missus has been locked up. I think he's going to die. I never meant for that to happen and I only wanted to help, so if you could set her free and throw me in the dungeon…" He started to shiver uncontrollably again.

"I don't believe you. I can't believe you. An adult put you up to this. It was either Margery or her husband. Which was it?"

The boy stared at her for a moment as if she was a simpleton. "It wasn't them." He hissed the words. Then he shouted, "It was me."

The guards who'd been hanging back leaped forward and grabbed the boy and one cuffed him on the cheek and scolded him for raising his voice to the countess. Ela wanted to remind him that in this instance she was the sheriff as much as the countess, but she restrained herself.

"Why are you so ready to die to protect another?" She was truly perplexed by his behavior.

"They're good people who never did anything bad." He stared sullenly at the floor.

Ela already knew that wasn't true. At the very least Margery was an adulterer and a fornicator and she might even have murdered her dead lover. "If Margery didn't poison the pie, why did she bring it here?"

"I don't know." He was angry now and wouldn't meet her gaze.

"I have a great kitchen filled with people rolling pastry and baking and stirring soups and stews. I never even saw the pie. It's more likely that you would have killed one of my servants with it."

He stared at the floor.

"Except that a foolish young ward of mine and my son saw fit to take it from the kitchen and eat it."

"I'm sorry about that," he mumbled.

Ela saw Stephen and Richard amble in with Bill Talbot in tow. An idea occurred to her. "Richard, I'd like you to talk to this young man and get the truth out of him."

She looked back at the lad. "My son was your age not long ago. He'll know if you're lying or not."

She muttered to the guards to watch and listen closely.

Bill stood looking curiously at them as they walked away to a nearby table. Ela beckoned Bill to her and explained the situation. "He swears Margery is innocent, and that now her old sick husband is dying without her."

Bill sighed. "One person's word against another's, that's what justice comes down to."

"Am I to summon jurors late into the evening to listen to a boy's wild ramblings?"

"I think you'd be within your rights to send him down to the dungeon to tend to his beloved mistress until morning."

Ela's stomach churned. She already worried about Margery down there with the damp and foul air. The poor woman had suffered a lot in her life. And if she truly hadn't poisoned the pie…. "Margery's not stupid enough to bring a pie she's poisoned herself, is she?"

Bill grimaced. "People are capable of astonishing acts of foolishness when they're driven by fear."

"But it's not likely. She seemed grateful that I was keeping her secret."

"That she was married before?"

Ela nodded. "I suppose I'm not doing such a good job of keeping it, am I? Now Rufus Clerebold knows, and perhaps others. And her first husband is alive, and has remarried. So now they're both adulterers." She looked around, making sure no one could hear. Luckily the usual evening din in the hall covered her speech. "Am I supposed to ignore their bold affront to one of the Ten Commandments of our Lord?"

Bill blinked innocently as if he knew better than to answer such a question.

"I suppose it's a matter for the ecclesiastical courts, not the jurors of the hundred," she reflected. "I wonder if there are grounds for the annulment of the marriage?"

"In my experience, grounds for annulment can almost always be found."

"I suspect the fertility of the grounds in those cases is directly related to the amount of money spent on legal advice by the parties involved."

"True," said Bill. "Ordinary people like Margery handle the matter exactly as she did, by putting as much distance between herself and her unwanted husband as she could manage."

"It wasn't enough distance at all, though. He lived less than twenty miles away. And did she have to remarry?"

"Women nearly always have to remarry," said Bill quietly. "Unless they're fortunate enough to have independent means."

"Indeed." She sighed. She knew how rare her own situation was. A woman like Margery truly found herself in a bind if her husband turned out to be cruel. "I'm undecided about what to do with Margery and her marriage, but for now we must summon a jury to acquit or convict someone of attempted poisoning. And at the same time we can discuss the matter of Bertram Beck and whether he has culpability in the death of Wilf Crowder."

"And while you're at it, you might as well discuss if there's cause to accuse anyone of murdering old Oddo."

"The coroner is convinced that he died of natural causes." Ela looked over at Richard to see how he fared with the boy. "And I see no reason to disagree with him."

"Then at least you can air that information to the jury and prevent it making a reappearance at some later time. This Lent has a smell of death about it, and I look forward to its end."

ELA WALKED OVER TO RICHARD, who rose as she approached. "What have you discovered about our confessed poisoner?"

"He says he poisoned the pie because he wanted you to leave his master and mistress alone."

"Then he had his mistress bring it here so she could incriminate herself?"

"No. He says you were supposed to eat it in the pie shop, then get sick later and no one would know how it happened." Richard looked at the boy, who sat sullenly at the table. "He says he went to visit his mother, and when he came back, she'd taken the pie."

"Why would he think I was coming to the pie shop to cause trouble for them? That's what I don't understand. He's a lad. What does he know about anything?" She'd hoped Richard could make more headway than she had. "Did he do it at his master's bidding?"

"He says it was all of his own accord." Richard moved closer to her. "He's not very sharp, Mama," he said soft enough for the boy not to hear it. "He seems like a younger boy than he is."

"If he's so dull, then what does he know of poison?"

"He said they use the stuff around the pie shop to keep the rats away from their stores." That at least made sense. "He thought you were going to take his mistress away, then his old master would die and he'd be out on the streets."

"And now"—she glanced at the boy—"thanks to his misdeeds, that's exactly what's happened."

"He's too young to be in prison, Mama."

"I do agree with you there," she said softly. "I shall send him to the Christian brothers. They'll keep him safe until I can figure out what to do with him."

"But what about my old master at home?" wailed the boy. "He'll die all alone. He can't even get up to use the chamber pot."

"I shall release your mistress from the prison tonight—" She paused, moved close to him and peered into his lightless eyes. "If you promise that you'll behave yourself with the brothers and do their bidding."

"I promise," he mumbled. "I'm a fool. They've always said I'm a fool."

An uncomfortable feeling tugged in Ela's chest. This world was no place for fools. And she didn't feel any inclination to show him further mercy or forgiveness right now when he could have killed or sickened anyone in her house-hold. "Pray for mercy, because you'll need it."

$$\backsim$$

MARGERY WAS BROUGHT up from the jail and into the great hall. Ela had told the guards to say nothing about the boy and his confession as she wanted to see her reaction to the news.

The small, plump woman's eyes were rimmed in red again. She seemed to have shrunk in stature and aged ten years in just a day.

"The lad has told us he tainted the pies himself with rat poison," said Ela. "To kill me."

"What?" Her shock appeared genuine. "Young Phil? Why would he do such a terrible thing?"

"I tried to extract that information from him, and so did my son Richard. He kept saying that he didn't want me to bring trouble to his mistress and master."

Margery's face crumpled. "The boy is simple. He doesn't understand things like you and I. Or even like an ordinary child. He latches on to an idea sometimes, and you can't shake it from his mind." She pressed a hand to her forehead. "He must have heard me telling my husband about your visit and how it could bring trouble for us."

"I'm letting you out tonight so you can go tend to your husband. But you must come here after the bells for Tierce tomorrow morning to stand in front of a jury. The boy will be here too."

"Where is he?"

"He'll be kept under watch by the brothers. He's too young for the jail."

Margery looked relieved. "He's not a bad boy. He tries so hard to help. Sometimes his judgment is poor."

"But you understand that when your poor judgment could kill someone that's a serious matter?"

Margery nodded. Ela remembered that Margery had lost a child and not been able to conceive since. Perhaps poor simple Phil was the closest thing she had to a child of her own. "He's a young boy and will be treated as such. And those he poisoned have recovered. Don't fret too much about him."

After Margery left, Ela retreated to her solar. She wanted to pray for good judgment in handling both the issue of the young poisoner and the matter of Margery's adultery. Both problems required a solution that would make their lives better, not ruin them altogether.

ELA ATTENDED TIERCE, along with Petronella, Richard and Stephen. Her youngest children went with their tutor to gather the morning's eggs that the castle hens had deposited around the garden. She didn't think that forcing children to sit through a service they didn't fully understand brought them any closer to God.

Her three remaining oldest children were to watch the jury proceedings. They were all old enough to learn how the affairs of men were dealt with by their peers.

As soon as service ended, they walked to the hall, where three long tables were arranged in a U shape. The men of the jury lined the edges of the table. She'd told the guards to raise twelve jurors—always a challenge on a busy morning when the burghers of Salisbury preferred to ply their trades. Eight men had arrived, and with Giles Haughton on his way and John Dacus there would be jury enough to deliberate the issues.

Ela took up her place at the head of the tables, with Giles

on one side of her and John on the other. "Our most pressing matter today is to discuss the culpability of Bertram Beck for the death of his neighbor Wilf Crowder. As you all know, Beck took pains to alter the boundaries of his farm to steal land from Crowder. He even diverted the course of a stream by digging it out. Crowder died while moving stones to mark the true border between their land. Our next matter is to determine his punishment for attempted theft of his neighbor's land." She asked the guards to bring Bertram Beck up from the jail.

John Dacus raised his hand. "Being somewhat new to this district, I find it odd that these men have fealty over their land. Is it not owned by a great lord or lady?" Ela wondered at him asking this question before the jury instead of just asking her.

"Land ownership by a yeoman farmer is not unusual in this part of Wiltshire. The ownership of many farms dates back to before the conquest."

"Such a dispute between neighbors wouldn't happen if they were both under the auspices and guidance of their lord," Dacus suggested.

Ela found his statement provoking. "Do you suggest I seize their land and declare them my tenants?"

"You'd be well within your rights, my lady. Crowder is dead with no heirs apparent, as he has no issue or surviving siblings. Beck has violated the laws of the land. It seems only fitting that both properties be forfeit to the great family that has ruled Salisbury in duty and benevolence for a hundred and fifty years."

First Haughton and now Dacus? Did these men think her greedy or did they think such actions would enhance her reputation? A female sheriff was an outlandish enough concept for most people to swallow. A female sheriff motivated by greed would be the talk of all England. "Thank you, Sir John. I'll take that under advisement."

Bertram Beck was brought in. People always looked terrible after even one night in the cold, damp dungeon, and he was no exception, his red cloak soiled and rumpled and skin ghostly gray. He was seated in the middle of the tables, and Ela asked the jurors if they had questions for him.

Stephen Hale the cordwainer raised his hand. "Was the body of the dead man, Simon of Oddo, found on Bertram Beck's land?"

Haughton replied. "Indeed it was. However, at the time of his death—in so far as we can determine it—the land still belonged to Simon's father, Oddo the Bald. Bertram Beck claims he had no knowledge of the body buried there."

Ela cleared her throat. "Our concern this morning is with the far more recent death of Wilf Crowder and whether Bertram Beck had a hand in it. He was at the scene either at the time of death or shortly afterward and reported it himself."

"I wouldn't have reported it if I'd killed him," protested Beck, with an uncharacteristically hoarse voice. The damp of the dungeon must be getting into his chest.

"Silence!" said Ela. "You will not speak unless you are directly addressed. The fact remains that Beck made deliberate efforts to steal his neighbor's land. He erected a fence far past the boundary in the woods on the hilltop, and redirected the course of a stream to steal another strip of land on the hillside. To my mind this demonstrates open hostility toward his neighbor Wilf Crowder. Let's leave the question of innocence or guilt in the murder for a moment and discuss the matter of punishment for his encroachments."

"You could take his land and give it to the king," said Stephen Hale, the cordwainer, directing his speech at Giles

Haughton, who would be presumed to be in favor based on his role of claiming funds and property due to the king. Haughton looked at Ela. She appreciated the act of deference.

"If Beck is found guilty of the murder, that is my recommended course of action," said Ela. "The encroachments in and of themselves, while irksome, were modest and perhaps don't merit such harsh punishment." She looked at Beck. "However, John Dacus has investigated the matter of your father's death and found that most of his fortune in gold and movable goods was missing from his residence when the sheriff's men arrived. It's the belief of the local sheriff that you stole them. What say you?"

"They stole my father's life and the estate that was my inheritance."

"So you felt justified in stealing from your king, who would be entitled to the spoils of your father's estate. He was found guilty of hiding funds in order to avoid taxes."

"Surely that merits a fine, rather than death," asked Peter Howard, the baker and one of the most stalwart and reliable jurors. "Unless it came on top of other offenses."

"I'm not aware of further offences, but perhaps Bertram Beck, or should I say Le Bec, knows of them," said Ela. The records hadn't yielded much information. They rather suggested that Le Bec was just unpopular in his shire and had fallen victim to a greedy sheriff. She couldn't really blame his son for taking what he could. However, in her official capacity she could hardly condone the behavior.

"Then he should pay a fine for his attempt to steal his neighbor's land," said Howard. "Perhaps a fine so high that he'll be forced to sell the land."

Other jurors nodded. No honest man wanted a cheat and a thief in their midst so she was hardly surprised their solution might involve ridding Salisbury of Bertram Beck.

"What amount does the jury suggest?" asked Ela.

"Fifty pounds," suggested Stephen Hale.

Bertram Beck flinched.

"Why not a hundred pounds?" asked Peter Howard.

Beck's mouth dropped open.

"Beck himself has stated that he paid thirty pounds for it."

"You could argue that its value has increased," said Will Dyer. "He's cleared scrub for grazing and improved the fields for crops."

"I'm to be punished for my hard work?" burst Beck.

"Silence!" said Ela. "The jury will decide the appropriate amount."

"In that case, perhaps fifty is fair," said Howard, weaving his hands together. The other jurors nodded and murmured agreement. Bertram Beck looked like he was about to faint.

"I'm in agreement," said Ela.

John Dacus stood up. "Bertram Beck shall pay fifty pounds to the high sheriff of Salisbury in penance for his crimes against his neighbor Wilf Crowder and against the peace and prosperity of the shire."

Ela had to admit that having a co-sheriff who could claim large fines for your without you seeming to grasp them yourself—had its advantages. "Then the matter of his encroachment is settled. The matter of whether he's culpable in the death of his neighbor is a matter for the traveling justice of the assizes so he can now return to the dungeon. And of course there's still the matter of who killed Simon of Oddo."

The guards moved forward to take him. Bertram Beck leaped to his feet, panic on his face. "I didn't kill anyone! I never even met Simon of Oddo." The guards seized his arms. "But I do know who killed him."

"Who?" Ela didn't believe him.

"I don't know his name," sniveled Beck. "I overheard him talk about killing a man on a farm in Salisbury."

215

Ela was in no mood for more of Bertram Beck's nonsense. He clearly felt that laws didn't apply to him. Now he wanted to waste the court's time with fool stories. "Save your pleas of innocence for the judge at the assizes. Lock him up, guards."

"I didn't do the murder. I just heard him speak of it."

Bertram Beck let out a wail of protest that continued as the guards dragged him from the hall. Ela wanted to cross herself but managed to keep her hands still. Beck would meet his final judge one day but for now his life was in the hands of his fellow men.

She looked over to one side of the hall where the boy, Phil Dawson, stood flanked by robed monks. She summoned them to bring him in front of the jury. She looked around for Margery, who would undoubtedly be the chief character witness for or against him, but she was nowhere to be seen.

Phil sat on the chair just vacated by Bertram Beck. His feet didn't reach the floor and he kicked his legs, staring at his lap.

Ela inhaled. "This boy works in the pie shop run by Margery Willoughby and her husband. I went to visit to question them about...a matter...and in anticipation of my arrival and the stress it perhaps caused, the boy decided I was their enemy and took it upon himself to poison a pie baked for me."

Phil Dawson looked around at them. His face didn't betray guilt or innocence or even a hint of apology.

"This pie was offered to Sir William Talbot and me when we visited the pie shop, but we did not partake. Margery Willoughby, unaware that the pie was poisoned, brought it to the castle that night. I sent it to the kitchen, not being in the habit of eating strange foods. There it was discovered by two of the children, who ate it and became very ill."

The jurors muttered and shook their heads.

"Happily, the children recovered, but young Phil must be punished for his crime. Given his age and what I suggest is a lack of wit and perception, I ask the jury to be compassionate in your deliberations."

"Where did you get the poison, lad?" asked Peter Howard the baker.

Phil blinked at him for what fell like an eternity before replying. "Mistress kept it in the store cupboard to kill rats."

"Well, I suppose at least he didn't take pains to obtain it," murmured one juror.

"Did you realize it could kill someone?" asked another.

"Yes. I wanted to kill the sheriff. I thought he was a bad man who'd hurt my friends."

The jurors stared at Ela. "As you can see, the boy is young and possibly also simple."

"Are you an apprentice at this shop?" asked Stephen Hale.

"I don't know," said Phil, after another long pause.

Margery came rushing in, apologetic for being late. "My husband was so ill I could hardly leave him."

"Is he resting comfortably now?" asked Ela.

"Nay, my lady. He's racked with pain this morning. He's upset that the pie shop is closed and that Phil is gone and he's quite beside himself that I was locked up—"

"We're here determining the matter of punishment for Phil. One of the jurors just asked if he's an apprentice in your shop."

The guards brought her into the midst of the tables, near Phil, and sat a stool there for her. Margery, chest still heaving with exertion, shook her head. "He's not an official apprentice. Just a lad whose widowed mother struggles to support all her children. He's lived in the shop with us for nigh on four years."

"And he does work to help you?" asked Ela.

"He tries his best," said Margery. "He's not good at

measuring ingredients, and I'd never trust him with hot things from the oven."

"Would you say he's…" Ela hesitated. "Like something of a son to you?"

Margery's mouth twitched. She glanced at Phil, who stared at the floor, kicking his legs. "I suppose you could say that. I've never had a child to care for. It would never have crossed my mind he'd try to poison anyone. If I'd have known—" She broke off, her eyes suddenly rimmed with red.

"I hope that if you'd known you'd have cuffed him soundly about the ears," bellowed old Matthew Hart.

Margery nodded. "If only…" Her voice broke into a sob. "Will he hang?"

"We're not in the habit of hanging children," cut in Ela quickly, before someone could answer in the affirmative. "But he must be punished." An idea occurred to her. "Margery, what would you consider the appropriate punishment for such a thing?" A mother, even an adopted one, knew her children better than anyone.

"I don't know."

Margery's wits weren't all that much sharper than poor Phil's, reflected Ela. "Do you think he'd benefit from a stay with the Christian brothers if they were willing to have him?" A sojourn in the quiet and discipline of the monastery might satisfy the jury without doing anything to ruin the boy's life.

"I don't know," muttered Margery. "I suspect he'd be a bother to them."

"They're scary," said Phil suddenly. "They don't talk, just stare at you."

"Is it a silent order?" asked Ela of the two brothers with him.

"No, my lady, but idle chatter is not encouraged." Both

brothers did indeed look slightly sinister. One's tonsure was a black ring that encircled his long, narrow head like a vice. The other's head was wide and block-like, his shaved hair growing back in strange tufts. Neither looked like the type of man you'd want to entrust with the raising of a tender young child, especially a simple one. "We'd flog some sense into the boy."

Ela flinched at the prospect. "I'm not sure that's what is needed. Margery, do you feel like you could punish him yourself?"

"I don't know."

Ela didn't know how they were going to get out of this hole.

"I've raised six sons," cut in Thomas Price, the old thatcher. "And I'd give him a whipping and have him live off gruel for a month. That would be a doubly cruel punishment in a pie shop."

"Has any of your children ever poisoned a person?" asked Stephen Hale.

"Not poisoned, but one of them choked his brother half to death in a stupid game, and another trapped his sister in a well. Either of these misadventures could have ended in death, and much like this one I'm glad it didn't. They're all good sensible grown men today who've learned from their mistakes."

Ela inhaled with relief at the straw of hope he'd handed Phil and Margery. "Margery Willoughby, what do you think of his suggestion. Would you be willing to execute such a punishment?"

Margery paled. "Execute?"

Ela drew in another breath. The woman was a simple as one of her pies. "Would you be willing to whip him and give him only gruel for a month?"

Margery looked around, clearly hoping the answer would

be plain on someone's face. "Yes," she said, with a question in her voice.

"I think that's settled then—if the jury is in agreement. What say you?" She looked at them.

"I've just realized something." Hal Price, the eldest son of the old thatcher who'd just offered the olive branch to young Phil, rose to his feet. Eyes wide, he pointed right at Margery. "It's her!" I didn't see it before but I see it now. Mistress Willoughby from the pie shop is the woman who used to live with Simon of Oddo."

Margery paled. She glanced at Ela, who wanted to say, "I didn't utter a word!" She held her tongue instead. It was rather surprising that no one had asked why Ela went to question Margery in the first place. Ela wondered if Hal was the one who'd trapped his sister in a well.

"It is! It's her! She's that much fatter now, I hardly recognize her," the sturdy young thatcher continued. "But now that we're sitting here staring right at her, I remember that sad slip of a girl who followed Simon of Oddo around in the weeks before he disappeared." He leaned over the table, toward where Margery stood in the center. "It is you, isn't it?"

Ela stared at Hal Price. He was barely five and twenty and must have been a lad of sixteen back when Simon of Oddo still lived.

Margery looked at Ela for a moment, in a plea for help. Then she lifted her chin and looked right at Hal Price. "Yes."

CHAPTER 20

$\mathcal{A}$ moment of stunned silence rose into a hum of shocked murmuring as the men of the jury consulted their memories and each other and decided they all recognized her.

"And you've lived in our midst these past nine years like a respectable woman," hissed Will Dyer, his eyes flashing with contempt.

Margery looked like she wanted to protest that she was a respectable woman. But both she and Ela knew she was an adulterer and a bigamist so she said nothing.

"She lived up there on the farm with him for weeks. Maybe months. One of my mates was relieved that lecherous Simon might finally stop chasing the woman he wanted as his wife."

"But how did you see her?" Ela's curiosity was getting the better of her. "If Simon kept her up there in his hut."

"Oh, but he didn't." Will Dyer said with a smirk on his weasel face. "He paraded her through the village like a trophy. Even put a gaudy ring on her finger!"

Another muttering arose from the jury as they all recalled

Ela's recent attempts to find the ring and as they realized—as Margery had originally feared—that it was one and the same ring. Of course Simon of Oddo had nothing to do with the ring—which was from her first husband—but that was neither here nor there.

Ela grew exasperated. "If all of you saw Margery waving her hands around in town with this ring, why did none of you mention it when I sought the ring's owner a few days ago?"

"Didn't remember it, did we?" said Hal Price. "The last time we noticed it were that long ago. And she looks completely different. She had a different name then, too."

"Gwynneth, or something," said Will Dyer.

"Or Gerarda," said Hal Price.

"Grizeldis," muttered Margery. "My name was Grizeldis."

"What kind of woman changes her first name?" asked Matthew Hart.

"One with something to hide, that's who," said Will Dyer.

The look on Margery's face made Ela's heart sink. She could see her careful deception crumbling to dust, along with her hard-won new life.

"She must have hidden away in the back of that pie shop until she grew plump and rosy enough to look like a different woman." Hal Price shook his head. "And all along we might have had a murderer in our midst."

Margery let out a whimper.

"Margery is not accused of murder."

"She should be! Probably killed him because he couldn't keep his hands off other women," sneered Dyer.

"If nothing else, she'd have known he was dead and buried up there," said Hal Price.

"She says she didn't know he was dead," retorted Ela. "Even his own father thought he went away to fight in the hope of returning a rich man."

"Anyone who drank ale with that layabout would know he'd be too lazy to fight his way out of a curtained bed."

"Aye. He weren't interested in anything unless it had tits and—" Hal Price broke off and blinked as he realized he was addressing Ela Longespée, Countess of Salisbury, instead of the usual stone-eared men of the shire. "Begging your pardon, my lady."

Ela let her withering glance linger on him for a moment before ignoring his apology and moving on. "No one knew he was dead until the property dispute erupted and we dug up the area looking for the ancient boundary marker."

"I'll bet she knew he was dead." Juror Will Dyer looked at Margery.

"I didn't know!" she said in a thin voice. "I waited and waited for him to come back. I went into town looking for him, but no one had seen him. Then I went to beg at the pie shop and Hugh Willoughby offered to let me wash the dishes in exchange for food and I stayed there."

"I bet he let you do something else, as well." Dyer thrust himself forward with a lewd glance.

"Silence! Enough of this idle chatter." Ela despised their insolence and cruel treatment of Margery. "But since Margery is here, and since she was indeed intimate with the dead man, we can address the matter." She turned to Margery. "Now that you know Simon is dead, instead of just gone away, do you have any suspicion about who might have killed him?"

Margery looked at the floor. Ela felt the jurors stir, probably wanting to cry out that she looked guilty, but mercifully they held their tongues. If Margery was on trial today she'd hang for sure. But luckily for her a murder must be tried at the assizes so there was no danger of that.

"No one liked him much," said Margery softly. "Not even his own father."

"Wasn't his father's knife found near the body?" offered John Dacus.

"It was," replied Ela. "Though in his recent appearance here he made it clear that it was gone from his possession before the murder happened."

"Well, he would say that, wouldn't he," muttered Hal Price.

"Old Oddo—known as the Bald—was well-liked and respected. Hardly anyone—if anyone—thinks him capable of killing his son." Ela paused. "And what reason would he have?"

"Perhaps he wanted to sell the farm and felt he couldn't as long as his son was waiting to inherit it," said Hugh Clifford the wine seller, a sensible man who'd been silent up to now.

Ela looked at Giles Haughton. "As coroner, what is your opinion of the possibility that Oddo the Bald killed his only son? We did find his knife near the body, after all."

Haughton leaned forward and rested his elbows on the linen cloth that covered the table. "I'm afraid there's no conclusive evidence one way or the other. His knife would point to guilt, but his reputation as a man of honor, and a good Christian, disputes it. I haven't heard a single man in Salisbury say they really believe he killed his son. If anything, they say he showed the lad excessive indulgence."

Ela sighed. It would be too convenient if the murderer could turn out to be a man already dead. She had to admit that Margery had the opportunity—but why would she kill the man who gave her shelter and succor in her time of need?

"Simon had angered his neighbor Wilf Crowder on more than one occasion," said Ela. "But similarly, no one sees Wilf Crowder as a likely murderer. The two old farmers grumbled about each other for decades, according to rumors, but there are no records of any violent disputes or even any legal proceedings until the recent one involving Bertram Beck."

"Of all the likely suspects, Margery has the misfortune of being the only one left alive," said Haughton, with a hint of sympathy in his voice.

"And she changed her name and hid among us all these years," said Matthew Hart, showing sudden animation. "Who was she and where did she come from before she turned up in Simon of Oddo's bed?"

IT TOOK ALL of Ela's persuasive powers to let the jury send Margery home to her ailing husband. Even that only happened on the promise that her first husband, Ebbo Fuller —yes, the truth about her first marriage and the fact that she was now a bigamist came out and caused an uproar of indignation—should appear in the court within the week. To Margery's horror, messengers were sent to summon him.

"MAMA, why are you so indulgent with Hilda?" asked Petronella when they sat alone in the peace of Ela's solar. A beeswax candle filled the room with soft light and honeyed fragrance and the whispers of their shared prayers still fluttered in the air. Ela wished they could drown out all the chattering voices and day-to-day cares. "You're far less strict with her than you were with any of us."

"Nonsense. You forget how often I scolded you when you were young. Hilda didn't have the benefit of a firm hand to guide her."

"Are her parents dead?"

"You know they're not. Her mother is Sibel's sister." Ela

sighed. Couldn't they just sit in quiet contemplation? "They're still angry with her for getting pregnant out of wedlock."

"As well they might be. What would you do if one of us did something so scandalous?"

"You wouldn't," said Ela briskly. "You know better. And she was led astray by a rascal as many young girls unfortunately are. Soon she'll be safely married and can put all that behind her."

"And enjoy the reward of a manor for her lascivious behavior."

"Petronella! I'm surprised at you."

"Well, won't she?"

"The Lord moves in strange and magnificent ways. It's not for you to decide who receives the joys of earthly reward. Does her gaining a manor take anything away from you?"

Petronella let out a huff. They sat in simple wood chairs before the crackling embers of the dying fire. "It just doesn't seem right."

"You'd prefer for her to starve on the road with her baby?"

"Well, no, but—"

"But nothing. Look to your own Christian charity and don't fret over the joys and triumphs of others."

"I don't understand why you paid all the legal bills to make this happen."

"I took personal satisfaction in wresting the manor away from the criminal occupying it." She'd taken further satisfaction at his meeting a grisly end some months later, but that was none of Petronella's concern.

"I suppose that is a good reason." Petronella pouted for a moment. "But I don't understand why you have to concern yourself with such matters. There are knights and soldiers and the jurors of the hundred to see to the transgressions of the common people."

"And sheriffs like Simon de Hal?" Ela spat the name of the man who'd sat in her place just a few months ago. His reputation for extortion and violence finally followed him south from Yorkshire and helped her unseat him from her family's hallowed halls. "I trust myself to do the work God guides me to."

"It would be so much more…dignified of you to take the veil." Petronella's lips pursed. "Many widows do, when they don't wish to marry again."

"Many are forced into it against their will, if you must know. Sometimes their family wants them out of the way." Petronella's words stung her more than she admitted. "And I believe I've comported myself in the role with dignity that befits our great family and the people of Salisbury."

"You could spend all your time in prayer for the people of Salisbury. And for the immortal soul of dear Papa."

A stinging retort hovered on Ela's lips. Petronella had always been somewhat distant from her father, a man who seized each day with both hands and was apt to neglect his prayers. But she shoved the harsh words back down her throat. "I pray day and night for your father's soul. And there are men and women in orders throughout the south of England praying and chanting that he might find eternal grace. Land is already cleared for the monastery at Snail's Meadow and I shall lay the first stone when the time comes. There monks shall dedicate hours every day to praying for his soul and for that of his father and my father and his father and—"

"I know, I know, my grandfather was a great king…I've heard it all before."

"Such history is a weighty burden to carry."

"And the cloister is the perfect place to carry it. When shall I enter it?"

Ela steadied herself. "The Lord will let us know when the time is right."

"When the new convent is built?"

"Perhaps." Ela didn't want to commit to anything. Petronella could be relentless in her persistence in pursuit of what she wanted. "I need your help with the little ones. My role as sheriff is demanding and takes me away from home."

"There are servants and tutors and all manner of other people to see to Nicky and Ellie."

"But none so ably as their loving sister." Even Petronella's stern nature melted somewhat in the presence of her sweet and playful younger siblings.

Petronella's eyes narrowed. "Hilda could have killed Nicky by making him steal that pie for her."

"God is merciful."

"And so are you, apparently."

"I seek to show mercy as often as I pray to receive it. Do not judge others, lest ye be judged."

"That's rich coming from the sheriff who sits in judgment on the people of Salisbury."

"My only goal is to promote justice and peace."

Petronella tilted her head. Even at home she always wore a scarf with never a wisp of hair showing. "Are you sure you aren't glad of an excuse to gallop about the countryside and make jaunts into London in the pursuit of justice?"

Ela's pulse quickened. In the moments when she was honest enough to look deep into her heart, she had to admit that she did enjoy the excitement and urgency of the role. "I simply seek to execute the role of sheriff with the same energy and efficiency as your father, and my father and all the good men of our family who've kept Salisbury peaceful and prosperous through the years.

Petronella looked doubtful. "Do you really want to become a nun one day or are you just saying that so people won't gossip about your not wanting to remarry?"

"A lot of rather insolent questions for your mother, don't you think?" In truth they cut rather close to the quick. "While I'd relish the peace of the cloister and the opportunity to spend my days in prayer, I still have young children to raise. When little Ellie and Nicky are safely married off like their older brothers and sisters, then I shall feel freed of my responsibilities and able to take the veil."

"I can't imagine why everyone doesn't want to," said Petronella wistfully. "To leave the cares of the mundane world behind, step inside the walls of a beautiful place dedicated entirely to the glory of God and live there insulated from the clamor and suffering of the world."

"I suppose you've seen rather more than most girls of the clamor and suffering of the world, since their representatives turn up daily in our hall looking for justice."

"My soul longs for the peace of the cloister," said Petronella, with unaccustomed passion. Her hazel eyes took on a dreamy look like a girl talking of her lover. "I long to take Christ as my bridegroom."

Ela blinked. "Are you sure such talk isn't sacrilegious?"

"Not at all. Nuns are brides of Christ."

Maybe Petronella wasn't so different from other girls. Except that her dream husband was divine. "The life of a nun is not all chanting and rejoicing, you know. The abbess might well decide to humble you by assigning you work in the garden or even washing pots or tending animals." This wasn't terribly likely. The communities that a nobleman's daughter like Petronella would enter had more servants than they had nuns.

"I shall mortify my pride with joy," said Petronella, with a deadly serious expression.

Ela had always sung the praises of the religious life to her children and encouraged them to attend services from an early age. She truly wanted them to take the veil or the tonsure at some point in their lives—preferably once their children had grown and their spouse died. It was a tradition in her family and a fine way to ensure the passage of your immortal soul to grace.

But she hadn't expected her eighteen-year-old daughter to beg so ardently to shut herself away in a cell for a life of celibacy.

"You must wait at least until the new convent at Lacock is built."

Petronella rose to her feet. "But why must I wait? Anything could happen. Papa is dead and you might die or be pushed into marriage by the king and then I'll find myself sold off like an ox to some red-faced baron who only wants my dowry." Her words erupted into the air, guttering the candle flame and bouncing off the stone walls.

"I have no intention of dying," said Ela, rather shocked that her daughter had aired her fears so boldly. "And as for remarriage, the Magna Carta ensures my right to remain in a widowed state. Your impatience is unbecoming and smacks of pride. Right now your duty is to your family."

"Hilda's not even family. Why do I have to embroider things for her dowry?"

Ela drew in an exasperated breath. "Look on it as an act of Christian charity. Let it prepare you for when the mother superior asks you to mend the shoes of your fellow sisters."

"Mend their shoes? How? Surely a cobbler does that?"

Ela shrugged. "The Lord has his own plan for all of us, and we must listen for his instruction."

Ebbo Fuller—Margery's first husband—energetically resisted the efforts of Ela's messenger to bring him to Salisbury. He ignored letters and had to be fetched by armed guards.

So it wasn't until the following Monday that the jury assembled again in the hall, with Fuller seated on a stool between the U shaped tables and Margery seated on another a few feet away from him.

Margery quaked in the man's presence and avoided laying her eyes on him as if doing so might turn her into a pillar of salt.

Ela had tasked John Dacus with initiating the proceedings, which were arranged to determine if Margery was an adulteress as well as a possible murderess.

Ebbo Fuller turned out to be a man of middling height with a broad, sturdy build. The thick muscles of his upper arms flexed visibly beneath his wool tunic. He looked younger than Ela expected—no more than thirty—but perhaps Margery's ordeals had aged her prematurely. A thatch of greasy hair topped his face, which currently glowed with protest.

"How was I to know the hag was still alive? She ran off years ago. Any man would assume she was dead."

Ela reflected that there was some truth to his statement. She'd also consulted with a lawyer and discovered that annulments of even the most disastrous marriages were rare to nonexistent among the ordinary people. Desertion and separation—often followed by illegal remarriage—were the normal manner of dealing with a marriage gone badly awry.

"She left the family home of her own accord?" asked John Dacus.

"Just ran off one morning before dawn."

"Did you try to find her?"

"Of course I did!" Fuller sounded indignant. "Who was

going to cook my supper and wash my clothes? And after I'd kept a roof over her head and clothes on her back for nigh on two years. Ungrateful!"

"Where did you seek her?" Dacus seemed unruffled by Fuller's displays of temper.

"In the village. Where else?"

"Which village was this?"

Fuller stared at Dacus as if her co-sheriff might be simple. "Devizes, Wiltshire. That's where my house and fulling mill are."

Ela knew that was where Clerebold Rufus had found him.

"So you're still living there?"

"Where else would I be?" Insolence rang in Fuller's every word. If Ela were leading the interrogation she'd have reprimanded Fuller by now. Dacus's indulgent nature allowed her to wield the power of the sheriff's office unimpeded, but it had its drawbacks as well.

"Did you find her in the village?"

"No. No one saw her leave, either. I searched in all the nearby villages, but she was nowhere to be found."

"And no one knew where she'd gone?"

"If they did, they weren't saying," he spat.

Dacus rose from his chair and walked around behind the tables before asking his next question. "Did you suspect her of running off to another man?"

Ela saw Fuller's cheek twitch. "Never. Her? She were skin and bone back then. You could have scrubbed your washing on her chest."

Ela glanced at Margery, who looked white as bone, her gaze fixed on the floor.

"Yet you still wanted her back." Dacus walked around the tables and peered at Fuller.

"A man's wife is his property, ain't she? It's not her right to take off and leave him when the house needs cleaning and there's piles of cloth that need fulling."

Ela's heart ached for Margery and her narrow existence as little more than a slave of this man, who saw her as a work animal. He showed no more concern than if she were an ass that had strayed and now he had no beast to pull his cart to market. And Margery said he'd used his fists on her, which wasn't hard to believe.

"Did you ever find her?" Dacus now stood quite close to Fuller and peered down on him from his considerable height.

Ela could swear she saw Fuller swallow quickly, before replying, "Never."

Ela looked at Margery, who, for the first time, raised her gaze to Fuller's face with a look of surprise.

Had he found her and didn't want the jury to know about it? If so, why hadn't Margery mentioned it?

"Do the jurors have any questions?" Dacus looked at the men seated along the two adjacent tables.

Stephen Hale the cordwainer raised his hand. "Why did you remarry when you couldn't be sure that your wife was dead?"

Fuller tilted his chin. "How would she not be dead? A lone woman with the brains of a parsnip and no living relations? Of course I thought she was dead."

Ela felt fury rising in her chest. He thought his wife was dead and was glad of it. As her husband he was legally entrusted with protecting her and providing for her and he'd all but driven her out to die.

Hal Price cleared his throat. "How long did you wait to remarry?"

"Almost six years." Fuller's eyes narrowed. "I think any man would consider that long enough."

Some murmuring from the jury indicated that they

233

agreed with him. Ela suspected it had taken him that long to find someone else desperate enough to marry him.

"You had no idea your wife took up with another man?" asked Will Dyer.

"Like I said, I'm shocked anyone would want her," spat Fuller.

Margery seemed to shrink inside her green wool gown.

"She took up with another man," repeated John Dacus as he made another circuit outside the tables. "And that man was murdered."

Again Ela thought she saw Fuller's jaw twitch.

He knows something.

"But no one knew he was murdered until this year." Dacus looked bemused by the information as if he'd just heard it. "When his body turned up during digging."

Fuller looked a little disconcerted. "What business is that of mine?"

"Don't you at least want to know who he was?"

"No. Why would I care?" Fuller shifted his weight. "I'd washed my hands of her by then."

"By when?" Dacus leaned in until Fuller could likely smell his breath.

Ela was intrigued. Dacus reminded her of an old judge who used to preside over the assizes many years ago who had a way of unsettling the accused until they were practically begging to blurt out their crimes. Had Dacus realized that Fuller was implicated in Simon of Oddo's death and now he was closing in on the brute, bringing him closer and closer to the brink of confession?

"By when he died," snarled Fuller.

Dacus stopped suddenly and glared at Fuller. "How do you know when he died?"

There was a silence, and Ela realized Fuller had just admitted knowledge of the murder.

CHAPTER 21

*E*la's senses pricked to attention. Fuller could feel the attention of the entire jury on him. In less than a minute he'd gone from having their sympathy as a man wronged by a feckless woman to being a murder suspect.

"Do you know the name of the man who died?"

"The guards told me when they dragged me here. Simon of Oddo, they said. Never heard of him before that."

An audible sigh of relief rose from the jury. The guards who brought him must have prattled on about the dead body or maybe just gossiped about Margery and her exploits in Salisbury. This wasn't supposed to be a murder inquiry. Ebbo Fuller was summoned in connection with Margery's bigamy and to determine fault in the dissolution of the marriage.

So far it was clear that every man in the room thought Margery at fault for the failure of her marriage. Ela watched John Dacus, wondering what his next move would be. He circled around the tables yet again, then moved in on Fuller. "Was this the first time you heard the name Simon of Oddo?"

"Yes." Fuller started to relax.

"What are your sentiments toward this man who took

your legally wedded wife into his bed?" Sir John asked the question with what appeared to be mild amusement.

Fuller hesitated, looking wary. "She ran off, didn't she? I wouldn't have no...*sentiments*." He mangled the word. Sir John's English was as good as his French, expressive and richer in vocabulary than half the native English speakers of Salisbury.

"It didn't upset you to know that another man had enjoyed your conjugal rights?"

Fuller frowned. He clearly had no idea what John was talking about in these unfamiliar words.

Again, John looked as if he found the whole proceeding entertaining rather than serious. "That he tupped your wife."

Fuller flinched. "She wasn't my wife then. Not to my mind, anyway."

Ela glanced at Margery, who, once again, was a vision of mortification.

Sir John turned to Margery. He offered her a slight smile before speaking. "Were you worried that your husband might track you down and take you home?"

She fussed for a moment, plucking at the hem of her right sleeve. "At first I was." She stole a glance at Fuller. Who glared at her. She spun away from him. "I thought he would find me and beat me like he always did."

"You'd run away before?" Dacus looked surprised.

"No," said Margery very quietly. "He just always beat me. He'd beat me for breathing too loud. That's why I ran away."

"And after a time you began to feel safe in Simon of Oddo's hut."

"It was high up in the woods. No one came there. Hardly anyone, at least. Old Crowder the farmer sometimes. He didn't cause trouble, though. He wasn't interested in Simon or in me. He just wanted to tend to his lambs and sometimes one would stray into the woods."

"We heard he didn't much like Simon."

"He didn't like it when Simon's sheep wandered onto his land, but mostly he left us alone."

"How long did you live up there?"

Margery fiddled with her cuff again. "I can't say. I'm not sure. I wasn't keeping track of the time."

Ela reflected that Margery was a very simple woman and ripe for exploitation.

"A month? A year?"

"Something in between that. It was almost winter when I arrived in Salisbury for the first time and flakes of snow followed me down the road. I wondered if I might die here." Margery stopped and blinked.

"And what time of year was it when Simon disappeared?"

"Almost summer. The grazing was thick, the trees heavy with leaves, bees buzzing in the air."

"And where did you think Simon had gone?"

Margery looked down at the floor. "I didn't know."

"Did you think he'd joined the king's army?"

Her chest rose as she drew in a shaky breath. "Not really, no. They didn't say that until later. I think it was his father who said that. I thought he'd—" She hesitated, and her brow crumpled. "That he'd gone into town to spend time with another woman."

"Were you worried about him?"

"Not at first, but as the days stretched on I did start to think he might have come to harm. I thought maybe he got into a brawl at the Bull and Bear. He wasn't well-liked. But in town no one had seen him at all."

Ela cleared her throat. "Why was the hue and cry not raised? A man went missing. Surely there was cause for alarm?" She'd been here nine years ago, and she didn't remember ever hearing the man's name before this year. She looked at Margery, then at the jurors and Giles Haughton.

Had none of them thought that the missing man might have come to harm?

Haughton stood. "There was no body, my lady. He was known to be a ne'er-do-well. No one had reason to think he'd done anything but shirk his responsibilities as usual. Him leaving the area on a whim wasn't hard to believe. And Margery never came forward. She just changed her name and disappeared into the pie shop."

Haughton's defense of the town's lack of interest rather surprised her. Maybe he felt partially culpable that a man had lain in their midst—dead and undiscovered—for nearly a decade.

Ela looked at the jurors. "None of you suspected that something was amiss?"

They shifted in their seats. One of them coughed. Finally old Peter Howard mumbled that since he wasn't liked, perhaps people were simply glad he wasn't around and didn't worry about where he'd gone.

"Someone killed him." Ela wished she could get up and stroll around the tables like John Dacus, but she knew that would be unseemly. She sat up straight in her chair. She turned her gaze to Ebbo Fuller, who looked almost bored by the proceedings. "And to my mind Master Fuller has as good a motive as anyone."

"What? No!"

"Silence. You're to speak only when you're asked a question." She was in no mood to let Fuller talk over her. "Men who beat their wives do it as a means of control. They want to make sure she's scared enough to do anything they want."

He looked like he wanted to protest. She was curious about what nonsense he intended to spout. "Why do you think men beat their wives, Master Fuller?"

"Because they're disobedient," he expostulated on a bead of spittle. "And don't heed their husband like they should."

"Is that why you beat Margery?"

"I didn't even beat her that much." His voice shrank. "But she was slow. And stupid."

Ela could almost feel Margery shriveling on the inside as she heard these words from her tormentor uttered in front of the gathered jurors. Worse yet, some of the jurors probably agreed with Fuller.

"But your wife wasn't too slow and stupid to find another man, was she?" Ela raised her voice. "She found Simon of Oddo and moved in with him within days of leaving you."

"Slut," spat Fuller.

"Does it make you angry to think of your disobedient wife leaving you and taking up with another?" Ela wished she could apologize to Margery for this line of questioning, but she wanted to scratch beneath the surface and see what Ebbo Fuller was made of.

"Of course it does," he growled. He shot a dark glance at her, and Ela watched Margery flinch as if he'd slapped her. "She had no right."

"And this other man stole your wife right out from under you," continued Ela. "And took her into his bed and enjoyed her body."

Margery looked like she was getting ready to fall unconscious with mortification.

But Ebbo Fuller looked like he might burst into angry flames. "Stealing another man's wife is as much a crime as stealing his cow or his ox. He should pay for it." Fury thickened his voice.

"How would you make him pay?" asked Ela, her attention fully focused on him.

Fuller's beady eyes narrowed. "He should pay with a purse of money, like he would for an ass or a sheep."

"And that would make it acceptable? If he gave you a bag

of coins, you'd have forgiven him for stealing your wife and making her groan with pleasure?"

"He didn't have a pot to piss in, let alone a bloody coin," yelled Fuller, eyes bulging.

Ela's heart almost stopped. Had Fuller—in his unhinged rage—unwittingly admitted that he went to the hut and found Simon?

CHAPTER 22

A hush descended over the hall. Even the soldiers stilled their muttering and the dogs stared mutely, ears cocked.

Ela focused all her attention on Fuller. She needed to keep him red hot with rage so that his anger would fry his brain and make him incautious. "Simon of Oddo was having sex with your wife. Making her do what he wanted. Things that she didn't want to do for you."

The jurors' mouths fell open. She knew they were no strangers to this kind of talk, as she'd been present for many trials over the years. But they'd never heard such bawdy words uttered by a woman, especially a countess. "What did he do when you asked him for payment?"

"Waved his knife at me, the fool."

Ela tried hard to keep her expression blank. She didn't want to startle him out of his fog of fury. "Did he want to hurt you?"

"He told me to get out, when he had my wife right there in his filthy hut. But he screamed like a woman when I stuck his own knife in his fool gut."

Margery fainted dead away and hit the stone floor with a thud. No one rushed to help her for a moment as they were all too stunned.

"Guards, fetch a maid to revive Mistress Willoughby," cried Ela. "And arrest Ebbo Fuller and place him in chains."

Fuller's flush of triumph at describing his act of revenge ebbed instantly. His head jerked as he looked around, realizing he'd stepped into a trap.

Ela drew in a shaking breath, glad of the two rows of witnesses. His confession truly puzzled her, though. "Did Margery see you stick the knife into Simon of Oddo?"

Fuller stared at her. The full import of his confession seemed to click in his brain as the iron chains tightened around his wrists. "Her name is Grizeldis, not Margery. And, yes, she was there."

Margery's limp form was heaved into a wooden chair with arms. She lay slumped there, still unconscious. Her scarf had slipped from her head, revealing greasy pale brown hair.

Why had she not said anything? They'd been chasing this killer since they found the body, and she'd come forward for the ring and not said that her despised and dreaded husband was the murderer? It made no sense.

The serving girl Becca hurried over with a sachet of strong-scented herbs and waved it under Margery's nose, and soon another girl brought a bowl of water and a cloth to dab her face.

Ela turned back to Fuller. "You took your rival's knife and killed him with it, and then buried him and the knife."

His face had settled into an odd sneer. "Are you asking me or telling me?"

"Don't be insolent. Did you bury him?"

"No." He said it without hesitation. "Why would I waste my time doing that?"

"Then who did?"

"How would I know?" His eyes blazed dark. "Maybe she did." He tilted his head in the direction of Margery. "She asked me to kill him."

What?

Ela stared at Margery, who blinked rapidly as the herbs jolted her back to wakefulness.

He's lying. He had to be lying.

Didn't he?

"Why would she want you to kill the man who protected and sheltered her?"

"Because she's a coward. She begged me to spare her. To take his life instead of hers."

"She thought you came there to kill her?"

"She's a stupid woman. You can see that."

Ela wished she could rise from her chair and slap Ebbo Fuller hard across his arrogant face. But she wrestled her emotions back under control. "How did you find out where she lived?"

"Talk."

That wasn't hard to believe. His village was close enough for word of a woman living in sin on a wooded hilltop to reach his ears. "Why did you come? Did you intend to bring her home?"

"God, no," he spat. "I already told you. He took my wife, and I wanted payment. If he'd taken my cart or my sow I'd want the same, wouldn't I?"

"What did Margery do when she saw you?" She couldn't bring herself to call the woman Grizeldis. She now fully sympathized with her making the hard decision to leave her old life behind.

"Screamed her silly head off." A leer creased his face. "Like she'd seen a ghost."

Becca and the other serving girl still fussed over Margery, pressing a damp cloth to her forehead and offering her a cup of wine. Ela grew impatient for her input. "Margery, are you able to rejoin us? Guards, please set her chair in the center of the tables."

Margery's chair was brought into the center of the tables again, just a few feet from where Ebbo Fuller was now chained to his chair. She still avoided his glance as if it might contain poisoned darts.

"Margery." Ela hesitated, part of her wanting to shake Margery to get the truth from her and part of her wanting to tread carefully about the poor distressed and abused woman. "Master Fuller tells us you were present when he killed Simon of Oddo."

She blinked like a simpleton.

Ela inhaled. "Did you see him kill Simon of Oddo?"

Margery looked around her as if the answer might be written in the air of the great hall. The jurors listened, rapt, not a man rustling or coughing to prick the silence.

"Were you there or not?" Ela couldn't hide the exasperation in her voice.

"I don't know," blurted Margery. "I can't remember."

"You remembered the ring you knew you'd lost in those woods. The ring that your husband gave you." Ela frowned. "But you don't remember if you saw your husband violently stab your lover with a knife?"

Margery swallowed. "I know you don't believe me. I hardly know what to believe myself. But I don't remember anything at all."

Ela glanced at Giles Haughton. She needed a rest, and it was time for him to bring his coroner's knowledge to bear.

He stepped forward and peered at Margery. "Who buried the body?"

"I don't know."

"And the knife?"

She shook her head. Her eyes stayed strangely dry, with a startled look.

Giles Haughton walked to Ebbo Fuller. "Thank you for your full and detailed confession in front of our jury here today. Your trial at the assizes will be swift as a result."

Fuller's eyes narrowed, and Ela could almost feel the hate simmering behind them. "I was tricked. Maybe I'm making it up. Maybe I don't remember." Fuller turned and shot a cold stare at Margery.

Who shrank from it as if it burned.

"How many times did you stab him?" asked Haughton.

"Does it matter?" Ebbo lifted his chin. "He's dead."

"I suppose not. The knife buried with him belonged to his father."

"Maybe his father killed him," growled Fuller, apparently forgetting he'd already confessed to the crime.

"We did wonder that, at first," said Haughton. "But he didn't have motive. Unlike you. You have all the motive any man needs to kill another man and get clean away with it."

Fuller's eyes brightened. "Because I was wronged. She's an adulteress, and he committed a crime against me by leading her astray. And he came at me with the knife! It was self-defense."

Haughton laughed. The odd sound startled Ela so much that she jumped in her chair. She hadn't realized until that moment how tense she was.

"Not in your case." Haughton let out another low chuckle. Ela was a little disturbed to see that his pleasure appeared genuine. "You've made it clear that you subjected your wife to countless miseries and beatings and belittlings that would have driven any mortal to the brink of madness and desperation. You gave her no choice but to leave you."

"Weak in body and weak in mind."

"The thing that surprises me"—Haughton frowned and

rubbed his chin between his thumb and finger. "Is that you didn't kill her too. Your anger aside, she witnessed the killing and could point the finger at you." He stared at Fuller. "Or were you so sure of your power over her that you knew she'd never dare tell?"

Fuller just gazed at him. His eyes glittered strangely, like someone in his cups.

"Margery, are you sure you were there?"

The poor woman looked like she was doing her best to search her poor addled mind for details. "I don't know. I don't remember."

Ela cleared her throat. "When Hilda, my maid, witnessed a murder at close quarters, she entirely lost her powers of speech for some days. From the shock, I presume. Could this be a similar phenomenon?"

Haughton looked doubtful. "Surely after all this time she would have remembered. This murder happened nine years ago."

Ela turned to Margery. "What do you remember of the last time you saw Simon of Oddo alive?"

She blinked again, her eyes almost vacant. "He was curled up with me, under the covers, in the hut." She frowned, like she needed to dredge the words out of a deep, dark well. "He said he'd protect me and take care of me."

Ela blinked herself. Poor Margery. From what they'd heard about Simon of Oddo these thoughtful words sounded more like figments of an overworked imagination.

"Were you then surprised that he disappeared and folk said that he'd gone off to fight?"

Margery's mouth twitched. "Not really."

Ela sighed. Margery, or Grizeldis, was used to men lying to her. She'd probably be shocked if one told the truth. No wonder putting up with a bedbound, invalid husband more than twice her age didn't seem like much of a hardship to her.

Ela apologized to Haughton for interrupting his questioning. He demurred politely. Then he peered down the length of his slightly crooked nose at Fuller. "You say you didn't bury him. What did you do with the body and the knife after he lay dead?"

Ela half expected Fuller to refuse to answer again. "Nothing."

"Did you kill him in the hut, or outside it?"

"In it. Blood everywhere, there was. Bled like a pig."

Margery swayed in her chair. Becca rushed in to fuss over her.

"And your former wife was in the hut at the time?"

"Screaming like a madwoman."

"Earlier you said she asked you to kill him. Why would she do that?"

"I don't claim to understand women and their whims."

"Then why did you kill him?"

"Because he stole from me and made me angry. He wouldn't pay for what he'd taken. And she told me to."

Haughton looked at Margery, who stared back at him as if he were a headless ghost. "Margery, did you ask Ebbo Fuller to kill Simon of Oddo?"

She stared at him, her lips quivering.

"You did, feckless cow," sneered Fuller. "You don't even remember, do you? You never remember anything. Brains of a weevil, she has."

"Silence!" cried Ela. She'd had enough of Fuller. "Do you remember nothing of that day, Margery?"

"I don't remember it at all. If it happened like that. And if I was there. Maybe I wasn't." Her voice had a pleading tone, as if she was begging to not be there.

They didn't really need her as a witness, since Fuller had

confessed all in front of a jury. But was she culpable? Had she actually asked Ebbo to kill her new lover? As an abused and cowed woman she might have seized on that ploy in self-defense.

Ela peered at Fuller, who had the decency to look agitated. "You were angry with your wife's lover for taking your property and using it for free." She inhaled. The whole situation and even her manner of describing it made her insides roil. "But surely you were angry with…Grizeldis, too. She left you and found a new lover. One who took better care of her than you did."

She hoped to reopen the raw wound of his anger again and let truth flow out.

He stared at her, hatred seething in his gaze.

She realized she hadn't actually asked a question. "Why did you leave her alive to be a witness?"

He glanced at Margery, who flinched under his stare.

Giles Haughton cleared his throat. "You killed her too, didn't you? Or at least you thought you did. You knocked her down or choked her or kicked her until she lay lifeless, then you left her there for dead." He had moved very close to Fuller, and he leaned in until their noses almost touched.

Fuller recoiled visibly, his throat working as he swallowed and his lack of response almost a silent admission of guilt.

"You must have done," said Haughton. "Because you'd hardly murder a man and leave a living witness to raise the hue and cry and get you hunted like a fox. Especially a witness who had reason to hate you and fear you and maybe even want you dead."

Ela said a quick prayer that he'd confess, but it soon became clear that he wasn't going to make it that easy again. She looked at the jurors. "Do any members of the jury have questions?"

Peter Howard the baker, raised his hand. "I wonder about the hut where this happened. Was it destroyed?"

"It's gone without a trace now," said Haughton. He turned to Margery. "When did you last see the hut standing?"

Margery stared at him, owl-eyed. "I don't know."

"But you stayed in it alone after you thought Simon was gone?"

She seemed to think for a moment, then shook her head. "I thought I did but if he was killed there and there was blood everywhere, then I can't have, can I?"

"Do you think you might have buried him?" Haughton spoke softly, as if talking to a skittish colt. "And buried the knife along with him?"

Margery just stared.

"If her memory was going to come back it would have happened by now," interjected Ela. She didn't see the point of plying Margery with questions when that part of her brain had been swept clean—probably an act of mercy. "Bertram Beck said the hut was gone when he took up farming the land, but he's been known to stretch the truth until it breaks. He's in the jail."

GUARDS WERE SENT to summon Beck from the dungeon. Before long he was brought up into the hall, looking very dispirited and worse for wear. The guards led him into the hall toward a third chair now placed next to Margery's, in the middle of the tables where the jurors sat.

He barely looked around and seemed so different from his previous cocky self that Ela hardly recognized him.

"Was there a hut in the woods on the top of the hill when you bought Simon of Oddo's farm?"

"There was no hut there," he said, in a small voice. "I think

I remember a piled of charred timbers but nothing substantial like you'd even think it was a building. It could have been the remains of a fire to roast a pig."

"So someone destroyed the hut," said Ela. "It could have been Simon's father. But if he found blood and disarray there at the time his son went missing, he'd have raised the hue and cry." She looked at Margery again. "You have no memory of leaving the hut, or of burning it to erase the bad memories?"

Margery shook her head. She seemed to be in some kind of shock. She still hadn't shed a single tear.

"She's a small woman," said John Hart, in his high-pitched voice. "How would she bury a body by herself?"

Bertram Beck's head jerked up, as if he just realized perhaps someone else was now accused of the murder he'd be imprisoned for. He stared at Margery, then his gaze wandered past her to fix on Ebbo Fuller.

"It's him!" The words exploded from Beck's mouth. "He's the one who told me he'd killed a man."

Ela stared at Beck, and his words that she'd taken for yet more bluster came back to her. "What do you mean?"

"This man right there—" He jutted his chin toward Fuller. He couldn't move his hands as—like Fuller's—they were chained to the sturdy wood chair. "Was bragging in the inn that he'd just killed the man who stole his wife."

Fuller stared at him, disbelief on his features. "I never—" He didn't continue, perhaps because he'd already made a confession in the hall.

"He was drunk as I've ever seen anyone so he may not remember, but he said he killed the man with his own knife on his own farm and then killed his cheating wife as well."

"Where did this happen?"

"In Devizes," said Beck. "I was living in the inn there that autumn, wondering what to do with myself. When I heard word that a farmer had just died, I decided to venture to Salisbury to see if there might be some land going cheap."

"But it wasn't Simon's farm."

"I found that out when I got here. I took a room in the Bull and Bear and settled in here. No one here had heard of a murder at all, so for a while I thought he'd made it up, then I got talking to old Oddo one day and found his son had gone missing. His son had lived in a hut on his farm and had a strange woman up there with him, then one day he was gone and no one knew where."

"Why didn't you report the murder to the sheriff?" asked Ela.

Beck blinked, probably realizing how bad his omission looked. "I didn't know if it was true or the drunken ramblings of a cuckold. And no one in Salisbury knew of a murder, so for all I knew maybe there wasn't one. Maybe Simon of Oddo did wander off. So I got to know his father— who came to drink in the Bull and Bear at least once a week —and planted the idea in his head that his son had gone off to fight. It was better than knowing he'd had his throat cut, wasn't it?"

Ela stared at him. "You should have told the sheriff."

"You seem to have forgotten that the sheriff of Yorkshire just had my father hanged," said Beck, with a touch of his old arrogance. "I wasn't too warmly disposed toward sheriffs."

"And still aren't, I wager," murmured one of the jurors. Ela looked up quickly but didn't catch which one.

"I didn't know the murdered man, or the one who murdered him, and I didn't care about any of that. I'd settled on the idea of buying myself a piece of land—"

"With the money you stole from the remains of your father's estate that was supposed to go to the crown," said Ela.

"My father committed no crimes," said Beck. "I just

wanted to live a quiet life and this seemed as good an opportunity as any."

"So you badgered Oddo the Bald until he agreed to sell you his land?" asked Ela.

"He was quite happy to go live with his daughter. And he was determined not to sell to his neighbor, old Wilf Crowder. It took me a year to convince him to sell, and in all that time I never heard any man mention the name of Simon of Oddo except his own father. When I bought the place I forgot all about him and got on with managing my farm."

His story lined up perfectly with Fuller's reluctant confession and tightened the noose around Fuller's neck. And also seemed to lift the noose from Margery's shoulders. "The drunk man in Devizes told you he'd killed his wife?"

"Yes. He said she'd pleaded with him to kill her and spare her lover, so he killed her first, then killed her lover as he tried to run away and save himself."

Ela crossed herself. Margery just stared. "You've just exonerated Margery for the crime of asking Fuller to kill her husband." She looked at Margery. "Does any of this sound familiar?"

Margery shook her head mutely.

Ela glared at Fuller. "Did you attempt to kill Margery first?"

"I might have. Clearly I didn't do a good job of it." His chin tilted in defiance, so sure of the noose that he didn't even bother to be polite.

Ela remembered something that Margery's second husband had said when she visited them above the pie shop. "Did you stab her in the stomach?"

Fuller stared back. "I don't know why it didn't kill her. I got a good thrust. It should have."

"That's the scar your new husband mentioned, isn't it?"

Margery just looked at her dumbly.

Ela could picture poor Margery—or Grizeldis as she was then—alone, badly injured and in shock—with the brutally murdered body of the man who'd tried to help her. She'd managed to do what she felt she needed to do, then that part of her life had somehow been locked away where it could no longer harm her.

One thing perplexed Ela. "Why wouldn't you want your husband—your first husband, Ebbo Fuller—arrested and tried?"

Margery snuck a glance at the man in question and then looked away quickly. "I don't know," she said in a voice barely more than a whisper. "I don't know why I don't remember anything."

Haughton drew in a deep breath. "She was terrified of her first husband and with good reason. She'd seen him kill a man in a burst of anger. She probably felt safer staying far away from him."

"If he'd learned you were still alive he could have come back and killed you," said Ela.

Margery watched in owlish silence.

"So that's why you came to the castle, at great risk to your reputation, to claim the ring. You didn't want him to hear the news and come claim the ring. You didn't want anything to bring him back here."

Margery stole a tiny glance sideways at her tormentor, her would-be murderer, who sat chained to a chair mere feet away. A visible shudder rocked her.

"You're safe now," said Ela. "We have many witnesses to his confession and justice will be served when he's tried at the assizes." It was a shame that the crime of murder couldn't be tried without the king's justice present as she'd love to pronounce the sentence for Ebbo Fuller right now. "He's sure to hang."

Ela felt sorry for everything that Margery had suffered,

but growing relief that today's events, including vivid testimony that her husband was a murderer who'd deliberately tried to kill her, should let her entirely off the hook for bigamy. "Giles Haughton, do you have any questions?"

He sat at the table, hands tented together. "I believe my questions have been answered. Culpability is clear. We must be grateful that Margery Willoughby escaped with her life."

"Indeed," said Ela. "And I think the jury can see that Margery was well motivated to leave her first husband, a murderous fiend, and to try to make a new life for herself. Do the men of the jury agree?"

They looked at each other and there was some mumbled and nodded assent.

"Then the matter of the accusations of bigamy are resolved. Margery Willoughby's husband tried to kill her—thus dissolving their marriage in the eyes of God and man—before she married her second husband." Ela wasn't entirely sure of the legal precedents involved, but she suspected this was close enough and very much doubted that anyone would have reason to present a challenge. "So, as High Sheriff of Wiltshire, I move to declare her second marriage legal."

The ruling was agreed and seconded and Margery was sent home to her ailing husband.

"Now we find ourselves in the presence of a proven murderer—Ebbo Fuller—and one who concealed a murder in order to profit from it. I propose that both men remain in the dungeon until the assizes to be tried for their crimes."

The jury agreed. Ela was glad to wash her hands of Bertram Beck and his devious ways. Perhaps he'd walk free or perhaps he'd hang, she didn't feel much attachment to either outcome. His property would undoubtedly be sold to pay his fines, and that was punishment enough for his crimes against his neighbor.

CHAPTER 23

Three weeks later

Hilda's wedding took place on a bright April morning at St. Andrew's Church in the sleepy village of Laverstock. Hilda traveled from the castle with a large group, including Ela's children and several of the staff. A light drizzle left raindrops in the trees, shining like scattered pearls.

Ela stood off to one side with Petronella as they waited for the last people to make their way up the lane.

"What are we waiting for?" asked Petronella, growing impatient.

"Sibel told me that Hilda's parents are coming. You know that Hilda's mother is Sibel's sister?"

"Of course I know that. But I thought they refused to speak to her again because she got pregnant without being married."

"I was hoping they'd calm down about that, and it seems they have. I suspect they're dying to see her baby."

"The baby's not even here."

"He's with a wet nurse at the castle. I didn't want him

crying and disturbing the ceremony or the Mass. The nurse is going to bring him to Fernlees for the celebration afterward."

Two more people appeared around the corner, walking up the lane toward the church.

"Is that them?" asked Petronella.

Ela peered into the dappled shade of the lane. A huge oak tree sheltered the walk up to the church. "No, her mother is heavier than that. It's probably more of the Miller's relatives. They seem to be one of the largest families in Wiltshire if this turnout is anything to go by."

Men and women dressed in their brightest finery stood in all directions around the church doorway, smiling and chattering and exclaiming over the lovely bride. Probably also muttering under their breath about her being a rather dubious sort of "widow."

"We've been standing here for an age," griped Petronella. "And where's the priest?"

Ela hesitated. Even a large application of coins had not been able to persuade prim Father Edulf to marry Hilda to Dunstan on account of her transgressions. He had at last agreed to perform the Mass afterward, but it would be left to his disheveled curate to pronounce the couple husband and wife. "He's inside preparing for Mass."

"Why are we even here? Did Bishop Poore refuse to marry Hilda at the cathedral because she conceived a child in sin?" asked Petronella in a whisper.

"He might well have, but I didn't ask him."

"She could have been married at the castle chapel, then. There would have been a lot less time wasted wandering to and fro."

"This small parish church is better suited. It's where Hilda was baptized. We don't need her getting airs."

"Is that why her dress is linen and not silk or velvet? Ida made it so lovely with her embroidery."

"Indeed she did." Ida had done penance for her jealousy of Hilda's baby by applying her needlework skills to sewing intricate borders of flowers on the cuffs and neckline of Hilda's dress.

Hilda stood outside the church, arrayed in her embroidered finery, a bouquet of fresh-picked bluebells in her hands and a giddy expression on her face.

Her handsome groom, face ruddy with excitement, kept sneaking glances at his bride from where he stood with his relatives. Ela had a feeling that they'd both enjoy their wedding night.

"Is that Hilda's parents?" Petronella peered down the lane as another group of people straggled around the corner next to the old stone gate.

"Yes!" exclaimed Ela. "It is, and those are her brothers and sisters." Ela's heart filled with joy, and her eyes almost flooded with tears. She knew how crushed Hilda had been by her parents' rejection and how overjoyed she'd be to see them at her wedding.

Unless they'd come here to pour cold water on the proceedings by objecting to the match for some reason.

Ela knew her heart would pound a little during that part of the ceremony. Gray clouds gathered behind the slate roof of the church and suddenly it looked as if the wedding would be interrupted by another sudden downpour.

As THE CLOUDS darkened the sky, Ela had an attendant announce that the ceremony would begin. A hush fell over the crowd as Hilda and Dunstan Miller stood facing each other—she on the left side of the church door, and he on the right.

The curate was an older man of three score and ten with white hair, a kindly expression and a loud, croaking voice. "Does anyone present know of a reason why this man and this woman should not be joined in holy matrimony?"

Ela held her breath and it seemed like everyone around her did too. This was the part of the ceremony where someone might shout out that Hilda was already married or that the couple were first cousins or that he was betrothed to another.

Hilda fretted that someone might call out unkind words about her "marriage" to the late Drogo Blount.

But no one said a peep except the birds, who twittered excitedly in the great oak.

The curate looked as relieved as anyone, and soon Dunstan pronounced, "I take you, Hilda Biggs, to be my wedded wife. To have and to hold from this day forward, in sickness and in health, for better and for worse, until death us do part."

Ela prayed he would live up to his word. He seemed a kind and steady young man, if a little too handsome for his own good. Since Hilda bore that same affliction, perhaps it made them a well-suited pair.

Hilda repeated the words, her eyes starry with excitement —or was it terror?—then Dunstan slid the ring onto Hilda's finger.

Hilda and Dunstan linked arms and led the crowd into St. Andrew's for the Mass.

The church was tiny and impossibly ancient, from the time when great stone crosses carved with curlicues loomed over every crossroads. A simpler time when men had lived closer to God. For all the grandness of her era's great cathedrals, Ela loved the intimacy of these tiny parish churches, where generation after generation of local villagers were baptized and worshiped and were buried in the churchyard. Only a fraction of the gathered assembly fit into the tiny building, and the others gathered around the door.

The rain that had threatened outside finally came as the priest repeated the Lord's Prayer. Ela watched Hilda turn and smile at her handsome new husband as the raindrops pattered on the roof. She prayed for their health and happiness and that they'd raise little Thomas with kindness and love and that he'd be treated just the same as their future children.

The service went on so long that sun poured down on them again as they left the church. Leaves and grass glistened and puddles shone in the lane as the group left the churchyard and headed the half mile or so along the road to Fernlees.

THE MILLER FAMILY had generously laid on a good portion of the feast at their son's new home. No doubt they wanted to show off his good fortune to their friends, who arrived on foot and horseback.

Ela had sent a cartload of roasted meats and pastries and sweetmeats from the castle—which had luckily avoided the rain—and the casks of wine already flowed by the time she arrived at Fernlees.

The wet nurse arrived with Hilda's crying baby, and Hilda abandoned her new husband and ran to comfort him. Then she excitedly showed him to her parents, who exclaimed over him as if they'd been happy for her all along.

Ela noticed Ida standing silently to one side while everyone fussed over the baby. She approached and offered Ida her own cup of wine.

"No, thanks." Her daughter attempted a false smile.

"You'll be pregnant before you know it."

"I doubt it. But if the Lord doesn't see fit to bless me with a child I shall do my best to bear it bravely."

"Try those things we talked about," Ela leaned in and whispered. "The marshmallow and mugwort, and the pessaries of musk."

"Mama," hissed Ida. "Not now!"

"I should tell Sibel about the pessaries," said Ela. She could see Sibel, her former lady's maid, standing to one side with her own fairly new husband and smiling at the young couple.

"Sibel's too old to have a child," snapped Ida. "Surely she knows that."

"Nonsense. She's younger than I am."

"Then you'll probably get married again and have a baby before I do," moaned Ida.

"I can assure you that won't happen. Your father was the only husband I shall ever want or need."

Ida's expression softened. "Do you still miss him?"

"Every day. Every hour." Ela inhaled deeply. "I'm sure some gossips think I enjoy my freedom to come and go as I please and to spend my money where I wish, but they forget that I now bear the full weight of the burdens we used to share."

"I do miss my husband," admitted Ida. "I miss holding him at night."

"It's time for you to go home to him."

Ida looked thoughtful. "I suppose it is. He might miss me, too. And the cook can be quite profligate with expensive and rare ingredients when I'm not there to supervise the menus."

Ela smiled. "Managing your household is a satisfying pursuit in itself. I always took pride in making sure our manors turned a profit. If a manor starts to lose money I visit it and work out how to find profits in the timber or improving the flocks or sowing a hillside with corn. You must familiarize yourself with every acre so that you can manage them well when your husband is away at war or on the king's business."

"I'm not businesslike like you, Mama," protested Ida. "I'd rather leave all that to Liam."

"Understanding these matters of business increases your worth to your husband. He'll be grateful to you for sharing his burdens and will find you indispensable."

"So he won't throw me aside if I don't bear him a son," mused Ida.

"That's not what I meant."

"But it's true."

"Look how sweet the newlyweds are," said Ela, keen to change the subject from her daughter's morose thoughts. "Dunstan just kissed little Thomas on the nose."

"Thomas is a very pretty baby," said Ida softly.

"All babies are pretty, but they'll grow up to cause you sleepless nights and silver hairs all the same," said Ela with a smile.

"I suspect Hilda's caused you more sleepless nights and silver hairs than all your own children put together."

"You may well be right." Ela chuckled. "But it's worth it all to see her well settled. And look how happy Sibel is." She could see Sibel talking animatedly with her sister—Hilda's mother—when they'd barely spoken for months. "Sibel served me so well for so long I could barely stand to let her go, and now I feel terrible that I stole so many years of her life. I pray every night that she'll be blessed with a child."

"Sometimes I feel you care more for everyone else around you than you care for your own children," said Ida. "You still have little ones at home, but you must be sheriff and worry about the concerns of every burgher and farmer in Salisbury. You could leave all that to John Dacus, you know?"

"I could, but I know I can do more good by playing an active role myself. I feel called to serve."

"By God?"

"By God, by your father, by my father, by all of our ancestors who brought me here and endowed me with the gifts and blessings I have."

Ida looked skeptical. "So basically you have dead people telling you what to do?"

Ela smiled sweetly. "Would you argue with them?"

THE END

AUTHOR'S NOTE

Ela Longespée became sheriff of Wiltshire for the first time in 1227. Local Wiltshire knight John Dacus, also mysteriously known as "The Dane," served as Ela's co-sheriff that year. Co-sheriffs were quite common in this era, giving the appointed noble the ability to travel or fulfill other duties. Since Dacus went on to serve as Ela's co-sheriff for several years in the 1230s, I suspect that they had a good working relationship.

Ela's daughter Ida, after a few childless years of marriage, went on to have six children—three boys and three girls—with her husband William de Beauchamp. While several of Ela's children, including Ida, Richard and Stephen, took holy orders in later life, Petronella Longespée was the only one to take the veil as a young woman. The others all married and had worldly careers before choosing a religious life. Ela herself would eventually become first a nun and then abbess of the convent she founded at Lacock in Wiltshire.

Stonehenge is the most famous ancient feature in the Salisbury area, but in fact the region contains many relics of ancient habitation. Just this summer a new discovery was announced: Giant shafts found at Durrington Walls reveal the outline of what is now the largest prehistoric monument ever discovered in Britain. It's quite possible that more of these artifacts were visible in Ela's time and have since been obliterated by agriculture. People in 1227 must have been just as curious about—and likely just as mystified by—these ancient monuments and the people who created them.

If you have questions or comments, please get in touch at jglewis@stoneheartpress.com.

Cover image includes: detail from Codex Manesse, ca. 1300, Heidelberg University Library; decorative detail from Beatus of Liébana, Fecundus Codex of 1047, Biblioteca Nacional de España; detail with Longespée coat of arms from Matthew Parris, *Historia Anglorum,* ca. 1250, British Museum.

Made in the USA
Middletown, DE
16 March 2023

26892363R00163